BEST BOOK OF
ANIMAL STORIES

The Cat That Walked By Himself

The Adventures of Old Mr. Toad

BEST BOOK
OF
ANIMAL STORIES

Edited by

PAULINE RUSH EVANS

Color Illustrations by

CHARLES McCURRY

Line Illustrations by

ROBERT BALL

Doubleday & Company, Inc., Garden City, New York

Library of Congress Catalog Card Number 64-16229

Preface

I have watched the *Best Book Series* in the making—and over
and over again I have wished that such books had been available
when my children were growing up. It seems to me that arrang-
ing stories by subject matter will be most appealing to children.
And certainly there is something here for every child. . . . Each
volume contains weeks and months of fine reading.

What I particularly like is that this is a series of books for
reading—not for looking. Every book is illustrated, and hand-
somely illustrated, but the emphasis is where it should be—on
the stories themselves. Today, as always, children want and need
reading that they can really get their teeth into.

The child who has this series to grow on is fortunate indeed.
It comes too late for my own children, but my younger grandchildren will be able to enjoy the *Best Book Series*—every one of
them.

Sidonie M. Gruenberg
Former Director, Child Study Association of America

The Best Book Series

Acknowledgments

Thanks are due to the following authors, publishers, publications and agents for permission to use the material indicated.

Mrs. Louise B. Baynes for permission to reprint "Jimmie, the Black Bear Cub" by Ernest Harold Baynes. Copyright 1923. Originally published by The Macmillan Company. Bobbs-Merrill Company, Inc. for "Our Friend Tasso" and "A Snow-White Rabbit" from GOOD COMRADES by Felix Salten, copyright © 1942, used by special permission of the publishers. Dodd, Mead & Company, Inc. for "Michael Who Missed His Train" from MICHAEL AND PATSY by Dorothy M. Bryan. Copyright © 1932, 1933 by Dorothy M. Bryan; MY FRIEND TOTO by Cherry Kearton; "How to Tell the Wild Animals" from BAUBLES by Carolyn Wells. Copyright © 1917 by Dodd, Mead & Company, Inc. Reprinted by permission of the publishers. Doubleday & Company, Inc. for "The Cat That Walked by Himself" from JUST SO STORIES by Rudyard Kipling; "Rikki-Tikki-Tavi" from THE JUNGLE BOOK by Rudyard Kipling, reprinted by permission of Mrs. George Bambridge, The Macmillan Company of Canada, and Doubleday & Company, Inc. "Animal Friends" from KILDEE HOUSE by Rutherford Montgomery. Copyright 1949 by Rutherford Montgomery; "Coaly-Bay—The Outlaw Horse" from WILD ANIMAL WAYS by Ernest Thompson Seton. Copyright 1916 by Ernest Thompson Seton. Reprinted by permission of the publishers. E. P. Dutton & Co., Inc. for "How Kari Saved Our Lives in the Jungle" from the book KARI THE ELEPHANT by Dhan Gopal Mukerji. Copyright, 1922, by E. P. Dutton & Co., Inc. Renewal, 1949, by Mrs. Dhan Mukerji. Reprinted by permission of the publishers. Faber and Faber Limited for "The Rum Tum Tugger" from OLD POSSUM'S BOOK OF PRACTICAL CATS by T. S. Eliot. Reprinted by permission of the publishers. Harcourt, Brace and Company, Inc. for "The Rum Tum Tugger" from OLD POSSUM'S BOOK OF PRACTICAL CATS, copyright, 1939, by T. S. Eliot; "The Dog of Pompeii" from THE DONKEY OF GOD And Other Stories by Louis Untermeyer, copyright 1932, by Harcourt, Brace and Company, Inc. Reprinted by permission of the publishers. Holiday House for "The General's Horse" from PADRE PORKO, THE GENTLEMANLY PIG by Robert Davis. Reprinted by permission of the publishers. Houghton Mifflin Company for STICKEEN, by John Muir, copyright 1909, reprinted by permission of an arrangement with Houghton Mifflin Company, the authorized publishers. Mr. Don Lang for permission to reprint his story, AN ELEPHANT NEVER FORGETS, originally published in Story Parade Magazine. J. B. Lippincott Company for "Animal Language" from THE STORY OF DOCTOR DOLITTLE by Hugh Lofting. Copyright 1920, by Hugh Lofting, 1948 by Josephine Lofting. Reprinted by permission of the publishers and Mrs. Lofting. "The Horse Who Lived Upstairs" by Phyllis McGinley. Copyright, 1944 by Phyllis McGinley; "Basta, A Holy Cat of Bubastis" from LAURA WAS MY CAMEL by Arthur Weigall. Copyright, 1933 by J. B. Lippincott Company. "A Kitten" from OVER THE GARDEN WALL by Eleanor Farjeon. Copyright 1933, 1951 by Eleanor Farjeon. Reprinted by permission of the publishers. Little,

Brown & Company for "Old Mr. Toad's Queer Tongue" and "Old Mr. Toad Shows His Tongue" from THE ADVENTURES OF OLD MR. TOAD by Thornton Burgess. Copyright 1916, by Thornton Burgess. Reprinted by permission of the publishers. The Macmillan Company for "Zinnia and Her Babies" from MORE ABOUT ANIMALS by Margery Bianco; "For the Love of a Man" from THE CALL OF THE WILD by Jack London. Copyright 1931 by The Macmillan Company. Reprinted by permission of the publishers. Charles Scribner's Sons for "Mr. Badger" from THE WIND IN THE WILLOWS by Kenneth Grahame, copyright 1908, 1933, by Charles Scribner's Sons. Reprinted by permission of the publisher. Simon and Schuster, Inc. for "How Bambi Discovered the Meadow" from BAMBI by Felix Salten. Copyright 1928, 1956 by Simon and Schuster, Inc. Reprinted by permission of the publishers. The Viking Press, Inc. for "Little Georgie Sings a Song" from RABBIT HILL by Robert Lawson. Copyright 1944 by Robert Lawson; "Serapina Takes Charge" from THE STORY OF SERAPINA by Anne H. White. Copyright 1951 by Anne H. White. Reprinted by permission of the publishers.

The editor and publisher have made diligent efforts to trace the ownership of all copyrighted material in this volume, and believe that all necessary permissions have been secured. If any errors have inadvertently been made, proper corrections will gladly be made in future editions.

Introduction

Children like all kinds of stories, but if there is one kind that is always immediately appealing it is surely a story about animals.

Perhaps that is why animal stories are among the oldest that have come down to us. Nobody knows when they began, but the earliest legends and folk tales of all countries are peopled with animals of all sorts. So is the Bible. The story of Noah and his ark is one of the first Bible stories that a child enjoys. And almost three thousand years ago Aesop, the legendary Greek slave, was telling little stories which are still retold in almost every language in the world.

These ancient stories were hardly ever about real animals. They were mostly fables—stories about animals who thought and talked and acted like people—and were intended to teach people simple moral lessons. After a while the animals all began to take on certain fixed characteristics: the fox was always sly and the turtle always sensible and plodding; the crow was sharp, the hare was scatterbrained, the owl was wise.

We still tell stories of imaginary animals, of course. Only now they are told just for fun and not to teach lessons. Some of the best of all stories are of this kind—*The Story of Dr. Dolittle, The Wind in the Willows, The Cat That Walked by Himself, Rabbit Hill,* and many, many others.

But today there are many more stories about real animals, and in some ways they are even better because they *are* real. Who could ever read *My Friend Toto* without wishing that some day he too could have such a pet? What human ever had greater courage and loyalty than the dog, Buck, in *Call of the*

Wild? Could any story ever make one feel so close to a wild animal as *Bambi?*

Fantasy or real, animals of all kinds are always peculiarly interesting to children, and stories about them have always been favorites. Here are some of the best.

P. R. E.

Danbury, Conn.

Contents

Animals: Mostly Real

Animals: Odd or Imaginary

The Horse Who Lived Upstairs

PHYLLIS McGINLEY

THERE was once a horse named Joey who was discontented. He was discontented because he didn't live in a red barn with a weathervane on top, and he didn't live in a green meadow where he could run about and kick up his heels.

Instead, he lived upstairs in a big brick building in New York. Joey worked for Mr. Polaski who sold fruits and vegetables to city people. Joey pulled the vegetable wagon through the city streets. And in New York, there isn't room for barns or meadows.

So every night when Joey came home, he stepped out from the shafts of the wagon, and into an elevator, and up he went to his stall on the fourth floor of the big brick building. It was a fine stall and Joey was very comfortable there. He had plenty of oats to eat and plenty of fresh straw to lie on.

He even had a window to look out of. But still Joey was discontented.

"How I long to sip fresh water from a babbling brook!" he often exclaimed.

And then he would sniff discontentedly at the old bathtub near the elevator which served him as a watering trough.

It wasn't that he had to work hard. Mr. Polaski was kind to him and brought him home at five o'clock every day.

In the winter Joey had a blanket to wear on his back to keep him warm.

And in the summertime Mr. Polaski got him a hat to wear on his head to keep him cool.

And every day he had many interesting adventures. Sometimes he met a Policeman who gave him sugar.

Sometimes ladies patted him on the nose and fed him carrots.

He was introduced to the highbred horses who drew the hansom cabs along the Plaza.

He saw the children playing in the playgrounds and the parks. But it made no difference to Joey.

"This is no life for a horse," he used to say to the Percheron who lived in the next stall to him. "We city horses don't know what real living is. I want to move to the country and sleep in a red barn with a weathervane on top, and kick up my heels in a green meadow."

So how happy he was when one day Mr. Polaski said to him, "Joey, I think I could sell more vegetables if I drove a truck. I will miss you, Joey, but you will like it on the farm where I am going to send you."

The next morning a big motor van rolled up. Joey got inside, and away he went to the country. Of course he said good-bye to the Percheron.

"Good-bye, Joey," called his friend. "I hope you will be contented on the farm."

When Joey reached the country, sure enough, there was the barn with its weathervane, and there was the meadow.

"This is the life!" cried Joey to himself.

But poor Joey! The barn was cold in winter and hot in summer. He didn't have a blanket and he didn't have a hat. And he had very little time to kick up his heels in the green meadow, for all day long he pulled a plow through the earth.

A plow is harder to pull than a wagon, and besides, the farmer worked from sunrise to sundown instead of the eight hours Joey was used to.

Sometimes they forgot to put fresh straw in his stall, and nobody thought to give him sugar or carrots.

There were plenty of children, but they climbed on his back and teased him when he wanted to eat. And instead of the Percheron, there was a cross old gray horse next door to him, who looked down his nose at Joey because Joey knew so little about farm life.

One day, when he wasn't pulling a plow, because it was Sunday, Joey saw several people picnicking in the meadow. He decided to join them, for they looked as if they came from the city, and he thought they might have a lump of sugar in one of their pockets.

When he reached the spot they had gone for a walk, so he ate up their lunch.

When they came back, they were very angry, and Joey was shut up in his stall for the rest of the day. He didn't even have a window to look out of.

He was lonely for his friends, the Policeman, and the ladies who patted him on the nose.

He was lonely for the highbred horses, and all the interesting sights of the city.

"I don't think I belong in the country after all," sighed Joey. "I am now more discontented than ever."

Next day he heard the honk of a horn. He looked from the door of the barn, and whom should he see but Mr. Polaski, getting out of the truck!

"I have come for Joey," Mr. Polaski told the farmer. "I think I'll sell fruit and vegetables from my wagon again."

My goodness, but Joey was happy!

He went back to the city with Mr. Polaski and got into the elevator and up he went to the fourth floor of the big brick building. There was his stall, and there was the window for him to look out of.

And there was the friendly Percheron. "Welcome back, Joey," exclaimed the Percheron. "I have missed you. The Policeman has missed you. The lady customers have missed you, and so have the children in the playgrounds and parks. Tell me, did you like the country?"

"The country is all right for country animals," Joey said, "but I guess I am just a city horse at heart."

And he was never discontented again.

FROM

The Story of Serapina

ANNE H. WHITE

Serapina, a cat with the most astonishing talents, adopts the Salinus family. How would you like to have a cat who can open doors, carry milk bottles with her tail, and even play baseball? At first Mrs. Salinus is uneasy about this almost human cat. She is soon won over, however, when Serapina proves that she cannot only amuse but discipline the children, and that she makes a perfect sitter when the parents are away.

Serapina Takes Charge

THE next day the astonishing story of Serapina continued. To begin with, Mr. Salinus was not waked up by his alarm clock. A soft, gargling sound in his left ear aroused him. It was Serapina, sitting on his pillow. Mr. Salinus, annoyed at being waked before the alarm went off, tried to push her aside, but Serapina did not push. She simply moved over to his right ear and gargled louder. Mr. Salinus sat up and glared at her. Then he looked at his clock. It was exactly six-forty-five and the alarm was turned off.

"That's strange," Mr. Salinus remarked, getting out of bed and into his wrapper and slippers. "I'm sure I set the alarm last night, but it's turned off."

"It's a good thing the cat happened to wake you," Mrs. Salinus murmured sleepily.

"Come to think of it, I don't think she did *happen* to," Mr.

Salinus said. "I'll bet she plans what she does, don't you, old girl?" he asked. But Serapina had vanished.

When he was dressed Mr. Salinus started his routine, but when he went into Sally's room he was too late. Serapina had just finished pulling the covers off Sally very neatly. With her front paws she pulled them back on one side, then jumped across Sally and pulled them back on the other side. Every time she jumped, Sally bounced gently on the mattress, so it was like being rocked awake instead of rocked asleep. When she had waked Sally, Serapina jumped off the bed and bustled into Peter's room. Peter was lying on his back reading a comic book, but Serapina stopped that. She sat on his stomach and thwacked the book with her tail so that Peter could not hold it still. When he turned over on his stomach, Serapina sat on his back and tickled him with her front paws. Peter got up, and Serapina went into Bobby's room. This particular morning Bobby was hiding in the bottom of his bed. Serapina went down to the bottom and shoveled him up to the top with her broad, hard head. As soon as she had got the children up she hurried to the kitchen to join Mr. and Mrs. Salinus. She opened the back door with no trouble at all and, wrapping the end of her tail firmly around the neck of a milk bottle, dragged it into the kitchen and stood it on the floor beside the refrigerator. When she had brought in all the milk she got the oranges by jumping into the vegetable bin and turning around a few times. The oranges flew out in all directions, and Serapina rolled them over to Mr. Salinus with her front paws. She paid no attention to the grownups while she did these chores, and when she had finished she hustled back upstairs to see about the children.

Of course Serapina could not actually dress the children, but Sally and Peter had dressed themselves for years. They just needed a little prodding and reminding, and Serapina was excellent at both. When she thought a child had dawdled enough she stretched out her tail the required number of notches and prodded firmly. She did not prick, poke, or push, but she prodded in a most unmistakable, hurry-up manner. She proved just as good at reminding too. Anxiously she watched Sally pass the bureau many times, always forgetting to brush her hair. So she waited until Sally bent down to tie her shoes. Her hair fell forward as she leaned, and Serapina quickly reached out her paw. Gently she clawed a lock of hair and stuck on a snarl.

"Why, Serapina!" Sally exclaimed, untangling hair and claw. "I will brush my hair right away so Mother can't send me back to do it."

Serapina waited till Sally picked up the brush, then she went into Peter's room. Peter also was tying his shoes. But instead of bending down to reach the laces, Peter bent up. He was lying on his back with one leg waving over his head. Serapina could not have asked for a better chance to remind him to wash his face. She sat close beside him and wiped his face with her toes. Peter said afterward it was a rough sort of washrag but he got the idea.

Presently Mrs. Salinus called everyone to breakfast, asking that somebody please find Bobby.

"I bet I know who will!" Sally sang out, and she was right. As the family sat down Bobby appeared. Serapina had found him in the coat closet and was conducting him to the dining room. Perhaps "bumping" him would be a better word for it. Bobby was just the right size for a large cat to bump, and Serapina succeeded in blocking every move he made *away* from the dining room by giving him a bump *toward* the dining room.

Mrs. Salinus began dishing up the cereal. "One of you help Bobby pull up his chair," she reminded the older children.

"We don't have to, Mummy," Peter and Sally said together. "Serapina—"

"No!" Mrs. Salinus almost screamed. "No, no! I won't believe it!" But she had to, poor woman, because there was Bobby pushing his chair, and there was Serapina pulling it, her tail crooked over the lower rung.

Mrs. Salinus clasped her head in her hands. "That finishes it!" she cried nervously. "James, there is something very strange about a cat that does all the things that cat does. And that tail! And those eyes! James, that is a very queer cat. In fact, for a cat, it is unheard of. Well," Mrs. Salinus rushed on, "I won't have something unheard of in my house. It makes me nervous. Besides, she is probably rare and valuable too. So you telephone The Unwanted Animal Society right away. Suppose Big Boy Bonzo got her! Suppose Fanny Fowler poisoned her!"

Sally and Peter turned a little pale at the mention of Big Boy Bonzo, who lived a few doors down the block and frightened everyone out of his wits when his owner, Mrs. Amanda Mac-Pherson, let him loose.

Mr. Salinus sighed. He was delighted with Serapina and did not mind having something unheard of in his house. He was an obliging man, however, and he went to the telephone and asked for The Unwanted Animal Society. Sally and Peter hovered at his elbow.

"Yes, yes," they heard a voice say, "we take cats if the owners do not want them."

"But," Mr. Salinus explained honestly, "I am not the owner."

"Then why," asked the voice, "do you own the cat?"

"I don't," Mr. Salinus answered. "I just have it."

"But you don't want it?"

"Yes, I do want it." Mr. Salinus spoke truthfully, but he did not look at his wife.

"Then why call us?" asked The Unwanted Animal Society and hung up.

Mr. Salinus, to please Mrs. Salinus, then called the police and reported he had a stray cat in his house. He talked to Officer Michael McCarthy, who did not pay very much attention to what Mr. Salinus was saying. Mike McCarthy was a young policeman and his ambition was to catch a criminal. He was not interested in animals, but he did look at the records in the Lost and Found Department. There was no mention of a lost cat so Mike could not be very helpful about a found one. He put Serapina's name down in the files and Mr. Salinus hung up. With a sigh of relief he turned to his anxious children.

"We will keep Serapina with a clear conscience until we get an answer to the advertisement," he declared. He looked at his watch and was horrified to see how late it was. "I must go!" he cried and snatched up his hat. "Take care of Serapina, my dears. She may be unheard of, or even valuable, but it strikes me she may be mighty useful too."

As the morning wore on Mrs. Salinus realized how very right Mr. Salinus could be. As she was sitting over her second cup of coffee and thinking some thoughts about cats, a slight, rattling noise attracted her attention. It was Serapina, the forgotten vitamin bottle held firmly in her tail, going in search of the children. In the excitement of the telephone calls everyone, except Serapina, had forgotten the vitamins. Mrs. Salinus finished her coffee, and gave up her thoughts. As she very sensibly put it, she really did not know what thoughts to think anyway.

She went on with her housework as usual, every now and then glancing out into the yard at the children. Serapina, when she was not playing with them, bunched herself up into a mound and watched them through half-closed eyes. Mrs. Salinus noticed that the cat always kept herself between Bobby and the gate. At eleven Mrs. Salinus went out with the tray of milk and cookies, but the telephone rang as she stepped out the door. She set the tray down and went to answer it. Knowing the children might forget to drink their milk, she went out when she finished talking and was just in time to see Serapina trotting across the yard with the last glass held carefully in her tail.

"Oh, dear," moaned Mrs. Salinus, "I suppose she thought that up all by herself!"

"Yes, she did," Sally replied. "We were playing and we didn't even see the tray was there."

"Do you think she will bring us the cookies too?" Bobby asked.

"Go on, Serapina," Peter commanded in a very lordly manner. "Get me the cookies like a good girl."

"You sound just like Grandpa sending me on an errand," Sally told her brother. "And if Serapina feels the way I do when I'm ordered around, she won't do it."

Serapina narrowed her green eyes at Peter, walked around behind him, and, ducking her head down and her chin in, gave him a good butt in the seat of his pants. Peter was pushed forward nearly onto his nose, to the great delight of his sister, his brother, and, I must confess, his mother.

"Ha, ha," crowed Sally. "That is what Serapina thinks of such a silly order. She knows perfectly well that you know she can't carry a flat plate."

"And you didn't say 'please,' either," Bobby said.

Mrs. Salinus gathered up the empty glasses and went back **into** the kitchen. At half-past eleven, as she was thinking of reminding Sally to come in, she heard a strange noise from the living room. It was a sort of scale being played on the piano, yet it was not quite a scale, not quite an arpeggio, not quite a run. Mrs. Salinus hurried in, and there was Serapina, walking carefully up the keyboard, her right paws playing white notes and her left ones playing black. Each time she covered the keyboard she went a little faster and a little louder, until an annoyed Sally burst into the hall. "Really, Mummy," Sally called, "you don't have to bang so hard. I heard you. What will the neighbors think!" And Sally came indignantly into the living room and saw who was doing the banging.

"At least, Serapina," Sally said reprovingly, "you might play quietly. I'm not deaf." But Serapina, like a great many mothers and fathers, could not be sure when children were deaf and when they were not. Sally sat down to practice, but Serapina flicked her wrists sharply. Sally sighed and went to wash her hands, telling Serapina in a low voice that she was nearly as tiresome as a mother could be.

At noontime Serapina went out into the yard to remind Peter and Bobby it was time for lunch, which was quite easy to do as both the boys were hungry. But reminding Peter to wash was not so easy. Serapina gave him every chance to take a hint. She sat practically under his nose and washed her own face; she tried to wash Peter's hands; she prodded; and finally she poked and pushed him, but Peter was too big for her and paid no attention.

"Peter!" Sally sounded cross with her brother's unhelpfulness. "Pay attention. Serapina is trying to tell you to get ready for lunch."

"I know," Peter explained patiently, "but I am conducting an experiment. I want to see what she will do if I pretend I *don't* understand. After all, if I was a very stupid person, which I am not, I wouldn't understand." Peter was very fond of experimenting, and he often found it interesting to do what was *not* expected of him. "Anyway," he added as an idea occurred to him, "we don't have to obey a cat."

Serapina, however, thought otherwise. She moved directly in front of Peter, arched her back into a very high peak, and, snapping her tail like a whip, began to express her feelings. It was astonishing how many feelings Serapina could express. First she made a low, sharp, annoyed sound, like an irritable uncle scolding a stupid nephew. Peter paid no attention. Serapina then made a little more noise and sounded like an irascible aunt scolding a lazy and careless nephew. Still Peter did not stir, but he looked interested. Serapina was not interested. She was mad. So she stopped sounding like an uncle or an aunt or a father or a mother or any person at all. She sounded like an angry cat, which sounds like a screaming seagull, a gargling tiger, a snarling leopard, a wailing banshee, and three angry fishwives all sounding off at once.

Bobby burst into tears, Sally turned pale, Peter jumped to his feet, and Serapina, hollering bloody murder, set off for the kitchen. She did not have to go far because Mrs. Salinus came running.

"What are you doing to Serapina?" she asked in alarm.

"Nothing," all three children answered promptly because they were not doing anything.

"Then what *did* you do?" asked Mrs. Salinus, who sometimes thought her children were a little too matter-of-fact. "You must have done something. She is certainly very angry with you."

"No," Peter explained, being both matter-of-fact and fair-minded, "we really did not *do* anything, but that's the trouble." And he told his mother about his experiment in not understanding Serapina. "I just wanted to see what she would do. I didn't know she would be such an old tattletale."

At these words Serapina went under the sofa, not in a huff but in an offended mood, which is quite different.

"It's very unfair of you to call her a tattletale," Sally objected. "Isn't it, Mummy? She can't push Peter around and she can't argue with him. If he won't cooperate with her, the only thing she can do is to call for help."

"But whoever heard of cooperating with a cat!" Peter exclaimed.

"Oh, dear," wailed Mrs. Salinus, "I don't suppose anyone we know has ever heard of such a thing. Perhaps someone will claim her tomorrow and end this very awkward situation we are in. So do just try to cooperate until she is claimed," Mrs. Salinus begged the children, "because the neighbors will object if you don't."

Sally and Peter had already decided to be more helpful to Serapina in the future. After lunch they invited her to come out from under the sofa, but she declined until later in the afternoon. Then she forgave them and joined them in the backyard, where they were playing tag with the two little Timminses. Serapina played tag enthusiastically although she was inclined to play by her own rules, which allowed her to be It all the time and do all the chasing. But she was so quick and so earnest about the game the children did not mind. She surprised and delighted the two little Timminses by bringing a glass of water to Sally in her tail. When she discovered, however, that Sally did not really want the water but only wanted her to show off, she dropped the glass crossly in the sandpile and went up on the roof.

"She's in a huff again," Sally explained to the Timminses. "She's quite sensitive for a cat and goes into a huff very easily."

"Well, let's get her out of it and make her do some more things," the older Timmins suggested.

"No," Sally said, "she's our cat, and if she does not want to do anything, we are not going to make her."

So the children left Serapina alone and ran off to play. Serapina, I think, was grateful. She had had a pretty strenuous day.

The Cat That Walked by Himself

RUDYARD KIPLING

Hear and attend and listen; for this befell and behappened and became and was, O my Best Beloved, when the Tame animals were wild. The Dog was wild, and the Horse was wild, and the Cow was wild, and the Sheep was wild, and the Pig was wild —as wild as wild could be—and they walked in the Wet Wild Woods by their wild lones. But the wildest of all the wild animals was the Cat. He walked by himself, and all places were alike to him.

Of course the Man was wild too. He was dreadfully wild. He didn't even begin to be tame till he met the Woman, and she told him that she did not like living in his wild ways. She picked out a nice dry Cave, instead of a heap of wet leaves, to lie down in; and she strewed clean sand on the floor; and she lit a nice fire of wood at the back of the Cave; and she hung a dried wild-horse skin, tail-down, across the opening of the Cave; and she said, "Wipe your feet, dear, when you come in, and now we'll keep house."

That night, Best Beloved, they ate wild sheep roasted on the hot stones, and flavoured with wild garlic and wild pepper; and wild duck stuffed with wild rice and wild fenugreek and wild coriander; and marrow-bones of wild oxen; and wild cherries, and wild grenadillas. Then the Man went to sleep in front of the fire ever so happy; but the Woman sat up, combing her hair. She took the bone of the shoulder of mutton—the big fat blade-bone —and she looked at the wonderful marks on it, and she threw more wood on the fire, and she made a Magic. She made the First Singing Magic in the world.

Out in the Wet Wild Woods all the wild animals gathered together where they could see the light of the fire a long way off, and they wondered what it meant.

The Wild Horse stamped with his wild foot and said, "O my Friends and O my Enemies, why have the Man and the Woman made that great light in that great Cave, and what harm will it do us?"

Wild Dog lifted up his wild nose and smelled the smell of roast mutton, and said, "I will go up and look, and say; for I think it is good. Cat, come with me."

"Nenni!" said the Cat. "I am the Cat who walks by himself, and all places are alike to me. I will not come."

"Then we can never be friends again," said Wild Dog, and he trotted off to the Cave. But when he had gone a little way the Cat said to himself, "All places are alike to me. Why should I not go too and see and look and come away at my own liking." So he slipped after Wild Dog softly, very softly, and hid himself where he could hear everything.

When Wild Dog reached the mouth of the Cave he lifted up the dried horse-skin with his nose and sniffed the beautiful smell of the roast mutton, and the Woman, looking at the blade-bone, heard him, and laughed, and said, "Here comes the first. Wild Thing out of the Wild Woods, what do you want?"

Wild Dog said, "O my Enemy and Wife of my Enemy, what is this that smells so good in the Wild Woods?"

Then the Woman picked up a roasted mutton-bone and threw it to Wild Dog, and said, "Wild Thing out of the Wild Woods, taste and try." Wild Dog gnawed the bone and it was more delicious than anything he had ever tasted, and he said, "O my Enemy and Wife of my Enemy, give me another."

The Woman said, "Wild Thing out of the Wild Woods, help my Man to hunt through the day and guard this Cave at night, and I will give you as many roast bones as you need."

"Ah!" said the Cat, listening. "This is a very wise Woman, but she is not so wise as I am."

Wild Dog crawled into the Cave and laid his head on the Woman's lap, and said, "O my Friend and Wife of my Friend, I will help your Man to hunt through the day, and at night I will guard your Cave."

"Ah!" said the Cat, listening. "That is a very foolish Dog." And he went back through the Wet Wild Woods waving his wild tail, and walking by his wild lone. But he never told anybody.

When the Man waked up he said, "What is Wild Dog doing here?" And the Woman said, "His name is not Wild Dog any more, but the First Friend, because he will be our friend for always and always and always. Take him with you when you go hunting."

Next night the Woman cut great green armfuls of fresh grass from the water-meadows, and dried it before the fire, so that it smelt like new-mown hay, and she sat at the mouth of the Cave and plaited a halter out of horse-hide, and she looked at the shoulder of mutton-bone—at the big broad blade-bone—and she made a Magic. She made the Second Singing Magic in the world.

Out in the Wild Woods all the wild animals wondered what had happened to Wild Dog, and at last Wild Horse stamped with his foot and said, "I will go and see and say why Wild Dog has not returned. Cat, come with me."

"Nenni!" said the Cat. "I am the Cat who walks by himself, and all places are alike to me. I will not come." But all the same he followed Wild Horse softly, very softly, and hid himself where he could hear everything.

When the Woman heard Wild Horse tripping and stumbling on his long mane, she laughed and said, "Here comes the second. Wild Thing out of the Wild Woods what do you want?"

Wild Horse said, "O my Enemy and Wife of my Enemy, where is Wild Dog?"

The Woman laughed, and picked up the blade-bone and looked at it, and said, "Wild Thing out of the Wild Woods, you did not come here for Wild Dog, but for the sake of this good grass."

And Wild Horse, tripping and stumbling on his long mane, said, "That is true; give it me to eat."

The Woman said, "Wild Thing out of the Wild Woods, bend your wild head and wear what I give you, and you shall eat the wonderful grass three times a day."

"Ah," said the Cat, listening, "this is a clever Woman, but she is not so clever as I am."

Wild Horse bent his wild head, and the Woman slipped the plaited hide halter over it, and Wild Horse breathed on the Woman's feet and said, "O my Mistress, and Wife of my Master, I will be your servant for the sake of the wonderful grass."

"Ah," said the Cat, listening, "that is a very foolish Horse." And he went back through the Wet Wild Woods, waving his wild tail and walking by his wild lone. But he never told anybody.

When the Man and the Dog came back from hunting, the Man said, "What is Wild Horse doing here?" And the Woman said, "His name is not Wild Horse any more, but the First Servant, because he will carry us from place to place for always and always and always. Ride on his back when you go hunting."

Next day, holding her wild head high that her wild horns should not catch in the wild trees, Wild Cow came up to the Cave, and the Cat followed, and hid himself just the same as before; and everything happened just the same as before; and the Cat said the same things as before, and when Wild Cow had promised to give her milk to the Woman every day in exchange for the wonderful grass, the Cat went back through the Wet Wild Woods waving his wild tail and walking by his wild lone, just the same as before. But he never told anybody. And when the Man and the Horse and the Dog came home from hunting and asked the same questions same as before, the Woman said, "Her name is not Wild Cow any more, but the Giver of Good Food. She will give us the warm white milk for always and always and always, and I will take care of her while you and the First Friend and the First Servant go hunting."

Next day the Cat waited to see if any other Wild thing would go up to the Cave, but no one moved in the Wet Wild Woods, so the Cat walked there by himself; and he saw the Woman milking the Cow, and he saw the light of the fire in the Cave, and he smelt the smell of the warm white milk.

Cat said, "O my Enemy and Wife of my Enemy, where did Wild Cow go?"

The Woman laughed and said, "Wild Thing out of the Wild Woods, go back to the Woods again, for I have braided up my hair, and I have put away the magic blade-bone, and we have no more need of either friends or servants in our Cave."

Cat said, "I am not a friend, and I am not a servant. I am the Cat who walks by himself, and I wish to come into your Cave."

Woman said, "Then why did you not come with First Friend on the first night?"

Cat grew very angry and said, "Has Wild Dog told tales of me?"

Then the Woman laughed and said, "You are the Cat who walks by himself, and all places are alike to you. You are neither a friend nor a servant. You have said it yourself. Go away and walk by yourself in all places alike."

Then Cat pretended to be sorry and said, "Must I never come into the Cave? Must I never sit by the warm fire? Must I never drink the warm white milk? You are very wise and very beautiful. You should not be cruel even to a Cat."

Woman said, "I knew I was wise, but I did not know I was beautiful. So I will make a bargain with you. If ever I say one word in your praise you may come into the Cave."

"And if you say two words in my praise?" said the Cat.

"I never shall," said the Woman, "but if I say two words in your praise, you may sit by the fire in the Cave."

"And if you say three words?" said the Cat.

"I never shall," said the Woman, "but if I say three words in your praise, you may drink the warm white milk three times a day for always and always and always."

Then the Cat arched his back and said, "Now let the Curtain at the mouth of the Cave, and the Fire at the back of the Cave, and the Milk-pots that stand beside the Fire, remember what my Enemy and the Wife of my Enemy has said." And he went away through the Wet Wild Woods waving his wild tail and walking by his wild lone.

That night when the Man and the Horse and the Dog came home from hunting, the Woman did not tell them of the bar-

gain that she had made with the Cat, because she was afraid
that they might not like it.

Cat went far and far away and hid himself in the Wet Wild
Woods by his wild lone for a long time till the Woman forgot
all about him. Only the Bat—the little upside-down Bat—that
hung inside the Cave, knew where Cat hid; and every evening
Bat would fly to Cat with news of what was happening.

One evening Bat said, "There is a Baby in the Cave. He is new
and pink and fat and small, and the Woman is very fond of
him."

"Ah," said the Cat, listening, "but what is the Baby fond of?"

"He is fond of things that are soft and tickle," said the Bat. "He is fond of warm things to hold in his arms when he goes to sleep. He is fond of being played with. He is fond of all those things."

"Ah," said the Cat, listening, "then my time has come."

Next night Cat walked through the Wet Wild Woods and hid very near the Cave till morning-time, and Man and Dog and Horse went hunting. The Woman was busy cooking that morning, and the Baby cried and interrupted. So she carried him outside the Cave and gave him a handful of pebbles to play with. But still the Baby cried.

Then the Cat put out his paddy paw and patted the Baby on the cheek, and it cooed; and the Cat rubbed against its fat knees and tickled it under its fat chin with his tail. And the Baby laughed; and the Woman heard him and smiled.

Then the Bat—the little upside-down Bat—that hung in the mouth of the Cave said, "O my Hostess and Wife of my Host and Mother of my Host's Son, a Wild Thing from the Wild Woods is most beautifully playing with your Baby."

"A blessing on that Wild Thing whoever he may be," said the Woman, straightening her back, "for I was a busy woman this morning and he has done me a service."

That very minute and second, Best Beloved, the dried horse-skin Curtain that was stretched tail-down at the mouth of the Cave fell down—*woosh!*—because it remembered the bargain she had made with the Cat, and when the Woman went to pick it up—lo and behold!—the Cat was sitting quite comfy inside the Cave.

"O my Enemy and Wife of my Enemy and Mother of my Enemy," said the Cat, "it is I: for you have spoken a word in my praise, and now I can sit within the Cave for always and always and always. But still I am the Cat who walks by himself, and all places are alike to me."

The Woman was very angry, and shut her lips tight and took up her spinning-wheel and began to spin.

But the Baby cried because the Cat had gone away, and the

Woman could not hush it, for it struggled and kicked and grew black in the face.

"O my Enemy and Wife of my Enemy and Mother of my Enemy," said the Cat, "take a strand of the wire that you are spinning and tie it to your spinning-whorl and drag it along the floor, and I will show you a magic that shall make your Baby laugh as loudly as he is now crying."

"I will do so," said the Woman, "because I am at my wits' end; but I will not thank you for it."

She tied the thread to the little clay spindle-whorl and drew it across the floor, and the Cat ran after it and patted it with his paws and rolled head over heels, and tossed it backward over his shoulder and chased it between his hind legs and pretended to lose it, and pounced down upon it again, till the Baby laughed as loudly as it had been crying, and scrambled after the Cat and frolicked all over the Cave till it grew tired and settled down to sleep with the Cat in its arms.

"Now," said the Cat, "I will sing the Baby a song that shall keep him asleep for an hour." And he began to purr, loud and low, low and loud, till the Baby fell fast asleep. The Woman smiled as she looked down upon the two of them and said, "That was wonderfully done. No question but you are very clever, O Cat."

That very minute and second, Best Beloved, the smoke of the fire at the back of the Cave came down in clouds from the roof—*puff!*—because it remembered the bargain she had made with the Cat, and when it had cleared away—lo and behold!—the Cat was sitting quite comfy close to the fire.

"O my Enemy and Wife of my Enemy and Mother of my Enemy," said the Cat, "it is I, for you have spoken a second word in my praise, and now I can sit by the warm fire at the back of the Cave for always and always and always. But still I am the Cat who walks by himself, and all places are alike to me."

Then the Woman was very very angry, and let down her hair and put more wood on the fire and brought out the broad blade-bone of the shoulder of mutton and began to make a Magic that should prevent her from saying a third word in praise of the Cat. It was not a Singing Magic, Best Beloved, it was a Still Magic;

and by and by the Cave grew so still that a little wee-wee mouse crept out of a corner and ran across the floor.

"O my Enemy and Wife of my Enemy and Mother of my Enemy," said the Cat, "is that little mouse part of your magic?"

"Ouh! Chee! No indeed!" said the Woman, and she dropped the blade-bone and jumped upon the footstool in front of the fire and braided up her hair very quick for fear that the mouse should run up it.

"Ah," said the Cat, watching, "then the mouse will do me no harm if I eat it?"

"No," said the Woman, braiding up her hair, "eat it quickly and I will ever be grateful to you."

Cat made one jump and caught the little mouse, and the Woman said, "A hundred thanks. Even the First Friend is not quick enough to catch little mice as you have done. You must be very wise."

That very moment and second, O Best Beloved, the Milk-pot that stood by the fire cracked in two pieces—*ffft*—because it remembered the bargain she had made with the Cat, and when the Woman jumped down from the footstool—lo and behold!—the Cat was lapping up the warm white milk that lay in one of the broken pieces.

"O my Enemy and Wife of my Enemy and Mother of my Enemy," said the Cat, "it is I: for you have spoken three words in my praise, and now I can drink the warm white milk three times a day for always and always and always. But *still* I am the Cat who walks by himself, and all places are alike to me."

Then the Woman laughed and set the Cat a bowl of the warm white milk and said, "O Cat, you are as clever as a man, but remember that your bargain was not made with the Man or the Dog, and I do not know what they will do when they come home."

"What is that to me?" said the Cat. "If I have my place in the Cave by the fire and my warm white milk three times a day I do not care what the Man or the Dog can do."

That evening when the Man and the Dog came into the Cave, the Woman told them all the story of the bargain while the Cat sat by the fire and smiled. Then the Man said, "Yes, but he has

not made a bargain with *me* or with all proper Men after me."
Then he took off his two leather boots and he took up his little
stone axe (that makes three) and he fetched a piece of wood
and a hatchet (that is five altogether), and he set them out in a
row and he said, "Now we will make *our* bargain. If you do not
catch mice when you are in the Cave for always and always and
always, I will throw these five things at you whenever I see you,
and so shall all proper Men do after me."

"Ah," said the Woman, listening, "this is a very clever Cat, but
he is not so clever as my Man."

The Cat counted the five things (and they looked very
knobby) and he said, "I will catch mice when I am in the Cave
for always and always and always; but *still* I am the Cat who
walks by himself, and all places are alike to me."

"Not when I am near," said the Man. "If you had not said
that last I would have put all these things away for always and
always and always; but I am now going to throw my two boots
and my little stone axe (that makes three) at you whenever I
meet you. And so shall all proper Men do afer me!"

Then the Dog said, "Wait a minute. He has not made a
bargain with *me* or with all proper Dogs after me." And he
showed his teeth and said, "If you are not kind to the Baby while
I am in the Cave for always and always and always, I will hunt
you till I catch you, and when I catch you I will bite you. And
so shall all proper Dogs do after me."

"Oh," said the Woman, listening, "this is a very clever Cat,
but he is not so clever as the Dog."

Cat counted the Dog's teeth (and they looked very pointed)
and he said, "I will be kind to the Baby while I am in the Cave,
as long as he does not pull my tail too hard, for always and always
and always. But *still* I am the Cat that walks by himself, and all
places are alike to me."

"Not when I am near," said the Dog. "If you had not said
that last I would have shut my mouth for always and always
and always; but *now* I am going to hunt you up a tree whenever
I meet you. And so shall all proper Dogs do after me."

Then the Man threw his two boots and his little stone axe
(that makes three) at the Cat, and the Cat ran out of the Cave

and the Dog chased him up a tree; and from that day to this, Best Beloved, three proper Men out of five will always throw things at a Cat whenever they meet him, and all proper Dogs will chase him up a tree. But the Cat keeps his side of the bargain too. He will kill mice and he will be kind to Babies when he is in the house, just as long as they do not pull his tail too hard. But when he has done that, and between times, and when the moon gets up and night comes, he is the Cat that walks by himself, and all places are alike to him. Then he goes out to the Wet Wild Woods or up the Wet Wild Trees or on the Wet Wild Roofs, waving his wild tail and walking by his wild lone.

FROM

Rabbit Hill

ROBERT LAWSON

The Rabbits and other small animals on Rabbit Hill are anxiously waiting to find out what sort of people the new folks moving into the Big House will be. They turn out to be most kindly disposed to all the little creatures. As he starts out on his journey, Little Georgie still has his old dog enemies to fear, but, to tell the truth, he really enjoys the dangerous game of outwitting them.

Little Georgie Sings A Song

Iт was barely daylight when Little Georgie started his journey. In spite of her worrying, Mother had managed to put up a small but nourishing lunch. This, along with a letter to Uncle Analdas, was packed in a little knapsack and slung over his shoulder. Father went along as far as the Twin Bridges. As they stepped briskly down the Hill, the whole valley was a lake of mist on which rounded treetops swam like floating islands. From old orchards rose a mounting chorus as the birds greeted the new day. Mothers chirped and chuckled and scolded as they swept and tidied the nests. On the topmost branches their menfolk warbled and shrilled and mocked one another.

The houses were all asleep, even the dogs of the Fat-Man-at-the-Crossroads were quiet, but the Little Animals were up and about. They met the Gray Fox returning from a night up Weston way. He looked footsore and sleepy and a few chicken feathers still clung to his ruff. The Red Buck trotted daintily across the Black Road to wish them good luck and good morning, but

Father, for once, had no time for long social conversation. This was Business, and no rabbit in the county knew his business any better than Father—few as well.

"Now, Son," he said firmly, "your mother is in a very nervous state and you are not to add to her worries by taking unnecessary risks or by carelessness. No dawdling and no foolishness. Keep close to the road but well off it. Watch your bridges and your crossings. What do you do when you come to a bridge?"

"I hide well," answered Georgie, "and wait a good long time. I look all around for dogs. I look up the road for cars and down the road for cars. When everything's clear, I run across—fast. I hide again and look around to be sure I've not been seen. Then I go on. The same thing for crossings."

"Good," said Father. "Now recite your dogs."

Little Georgie closed his eyes and dutifully recited: "Fat-Man-at-the-Crossroads: two Mongrels—Good Hill Road: Dalmatian —House on Long Hill: Collie, noisy, no wind—Norfield Church corner: Police Dog, stupid, no nose—On the High Ridge, red farmhouse: Bulldog and Setter, both fat, don't bother—Farmhouse with the big barns: Old Hound, very dangerous——" and so on he recited every dog on the route clear up to Danbury way. He did it without a mistake and swelled with pride at Father's approving nod.

"Excellent," said Father. "Now do you remember your checks and doublings?" Little Georgie closed his eyes again and rattled off, quite fast, "Sharp right and double left, double left and double right, dead stop and back flip, right jump, left jump, false trip and briar dive."

"Splendid," said Father. "Now attend carefully. Size up your dog; don't waste speed on a plodder, you may need it later. If he's a rusher, check, double, and freeze. Your freeze, by the way, is still rather bad. You have a tendency to flick your left ear, you must watch that. The High Ridge is very open country, so keep in the shadow of the stone walls and mark the earth piles. Porkey has lots of relatives along there and if you are pressed hard, any of them will gladly take you in. Just tell them who you are, and don't forget to thank them. After a chase, hide up and take at least ten minutes' rest. And if you have to *really* run, tighten that knapsack strap, lace back your ears, put your stomach to the ground, and RUN!

"Get along with you now and mind—no foolishness. We shall expect you and Uncle Analdas by tomorrow evening at the latest."

Little Georgie crossed the Twin Bridges in perfect form, returned Father's approving wave, and was off, on his own.

It was gray and misty as he crossed Good Hill Road, and the Dalmatian still slept. So, apparently, did the Collie up the road, for all was quiet as he plodded up Long Hill. People were beginning to stir as he approached Norfield Church corner, little plumes of blue smoke were rising from kitchen chimneys, and the air was pleasant with the smell of frying bacon.

As he expected, the Police Dog rushed him there, but he wasted little time on that affair. Loping along with tantalizing slowness until they were almost on an old fallen apple tree buried in briars, he executed a dead stop, a right jump, and a freeze. The bellowing brute overran him, and plunged headlong into the thorny tangle. His agonized howls were sweet music to Little Georgie as he hopped sedately along toward the High Ridge. He wished Father had been there to see how skillfully he had worked and to note that during the freeze his left ear hadn't flickered once.

The sun was well up when he emerged on the High Ridge. On the porch of the Red Farmhouse the fat Bulldog and the Setter slept soundly, soaking up its warmth. On any other occasion Little Georgie would have been tempted to wake them to enjoy their silly efforts at running, but mindful of Father's instructions he kept dutifully on his way.

The High Ridge was a long and open strip of country, very uninteresting to Little Georgie. The view, over miles and miles of rolling woods and meadows, was very beautiful, but he didn't care especially about views. The brilliant blue sky and the bright little cream-puff clouds were beautiful too. They made him feel good, so did the warm sun, but frankly he was becoming slightly bored. So to ease his boredom he began to make a little song.

The words had been rattling round in his head for some days now and the music was there too, but he couldn't quite get them straight and fitted together. So he hummed and he sang and he whistled. He tried the words this way and that way, he stopped and started and changed the notes around, and finally he got the first line so that it suited him. So Georgie sang that line over and over again to be sure that he wouldn't forget it when he started on the second line.

It must have been this preoccupation with his song that made Little Georgie careless and almost led to his undoing. He scarcely noticed that he had passed the house with the big barns, and he was just starting to sing his first line for the forty-seventh time when there came the roaring rush of the Old Hound right on his heels, so close that he could feel the hot breath.

Instinctively Little Georgie made several wild springs that carried him temporarily out of harm's way. He paused a fraction of a second to tighten the knapsack strap and then set off at a good steady pace. "Don't waste speed on a plodder" was Father's rule. He tried a few checks and doubles and circlings, although he knew they were pretty useless. The great fields were too bare and the Old Hound knew all the tricks. No matter how he turned and dodged, the Hound was always there, coming along at his heavy gallop. He looked for woodchuck burrows, but there were none in sight. "Well, I guess I'll have to run it out," said Little Georgie.

He pulled the knapsack strap tighter, laced back his ears, put his stomach to the ground, and RAN. And *how* he ran!

The warm sun had loosened his muscles, the air was invigorating, Little Georgie's leaps grew longer and longer. Never had he felt so young and strong. His legs were like coiled springs of steel that released themselves of their own accord. He was hardly conscious of any effort, only of his hind feet pounding the ground, and each time they hit, those wonderful springs released and shot him through the air. He sailed over fences and stone walls as though they were mole runs. Why, this was almost like flying! Now he understood what Zip the Swallow had been driving at when he tried to describe what it was like. He glanced back at the Old Hound, far behind now, but still coming along at his plodding gallop. He was old and must be tiring while he, Little Georgie, felt stronger and more vigorous at every leap. Why didn't the old fool give up and go home?

And then, as he shot over the brow of a slight rise, he suddenly knew. *He had forgotten Deadman's Brook!* There it lay before him, broad and deep, curving out in a great silvery loop. He, the son of Father, gentleman hunter from the Bluegrass, had been driven into a trap, a trap that even Porkey should have been able to avoid! Whether he turned to right or left, the loop of the creek hemmed him in and the Old Hound could easily cut him off. There was nothing for it but to jump!

This sickening realization had not reduced his speed; now he redoubled it. The slope helped and his soaring leaps became prodigious. The wind whistled through his laced-back ears. Still he kept his head, as Father would have wished him to. He picked a spot where the bank was high and firm; he spaced his jumps so they would come out exactly right.

The take-off was perfect. He put every ounce of leg muscle into that final kick and sailed out into space. Below him he could see the cream-puff clouds mirrored in the dark water; he could see the pebbles on the bottom and the silver flash of frightened minnows, dashing away from his flying shadow. Then, with a breath-taking thump, he landed, turned seven somersaults, and came up sitting in a clump of soft lush grass.

He froze, motionless except for heaving sides, and watched the Old Hound come thundering down the slope, slide to a stop and, after eyeing the water disgustedly, take his way slowly homeward, his dripping tongue almost dragging the ground.

Little Georgie did not need to remember Father's rule for a ten-minute rest after a good run. He was blown and he knew it, but he did remember his lunch, so he unstrapped the little knapsack and combined lunch and rest. He had been really scared for a moment, but as his wind came back and his lunch went down, his spirits came up.

Father would be angry, and rightly, for he had made two very stupid mistakes: he had let himself be surprised and he had run right into a dangerous trap. But that leap! Never in the history of the county had any rabbit jumped Deadman's Brook, not even Father. He marked the exact spot and calculated the width of the stream there—at least eighteen feet! And with his rising spirits the words and the notes of his song suddenly tumbled into place.

Little Georgie lay back in the warm grass and sang his song—

> *New Folks coming, Oh My!*
> *New Folks coming, Oh My!*
> *New Folks coming, Oh My!*
> *Oh my! Oh my!*

There weren't many words and there weren't many notes, and the notes just went up a little and down a little and ended where they began. Lots of people might have thought it monotonous, but it suited Little Georgie completely. He sang it loud and he sang it soft, he sang it as a paean of triumph, a saga of perils met and overcome. He sang it over and over again.

Red-Bellied Robin, flying northward, paused in a sapling and called down, "Hi, Little Georgie, what're you doing way up here?"

"Going to fetch Uncle Analdas. Have you been by the Hill?"

"Just left there," Robin answered. "Everybody's excited. Seems there's new Folks coming."

"Yes, I know," cried Little Georgie eagerly. "I've just made a song about it. Wouldn't you like to hear it? It goes like——"

"No, thanks," called Robin. "Getting along——" and flew on.

Not in the least discouraged, Little Georgie sang his song a few times more while he strapped on his knapsack and took up his journey. It was a good song to walk to, too, so he sang it as he tramped the rest of the High Ridge, as he went down the Windy Hill and circled around Georgetown. He was still singing it in the late afternoon when he got clear up Danbury way.

He had just finished "Oh my!" for the four thousandth time when a sharp voice from the bushes broke in with "Oh my— *what?*"

Little Georgie whirled. "Oh my—*goodness!*" he cried. "Why —why, it's Uncle Analdas."

"Sure *is,*" the voice chuckled. "Uncle Analdas as ever was. Come in, Little Georgie, come in—you're a long way from home.

Ef I'd been a dog, I'd got you. Surprised yer Old Man ain't learned you more care—come in, anyhow."

Although Mother had worried about the state of Uncle Analdas's home with no feminine hands around to keep things neat, she could never, in her most pessimistic moments, have

pictured anything quite so disorderly as the burrow to which Little Georgie was welcomed.

It was a man's home, there could be no doubt about that, and while Little Georgie rather admired the bachelor freedom of the place, he was forced to admit that it really was extremely dirty and the fleas numerous and active. After his day in the open air, the atmosphere indoors seemed stifling and not at all fragrant. Perhaps it was the sort of tobacco that Uncle Analdas smoked—Little Georgie hoped so. His Uncle's cooking too left something to be desired—their supper consisted of one very ancient and dried-up turnip. After this meager meal, they sat outside, at Little Georgie's suggestion, and Mother's letter was produced.

"S'pose you read it to me, Georgie," said Uncle Analdas. "Seem to've mislaid them dingblasted spectacles." Little Georgie knew that he hadn't mislaid them, in fact that he didn't own any; he'd just never learned to read, but this formality always had to be gone through with, so he dutifully read:

> *Dear Uncle Analdas:*
> I hope this finds you well but I know you are lonesome with Mildred married and gone away and all and we are hoping you will spend the summer with us, as we have new Folks coming and we hope they are planting Folks and if they are we will all eat good but they may have dogs or poison or traps and spring-guns and maybe you shouldn't risk your life although you haven't much of it left but we will be looking forward to seeing you anyway.
>
> > *Your loving niece,*
> > MOLLIE

There was a postscript which said, "P.S. Please don't let Little Georgie get his feet wet," but Georgie didn't read that out loud. The idea! He, Little Georgie, who had jumped Deadman's Brook, Little Georgie the Leaper, getting his feet wet!

"Well, now," cried Uncle Analdas. "Well, now, that's a real nice letter, real nice. Don't know but what I will. Certainly is dingblasted lonesome 'round here now, with Millie gone and all. And as for food— Of all the carrot-pinchin', stingy folks I ever see, the folks around here is the stingiest, carrot-pinchin'est. Yes sir, I think I will. 'Course new Folks coming may be good and it may be bad. Either way I don't trust 'em. Don't trust old Folks neither. But with old Folks you kin tell just how much you *can't* trust 'em and with new Folks you can't tell *nothing.* Think I'll do it though, think I will. Does yer Maw still make that peavine and lettuce soup as good as she used to?"

Little Georgie assured him that she still did and wished he had a bowl of it right then. "I've made up a song about the new Folks," he added eagerly. "Would you like to hear it?"

"Don't think I would," answered Uncle Analdas. "Sleep anywheres you've a mind to, Georgie. I've got a few knickknacks to pack up and we'd ought to get an early start. I'll wake you."

Little Georgie decided to sleep outside under the bushes. The evening was quite warm and the burrow was really pretty strong. He hummed his song, as a lullaby now, and it was a good lullaby, for before he'd finished it the third time he was sound asleep.

FROM

The Adventures of Old Mr. Toad

THORNTON BURGESS

Old Mother Nature doth provide
For all her children, large or small.
Her wisdom foresees all their needs
And makes provision for them all.

Old Mr. Toad's Queer Tongue

I<small>F YOU</small> don't believe it, just you go ask Old Mr. Toad, as Peter Rabbit did, how such a slow-moving fellow as he is can catch enough bugs and insects to keep him alive. Perhaps you'll learn something just as Peter did. Peter and Old Mr. Toad sat in the rain watching the tiny Toads, who, you know, were Mr. Toad's children, leaving their kindergarten in the Smiling Pool and starting out to see the Great World. When the last little Toad had passed them, Old Mr. Toad suddenly remembered that he was hungry, very hungry indeed.

"Didn't have time to eat much while I was in the Smiling Pool," he explained. "Couldn't eat and sing too, and while I was down there, I was supposed to sing. Now that it is time to quit singing, I begin to realize that I've got a stomach to look out for as well as a voice. See that bug over there on that leaf? Watch him."

Peter looked, and sure enough there was a fat bug crawling along on an old leaf. He was about two inches from Old Mr. Toad, and he was crawling very fast. And right while Peter was looking at him he disappeared. Peter turned to look at Old Mr. Toad. He hadn't budged. He was sitting exactly where he had been sitting all the time, but he was smacking his lips, and there was a twinkle of satisfaction in his eyes. Peter opened his eyes very wide.

"Wha—what—" he began.

"Nice bug," interrupted Old Mr. Toad. "Nicest bug I've eaten for a long time."

"But I didn't see you catch him!" protested Peter, looking at Old Mr. Toad as if he suspected him of joking.

"Anything wrong with your eyes?" inquired Old Mr. Toad.

"No," replied Peter just a wee bit crossly. "My eyes are just as good as ever."

"Then watch me catch that fly over yonder," said Old Mr. Toad. He hopped towards a fly which had lighted on a blade of grass just ahead. About two inches from it he stopped, and so far as Peter could see, he sat perfectly still. But the fly disappeared, and it wasn't because it flew away, either. Peter was sure of that. As he told Mrs. Peter about it afterwards, "It was there, and then it wasn't, and that was all there was to it."

Old Mr. Toad chuckled. "Didn't you see that one go, Peter?" he asked.

Peter shook his head. "I wish you would stop fooling me," said Peter. "The joke is on me, but now you've had your laugh at my expense, I wish you would tell me how you do it. Please, Mr. Toad."

Now when Peter said please that way, of course Old Mr. Toad couldn't resist him. Nobody could.

"Here comes an ant this way. Now you watch my mouth instead of the ant and see what happens," said Old Mr. Toad.

Peter looked and saw a big black ant coming. Then he kept his eyes on Old Mr. Toad's mouth. Suddenly there was a little flash of red from it, so tiny and so quick that Peter couldn't be absolutely sure that he saw it. But when he looked for the ant, it was nowhere to be seen. Peter looked at Old Mr. Toad very hard.

"Do you mean to tell me, Mr. Toad, that you've got a tongue long enough to reach way over to where that ant was?" he asked.

Old Mr. Toad chuckled again. With every insect swallowed he felt better-natured. "You've guessed it, Peter," said he. "Handy tongue, isn't it?"

"I think it's a very queer tongue," retorted Peter, "and I don't understand it at all. If it's so long as all that, where do you keep it when it isn't in use? I should think you'd have to swallow it to get it out of the way, or else leave it hanging out of your mouth."

"Ha, ha, ha, ha, ha!" laughed Old Mr. Toad. "My tongue never is in the way, and it's the handiest tongue in the world. I'll show it to you."

Old Mr. Toad Shows His Tongue

To show one's tongue, as you well know,
Is not considered nice to do;
But if it were like Mr. Toad's
I'd want to show it—wouldn't you?

I'm quite sure you would. You see, if it were like Old Mr. Toad's, it would be such a wonderful tongue that I suspect you would want everybody to see it. Old Mr. Toad thinks his tongue the most satisfactory tongue in the world. In fact, he is quite sure that without it he couldn't get along at all, and I don't know as he could. And yet very few of his neighbors know anything about that tongue and how different it is from most other tongues. Peter Rabbit didn't until Old Mr. Toad showed him after Peter had puzzled and puzzled over the mysterious way in which bugs and flies disappeared whenever they happened to come within two inches or less of Old Mr. Toad.

What Peter couldn't understand was what Old Mr. Toad did with a tongue that would reach two inches beyond his mouth. He said as much.

"I'll show you my tongue, and then you'll wish you had one just like it," said Old Mr. Toad, with a twinkle in his eyes.

He opened his big mouth and slowly ran his tongue out its full length. "Why! Why-ee!" exclaimed Peter. "It's fastened at the wrong end!"

"No such thing!" replied Old Mr. Toad indignantly. "If it was fastened at the other end, how could I run it out so far?"

"But mine and all other tongues that I ever have seen are fastened way down in the throat," protested Peter. "Yours is fastened at the other end, way in the very front of your mouth. I never heard of such a thing."

"There are a great many things you have never heard of, Peter Rabbit," replied Old Mr. Toad dryly. "Mine is the right way to have a tongue. Because it is fastened way up in the front of my mouth that way, I can use the whole of it. You see, it goes out its full length. Then, when I draw it in with a bug on the end of it, I just turn it over so that the end that was out goes way back in my throat and takes the bug with it to just the right place to swallow."

Peter thought this over for a few minutes before he ventured another question. "I begin to understand," said he, "but how do you hold on to the bug with your tongue?"

"My tongue is sticky, of course, Mr. Stupid," replied Old Mr. Toad, looking very much disgusted. "Just let me touch a bug with it, and he's mine every time."

Peter thought this over. Then he felt of his own tongue. "Mine isn't sticky," said he very innocently.

Old Mr. Toad laughed right out. "Perhaps if it was, you couldn't ask so many questions," said he. "Now watch me catch that fly." His funny little tongue darted out, and the fly was gone.

"It certainly is very handy," said Peter politely. "I think we are going to have more rain, and I'd better be getting back to the dear Old Briar-patch. Very much obliged to you, Mr. Toad. I think you are very wonderful."

"Not at all," replied Old Mr. Toad. "I've simply got the things I need in order to live, just as you have the things you need. I couldn't get along with your kind of a tongue, but no more could you get along with mine. If you live long enough, you will learn that Old Mother Nature makes no mistakes. She gives each of us what we need, and each one has different needs."

FROM

The Story of Doctor Dolittle

HUGH LOFTING

Doctor Dolittle is a kindly animal-loving old doctor who pays so much attention to his pets, and so little to his patients that he finally loses them all. After his grateful parrot Polynesia has taught him how to understand animal language, however, he becomes famous all over the world as the animal's own doctor.

Animal Language

IT HAPPENED one day that the Doctor was sitting in his kitchen talking with the Cat's-meat-Man who had come to see him with a stomach-ache.

"Why don't you give up being a people's doctor, and be an animal-doctor?" asked the Cat's-meat-Man.

The parrot, Polynesia, was sitting in the window looking out at the rain and singing a sailor-song to herself. She stopped singing and started to listen.

"You see, Doctor," the Cat's-meat-Man went on, "you know all about animals—much more than what these here vets do. That book you wrote—about cats, why, it's wonderful! I can't read or write myself—or maybe *I'd* write some books. But my wife, Theodosia, she's a scholar, she is. And she read your book to me. Well, it's wonderful—that's all can be said—wonderful. You might have been a cat yourself. You know the way they think. And listen: you can make a lot of money doctoring animals. Do you know that? You see, I'd send all the old women who had sick cats or dogs to you. And if they didn't get sick fast enough, I could put something in the meat I sell 'em to make 'em sick, see?"

"Oh, no," said the Doctor quickly. "You mustn't do that. That wouldn't be right."

"Oh, I didn't mean real sick," answered the Cat's-meat-Man. "Just a little something to make them droopy-like was what I had reference to. But as you say, maybe it ain't quite fair on the animals. But they'll get sick anyway, because the old women always give 'em too much to eat. And look, all the farmers round about who had lame horses and weak lambs—they'd come. Be an animal-doctor."

When the Cat's-meat-Man had gone the parrot flew off the window on to the Doctor's table and said:

"That man's got sense. That's what you ought to do. Be an animal-doctor. Give the silly people up—if they haven't brains enough to see you're the best doctor in the world. Take care of animals instead—*they'll* soon find it out. Be an animal-doctor."

"Oh, there are plenty of animal-doctors," said John Dolittle, putting the flower-pots outside on the window-sill to get the rain.

"Yes, there *are* plenty," said Polynesia. "But none of them are any good at all. Now listen, Doctor, and I'll tell you something. Did you know that animals can talk?"

"I knew that parrots can talk," said the Doctor.

"Oh, we parrots can talk in two languages—people's language and bird-language," said Polynesia proudly. "If I say, 'Polly wants a cracker,' you understand me. But hear this: *Ka-ka oi-ee, fee-fee?*"

"Good Gracious!" cried the Doctor. "What does that mean?"

"That means, 'Is the porridge hot yet?'—in bird-language."

"My! You don't say so!" said the Doctor. "You never talked that way to me before."

"What would have been the good?" said Polynesia, dusting some cracker-crumbs off her left wing. "You wouldn't have understood me if I had."

"Tell me some more," said the Doctor, all excited; and he

rushed over to the dresser-drawer and came back with the butcher's book and a pencil. "Now don't go too fast—and I'll write it down. This is interesting—very interesting—something quite new. Give me the Birds' A.B.C.'s first—slowly now."

So that was the way the Doctor came to know that animals had a language of their own and could talk to one another. And all that afternoon, while it was raining, Polynesia sat on the kitchen table giving him bird words to put down in the book.

At tea-time, when the dog, Jip, came in, the parrot said to the Doctor, "See, *he's* talking to you."

"Looks to me as though he were scratching his ear," said the Doctor.

"But animals don't always speak with their mouths," said the parrot in a high voice, raising her eyebrows. "They talk with their ears, with their feet, with their tails—with everything. Sometimes they don't *want* to make a noise. Do you see now the way he's twitching up one side of his nose?"

"What's that mean?" asked the Doctor.

"That means, 'Can't you see that it has stopped raining?'" Polynesia answered. "He is asking you a question. Dogs nearly always use their noses for asking questions."

After a while, with the parrot's help, the Doctor got to learn the language of the animals so well that he could talk to them himself and understand everything they said. Then he gave up being a people's doctor altogether.

As soon as the Cat's-meat-Man had told every one that John Dolittle was going to become an animal-doctor, old ladies began to bring him their pet pugs and poodles who had eaten too much cake; and farmers came many miles to show him sick cows and sheep.

One day a plow-horse was brought to him; and the poor thing was terribly glad to find a man who could talk in horse-language.

"You know, Doctor," said the horse, "that vet over the hill knows nothing at all. He has been treating me six weeks now— for spavins. What I need is *spectacles*. I am going blind in one eye. There's no reason why horses shouldn't wear glasses, the same as people. But that stupid man over the hill never even looked at my eyes. He kept on giving me big pills. I tried to tell him; but he couldn't understand a word of horse-language. What I need is spectacles."

"Of course—of course," said the Doctor. "I'll get you some at once."

"I would like a pair like yours," said the horse—"only green. They'll keep the sun out of my eyes while I'm plowing the Fifty-Acre Field."

"Certainly," said the Doctor. "Green ones you shall have."

"You know, the trouble is, Sir," said the plow-horse as the Doctor opened the front door to let him out—"the trouble is that *anybody* thinks he can doctor animals—just because the animals don't complain. As a matter of fact it takes a much cleverer man to be a really good animal-doctor than it does to be a good people's doctor. My farmer's boy thinks he knows all about horses. I wish you could see him—his face is so fat he looks as though he had no eyes—and he has got as much brain as a potato-bug. He tried to put a mustard-plaster on me last week."

"Where did he put it?" asked the Doctor.

"Oh, he didn't put it anywhere—on me," said the horse. "He only tried to. I kicked him into the duck-pond."

"Well, well!" said the Doctor.

"I'm a pretty quiet creature as a rule," said the horse—"very patient with people—don't make much fuss. But it was bad enough to have that vet giving me the wrong medicine. And when that red-faced booby started to monkey with me, I just couldn't bear it any more."

"Did you hurt the boy much?" asked the Doctor.

"Oh, no," said the horse. "I kicked him in the right place. The vet's looking after him now. When will my glasses be ready?"

"I'll have them for you next week," said the Doctor. "Come in again Tuesday— Good morning!"

Then John Dolittle got a fine, big pair of green spectacles; and the plow-horse stopped going blind in one eye and could see as well as ever.

And soon it became a common sight to see farm-animals wearing glasses in the country round Puddleby; and a blind horse was a thing unknown.

And so it was with all the other animals that were brought to him. As soon as they found that he could talk their language, they told him where the pain was and how they felt, and of course it was easy for him to cure them.

Now all these animals went back and told their brothers and friends that there was a doctor in the little house with a big

Illustration by Hugh Lofting

garden who really *was* a doctor. And whenever any creatures got sick—not only horses and cows and dogs—but all the little things of the fields, like harvest-mice and water-voles, badgers and bats, they came at once to his house on the edge of the town, so that his big garden was nearly always crowded with animals trying to get in to see him.

There were so many that came that he had to have special doors made for the different kinds. He wrote "HORSES" over the front door, "COWS" over the side door, and "SHEEP" on the kitchen door. Each kind of animal had a separate door —even the mice had a tiny tunnel made for them into the cellar, where they waited patiently in rows for the Doctor to come round to them.

And so, in a few years' time, every living thing for miles and miles got to know about John Dolittle, M.D. And the birds who flew to other countries in the winter told the animals in foreign lands of the wonderful doctor of Puddleby-on-the-Marsh, who could understand their talk and help them in their troubles. In this way he became famous among the animals—all over the world—better known even than he had been among the folks of the West Country. And he was happy and liked his life very much.

One afternoon when the Doctor was busy writing in a book, Polynesia sat in the window—as she nearly always did—looking out at the leaves blowing about in the garden. Presently she laughed aloud.

"What is it, Polynesia?" asked the Doctor, looking up from his book.

"I was just thinking," said the parrot; and she went on looking at the leaves.

"What were you thinking?"

"I was thinking about people," said Polynesia. "People make me sick. They think they're so wonderful. The world has been going on now for thousands of years, hasn't it? And the only thing in animal-language that *people* have learned to understand is that when a dog wags his tail he means 'I'm glad!'—It's funny, isn't it? You are the very first man to talk like us. Oh, sometimes people annoy me dreadfully—such airs they put on—talking about 'the dumb animals.' *Dumb!*—Huh! Why I knew a macaw once who could say 'Good morning!' in seven different ways without once opening his mouth. He could talk every language —and Greek. An old professor with a gray beard bought him. But he didn't stay. He said the old man didn't talk Greek right, and he couldn't stand listening to him teach the language wrong. I often wonder what's become of him. That bird knew more geography than people will ever know.—*People*, Golly! I suppose if people ever learn to fly—like any common hedge-sparrow—we shall never hear the end of it!"

"You're a wise old bird," said the Doctor. "How old are you really? I know that parrots and elephants sometimes live to be very, very old."

"I can never be quite sure of my age," said Polynesia. "It's either a hundred and eighty-three or a hundred and eighty-two. But I know that when I first came here from Africa, King Charles was still hiding in the oak-tree—because I saw him. He looked scared to death."

FROM

The Wind in the Willows

KENNETH GRAHAME

The Mole is rescued from the dangers of the Wild Wood by his friend, the Water Rat. But now a snowstorm comes up suddenly and they are both about to be lost. Luckily Ratty discovers the entrance to the underground home of Mr. Badger—one of the wisest and kindest of all the delightful animals in The Wind in the Willows.

Mr. Badger

THEY waited patiently for what seemed a very long time, stamping in the snow to keep their feet warm. At last they heard the sound of slow shuffling footsteps approaching the door from the inside. It seemed, as the Mole remarked to the Rat, like some one walking in carpet slippers that were too large for him and down-at-heel; which was intelligent of Mole, because that was exactly what it was.

There was the noise of a bolt shot back, and the door opened a few inches, enough to show a long snout and a pair of sleepy, blinking eyes.

"Now, the *very* next time this happens," said a gruff and suspicious voice, "I shall be exceedingly angry. Who is it *this* time, disturbing people on such a night? Speak up!"

"O, Badger," cried the Rat, "let us in, please. It's me, Rat, and my friend Mole, and we've lost our way in the snow."

"What, Ratty, my dear little man!" exclaimed the Badger, in quite a different voice. "Come along in, both of you, at once. Why, you must be perished. Well I never! Lost in the snow! And in the Wild Wood, too, and at this time of night! But come in with you."

The two animals tumbled over each other in their eagerness to get inside, and heard the door shut behind them with great joy and relief.

The Badger, who wore a long dressing-gown, and whose slippers were indeed very down-at-heel, carried a flat candlestick in his paw and had probably been on his way to bed when their summons sounded. He looked kindly down on them and patted both their heads. "This is not the sort of night for small animals to be out," he said paternally. "I'm afraid you've been up to some of your pranks again, Ratty. But come along; come into the kitchen. There's a first-rate fire there, and supper and everything."

He shuffled on in front of them, carrying the light, and they followed him, nudging each other in an anticipating sort of way, down a long, gloomy, and, to tell the truth, decidedly shabby passage, into a sort of a central hall, out of which they could dimly see other long tunnel-like passages branching, passages mysterious and without apparent end. But there were doors in the hall as well—stout oaken comfortable-looking doors. One of these the Badger flung open, and at once they found themselves in all the glow and warmth of a large fire-lit kitchen.

Illustration by E. H. Shepard

The floor was well-worn red brick, and on the wide hearth burnt a fire of logs, between two attractive chimney-corners tucked away in the wall, well out of any suspicion of draught.

A couple of high-backed settles, facing each other on either side of the fire, gave further sitting accommodation for the sociably disposed. In the middle of the room stood a long table of plain boards placed on trestles, with benches down each side. At one end of it, where an arm-chair stood pushed back, were spread the remains of the Badger's plain but ample supper. Rows of spotless plates winked from the shelves of the dresser at the far end of the room, and from the rafters overhead hung hams, bundles of dried herbs, nets of onions, and baskets of eggs. It seemed a place where heroes could fitly feast after victory, where weary harvesters could line up in scores along the table and keep their Harvest Home with mirth and song, or where two or three friends of simple tastes could sit about as they pleased and eat and smoke and talk in comfort and contentment. The ruddy brick floor smiled up at the smoky ceiling; the oaken settles, shiny with long wear, exchanged cheerful glances with each other; plates on the dresser grinned at pots on the shelf, and the merry firelight flickered and played over everything without distinction.

The kindly Badger thrust them down on a settle to toast themselves at the fire, and bade them remove their wet coats and boots. Then he fetched them dressing-gowns and slippers, and himself bathed the Mole's shin with warm water and mended the cut with sticking-plaster till the whole thing was just as good as new, if not better. In the embracing light and warmth, warm and dry at last, with weary legs propped up in front of them, and a suggestive clink of plates being arranged on the table behind, it seemed to the storm-driven animals, now in safe anchorage, that the cold and trackless Wild Wood just left outside was miles and miles away, and all that they had suffered in it a half-forgotten dream.

When at last they were thoroughly toasted, the Badger summoned them to the table, where he had been busy laying a repast. They had felt pretty hungry before, but when they actually saw at last the supper that was spread for them, really it seemed only a question of what they should attack first where all was so attractive, and whether the other things would obligingly wait for them till they had time to give them attention. Conversation was impossible for a long time; and when it was slowly resumed, it was that regrettable sort of conversation that results from talking with your mouth full. The Badger did not mind that sort of thing at all, nor did he take any notice of elbows on the table, or everybody speaking at once. As he did not go into Society himself, he had got an idea that these things belonged to the things that didn't really matter. (We know of course that he was wrong, and took too narrow a view; because they do matter very much, though it would take too long to explain why.) He sat in his arm-chair at the head of the table, and nodded gravely at intervals as the animals told their story; and he did not seem surprised or shocked at anything, and he never said, "I told you so," or, "Just what I always said," or remarked that they ought to have done so-and-so, or ought not to have done something else. The Mole began to feel very friendly towards him.

When supper was really finished at last, and each animal felt that his skin was now as tight as was decently safe, and that by this time he didn't care a hang for anybody or anything, they gathered round the glowing embers of the great wood fire, and thought how jolly it was to be sitting up *so* late, and *so* independent, and *so* full; and after they had chatted for a time about things in general, the Badger said heartily, "Now then! tell us the news from your part of the world. How's old Toad going on?"

"O, from bad to worse," said the Rat gravely, while the Mole, cocked up on a settle and basking in the firelight, his heels higher than his head, tried to look properly mournful. "Another smash-up only last week, and a bad one. You see, he will insist on driving himself, and he's hopelessly incapable. If he'd only employ a decent, steady, well-trained animal, pay him good wages, and leave everything to him, he'd get on all right. But no; he's convinced he's a heaven-born driver, and nobody can teach him anything; and all the rest follows."

"How many has he had?" inquired the Badger gloomily.

"Smashes, or machines?" asked the Rat. "O, well, after all, it's the same thing—with Toad. This is the seventh. As for the others—you know that coach-house of his? Well, it's piled up —literally piled up to the roof—with fragments of motor-cars none of them bigger than your hat! That accounts for the other six—so far as they can be accounted for."

"He's been in hospital three times," put in the Mole; "and as for the fines he's had to pay, it's simply awful to think of."

"Yes, and that's part of the trouble," continued the Rat. "Toad's rich, we all know; but he's not a millionaire. And he's a hopelessly bad driver, and quite regardless of law and order. Killed or ruined—it's got to be one of the two things, sooner or later. Badger! we're his friends—oughtn't we to do something?"

The Badger went through a bit of hard thinking. "Now look here!" he said at last, rather severely; "of course you know I can't do anything *now?*"

His two friends assented, quite understanding his point. No animal, according to the rules of animal-etiquette, is ever expected to do anything strenuous, or heroic, or even moderately active during the off-season of winter. All are sleepy—some actually asleep. All are weather-bound, more or less; and all are resting from arduous days and nights, during which every muscle in them has been severely tested, and every energy kept at full stretch.

"Very well then!" continued the Badger. "*But,* when once the year has really turned, and the nights are shorter, and half-way through them one rouses and feels fidgety and wanting to be up and doing by sunrise, if not before—*you* know!——"

Both animals nodded gravely. *They* knew!

"Well, *then,*" went on the Badger, "we—that is, you and me and our friend the Mole here—we'll take Toad seriously in hand. We'll stand no nonsense whatever. We'll bring him back to reason, by force if need be. We'll *make* him be a sensible Toad. We'll—you're asleep, Rat!"

"Not me!" said the Rat, waking up with a jerk.

"He's been asleep two or three times since supper," said the Mole, laughing. He himself was feeling quite wakeful and even lively, though he didn't know why. The reason was, of course, that he being naturally an underground animal by birth and breeding, the situation of Badger's house exactly suited him and made him feel at home; while the Rat, who slept every night in a bedroom the windows of which opened on a breezy river, naturally felt the atmosphere still and oppressive.

"Well, it's time we were all in bed," said the Badger, getting up and fetching flat candlesticks. "Come along, you two, and I'll show you your quarters. And take your time to-morrow morning —breakfast at any hour you please!"

He conducted the two animals to a long room that seemed half bedchamber and half loft. The Badger's winter stores, which indeed were visible everywhere, took up half the room—piles of apples, turnips, and potatoes, baskets full of nuts, and jars of honey; but the two little white beds on the remainder of the floor looked soft and inviting, and the linen on them, though coarse, was clean and smelt beautifully of lavender; and the Mole and the Water Rat, shaking off their garments in some thirty seconds, tumbled in between the sheets in great joy and contentment.

In accordance with the kindly Badger's injunctions, the two tired animals came down to breakfast very late next morning, and found a bright fire burning in the kitchen, and two young hedgehogs sitting on a bench at the table, eating oatmeal porridge out of wooden bowls. The hedgehogs dropped their spoons, rose to their feet, and ducked their heads respectfully as the two entered.

"There, sit down, sit down," said the Rat pleasantly, "and go on with your porridge. Where have you youngsters come from? Lost your way in the snow, I suppose?"

"Yes, please, sir," said the elder of the two hedgehogs respectfully. "Me and little Billy here, we was trying to find our way to school—mother *would* have us go, was the weather ever so—and of course we lost ourselves, sir, and Billy he got frightened and took and cried, being young and faint-hearted. And at last we happened up against Mr. Badger's back door, and made so bold as to knock, sir, for Mr. Badger he's a kind-hearted gentleman, as every one knows——"

"I understand," said the Rat, cutting himself some rashers from a side of bacon, while the Mole dropped some eggs into a saucepan. "And what's the weather like outside? You needn't 'sir' me quite so much," he added.

"O, terrible, bad, sir, terrible deep the snow is," said the hedge-hog. "No getting out for the likes of you gentlemen to-day."

"Where's Mr. Badger?" inquired the Mole, as he warmed the coffee-pot before the fire.

Illustration by E. H. Shepard

"The master's gone into his study, sir," replied the hedgehog, "and he said as how he was going to be particular busy this morning, and on no account was he to be disturbed."

This explanation, of course, was thoroughly understood by every one present. The fact is, as already set forth, when you live a life of intense activity for six months in the year, and of comparative or actual somnolence for the other six, during the latter period you cannot be continually pleading sleepiness when there are people about or things to be done. The excuse gets monotonous. The animals well knew that Badger, having eaten a hearty breakfast, had retired to his study and settled himself in an arm-chair with his legs up on another and a red cotton hand-kerchief over his face, and was being "busy" in the usual way at this time of the year.

The front-door bell clanged loudly, and the Rat, who was very greasy with buttered toast, sent Billy, the smaller hedgehog, to see who it might be. There was a sound of much stamping in the hall, and presently Billy returned in front of the Otter, who threw himself on the Rat with an embrace and a shout of affectionate greeting.

"Get off!" spluttered the Rat, with his mouth full.

"Thought I should find you here all right," said the Otter cheerfully. "They were all in a great state of alarm along River Bank when I arrived this morning. Rat never been home all night —nor Mole either—something dreadful must have happened, they said; and the snow had covered up all your tracks, of course. But I knew that when people were in any fix they mostly went to Badger, or else Badger got to know of it somehow, so I came straight off here, through the Wild Wood and the snow! My! it was fine, coming through the snow as the red sun was rising and showing against the black tree-trunks! As you went along in the stillness, every now and then masses of snow slid off the branches suddenly with a flop! making you jump and run for cover. Snow-castles and snow-caverns had sprung up out of nowhere in the night—and snow bridges, terraces, ramparts—I could have stayed and played with them for hours. Here and there great branches had been torn away by the sheer weight of the snow, and robins perched and hopped on them in their perky conceited way, just as if they had done it themselves. A ragged string of wild geese passed overhead, high on the grey sky, and a few rooks whirled over the trees, inspected, and flapped off homewards with a disgusted expression; but I met no sensible being to ask the news of. About halfway across I came on a rabbit sitting on a stump, cleaning his silly face with his paws. He was a pretty scared animal when I crept up behind him and placed a heavy fore-paw on his shoulder. I had to cuff his head once or twice to get any sense out of it at all. At last I managed to extract from him that Mole had been seen in the Wild Wood last night by one of them. It was the talk of the burrows, he said, how Mole, Mr. Rat's particular friend, was in a bad fix; how he had lost his way, and 'They' were up and out hunting, and were chivvying him round and round. 'Then why didn't any of you *do* something?' I asked. 'You mayn't be blest with brains, but there are hundreds and hundreds of you, big stout fellows, as fat as butter, and your burrows running in all directions, and you could have taken him in and made him safe and comfortable, or tried to, at all events. 'What, us?' he merely said: '*do* something? us rabbits?' So I cuffed him again and left him. There was nothing else to be done. At any rate, I had learnt something; and if I had had the luck to meet any of 'Them' I'd have learnt something more—or *they* would."

"Weren't you at all—er—nervous?" asked the Mole, some of

yesterday's terror coming back to him at the mention of the Wild Wood.

"Nervous?" The Otter showed a gleaming set of strong white teeth as he laughed. "I'd give 'em nerves if any of them tried anything on with me. Here, Mole, fry me some slices of ham, like the good little chap you are. I'm frightfully hungry, and I've got any amount to say to Ratty here. Haven't seen him for an age."

So the good-natured Mole, having cut some slices of ham, set the hedgehogs to fry it, and returned to his own breakfast, while the Otter and the Rat, their heads together, eagerly talked river-shop, which is long shop and talk that is endless, running on like the babbling river itself.

A plate of fried ham had just been cleared and sent back for more, when the Badger entered, yawning and rubbing his eyes, and greeted them all in his quiet, simple way, with kind inquiries for every one. "It must be getting on for luncheon time," he remarked to the Otter. "Better stop and have it with us. You must be hungry, this cold morning."

"Rather!" replied the Otter, winking at the Mole. "The sight of these greedy young hedgehogs stuffing themselves with fried ham makes me feel positively famished."

The hedgehogs, who were just beginning to feel hungry again after their porridge, and after working so hard at their frying, looked timidly up at Mr. Badger, but were too shy to say anything.

"Here, you two youngsters be off home to your mother," said the Badger kindly. "I'll send some one with you to show you the way. You won't want any dinner to-day, I'll be bound."

He gave them sixpence apiece and a pat on the head, and they went off with much respectful swinging of caps and touching of forelocks.

Presently they all sat down to luncheon together. The Mole found himself placed next to Mr. Badger, and, as the other two were still deep in river-gossip from which nothing could divert them, he took the opportunity to tell Badger how comfortable and home-like it all felt to him. "Once well underground," he said, "you know exactly where you are. Nothing can happen to you, and nothing can get at you. You're entirely your own master, and you don't have to consult anybody or mind what they say. Things go on all the same overhead, and you let 'em, and don't bother about 'em. When you want to, up you go, and there the things are, waiting for you."

The Badger simply beamed on him. "That's exactly what I say," he replied. "There's no security, or peace and tranquillity, except underground. And then, if your ideas get larger and you want to expand—why, a dig and a scrape, and there you are! If you feel your house is a bit too big, you stop up a hole or two, and there you are again! No builders, no tradesmen, no remarks passed on you by fellows looking over your wall, and, above all, no *weather*. Look at Rat, now. A couple of feet of flood-water, and he's got to move into hired lodgings; uncomfortable, inconveniently situated, and horribly expensive. Take Toad. I say nothing against Toad Hall; quite the best house in these parts, *as* a house. But supposing a fire breaks out—where's Toad? Supposing tiles are blown off, or walls sink or crack, or windows get broken—where's Toad? Supposing the rooms are draughty —I *hate* a draught myself—where's Toad? No, up and out of doors is good enough to roam about and get one's living in; but underground to come back to at last—that's my idea of *home!*"

The Mole assented heartily; and the Badger in consequence got very friendly with him. "When lunch is over," he said, "I'll take you all round this little place of mine. I can see you'll appreciate it. You understand what domestic architecture ought to be, you do."

After luncheon, accordingly, when the other two had settled themselves into the chimney-corner and had started a heated argument on the subject of *eels*, the Badger lighted a lantern and bade the Mole follow him. Crossing the hall, they passed down one of the principal tunnels, and the wavering light of the lantern gave glimpses on either side of rooms both large and small, some mere cupboards, others nearly as broad and imposing as Toad's dining-hall. A narrow passage at right angles led them into another corridor, and here the same thing was repeated. The Mole was staggered at the size, the extent, the ramifications of it all; at the length of the dim passages, the solid vaultings of the crammed store-chambers, the masonry everywhere, the pillars, the arches, the pavements. "How on earth, Badger," he said at last, "did you ever find time and strength to do all this? It's astonishing!"

"It *would* be astonishing indeed," said the Badger simply, "if I *had* done it. But as a matter of fact I did none of it—only cleaned out the passages and chambers, as far as I had need of them. There's lots more of it, all round about. I see you don't understand, and I must explain it to you. Well, very long ago, on the spot where the Wild Wood waves now, before ever it had planted itself and grown up to what it now is, there was a city —a city of people, you know. Here, where we are standing, they lived, and walked, and talked, and slept, and carried on their business. Here they stabled their horses and feasted, from here they rode out to fight or drove out to trade. They were a power-ful people, and rich, and great builders. They built to last, for they thought their city would last for ever."

"But what has become of them all?" asked the Mole.

"Who can tell?" said the Badger. "People come—they stay for a while, they flourish, they build—and they go. It is their way. But we remain. There were badgers here, I've been told, long before that same city ever came to be. And now there are badgers here again. We are an enduring lot, and we may move out for a time, but we wait, and are patient, and back we come. And so it will ever be."

"Well, and when they went at last, those people?" said the Mole.

"When they went," continued the Badger, "the strong winds and persistent rains took the matter in hand, patiently, cease-lessly, year after year. Perhaps we badgers too, in our small way, helped a little—who knows? It was all down, down, down, grad-ually—ruin and levelling and disappearance. Then it was all up, up, up, gradually, as seeds grew to saplings, and saplings to forest trees, and bramble and fern came creeping in to help. Leaf-mould rose and obliterated, streams in their winter freshets brought sand and soil to clog and to cover, and in course of time our home was ready for us again, and we moved in. Up above us, on the surface, the same thing happened. Animals arrived, liked the look of the place, took up their quarters, settled down, spread, and flourished. They didn't bother themselves about the past—they never do; they're too busy. The place was a bit humpy and hillocky, naturally, and full of holes; but that was rather an advantage. And they don't bother about the future, either—the future when perhaps the people will move in again— for a time—as may very well be. The Wild Wood is pretty well populated by now; with all the usual lot, good, bad, and indiffer- ent—I name no names. It takes all sorts to make a world. But I fancy you know something about them yourself by this time."

"I do indeed," said the Mole, with a slight shiver.

"Well, well," said the Badger, patting him on the shoulder, "it was your first experience of them, you see. They're not so bad really; and we must all live and let live. But I'll pass the word round to-morrow, and I think you'll have no further trouble. Any friend of *mine* walks where he likes in this coun- try, or I'll know the reason why!"

When they got back to the kitchen again, they found the Rat walking up and down, very restless. The underground atmos- phere was oppressing him and getting on his nerves, and he seemed really to be afraid that the river would run away if he wasn't there to look after it. So he had his overcoat on, and his pistols thrust into his belt again. "Come along, Mole," he said anxiously, as soon as he caught sight of them. "We must get off while it's daylight. Don't want to spend another night in the Wild Wood again."

"It'll be all right, my fine fellow," said the Otter. "I'm com- ing along with you, and I know every path blindfold; and if there's a head that needs to be punched, you can confidently rely upon me to punch it."

"You really needn't fret, Ratty," added the Badger placidly. "My passages run further than you think, and I've bolt-holes to the edge of the wood in several directions, though I don't care for everybody to know about them. When you really have to go, you shall leave by one of my short cuts. Meantime, make your- self easy, and sit down again."

The Rat was nevertheless still anxious to be off and attend to his river, so the Badger, taking up his lantern again, led the way along a damp and airless tunnel that wound and dipped, part vaulted, part hewn through solid rock, for a weary distance that seemed to be miles. At last daylight began to show itself confusedly through tangled growth overhanging the mouth of the passage; and the Badger, bidding them a hasty good-bye, pushed them hurriedly through the opening, made everything look as natural as possible again, with creepers, brushwood, and dead leaves, and retreated.

They found themselves standing on the very edge of the Wild Wood. Rocks and brambles and tree-roots behind them, confusedly heaped and tangled; in front, a great space of quiet fields, hemmed by lines of hedges black on the snow, and, far ahead, a glint of the familiar old river, while the wintry sun hung red and low on the horizon. The Otter, as knowing all the paths, took charge of the party, and they trailed out on a bee-line for a distant stile. Pausing there a moment and looking back, they saw the whole mass of the Wild Wood, dense, menacing, compact, grimly set in vast white surroundings; simultaneously they turned and made swiftly for home, for firelight and the familiar things it played on, for the voice, sounding cheerily outside their window, of the river that they knew and trusted in all its moods, that never made them afraid with any amazement.

As he hurried along, eagerly anticipating the moment when he would be at home again among the things he knew and liked, the Mole saw clearly that he was an animal of tilled field and hedgerow, linked to the ploughed furrow, the frequented pasture, the lane of evening lingerings, the cultivated garden-plot. For others the asperities, the stubborn endurance, or the clash of actual conflict, that went with Nature in the rough; he must be wise, must keep to the pleasant places in which his lines were laid and which held adventure enough, in their way, to last for a lifetime.

How to Tell
the Wild Animals

CAROLYN WELLS

If ever you should go by chance
To jungles in the east;
And if there should to you advance
A large and tawny beast,
If he roars at you as you're dyin'
You'll know it is the Asian Lion . . .

Or if some time when roaming round,
A noble wild beast greets you,
With black strips on a yellow ground,
Just notice if he eats you.
This simple rule may help you learn
The Bengal Tiger to discern.

If strolling forth, a beast you view,
Whose hide with spots is peppered,
As soon as he has lept on you,
You'll know it is the Leopard.
'Twill do no good to roar with pain,
He'll only lep and lep again.

If when you're walking round your yard
You meet a creature there,
Who hugs you very, very hard,
Be sure it is a Bear.
If you have any doubts, I guess
He'll give you just one more caress.

Though to distinguish beasts of prey
A novice might nonplus,
The Crocodile you always may
Tell from the Hyena thus:
Hyenas come with merry smiles;
But if they weep they're Crocodiles.

The true Chameleon is small,
A lizard sort of thing;
He hasn't any ears at all,
And not a single wing.
If there is nothing on the tree,
'Tis the Chameleon you see.

Padre Porko,
The Gentlemanly Pig

ROBERT DAVIS

Padre Porko is a famous and beloved character in Spanish folklore—a wise, witty and kindly pig who devotes his life to helping the animals, and humans too. In this story he ingeniously solves the problem of the stable boy and the General's lame horse.

The General's Horse

IT WAS a misty-moisty evening. The drops of rain fell from the tips of the leaves, with a "plop," into the puddles underneath. The wind blew the branches of the umbrella pine against the windows of the Padre's house. It was the sort of weather when no person or animal was willingly out-of-doors. The honest creatures of the air, the forest and the earth had long been asleep.

The Widow Hedge-Hog had washed the supper dishes, swept the hearth with her tail, warmed the Padre's flannel pajamas, and gone home to her family under the apple tree.

Before his fire the Padre dozed. He had eaten three plates of heavenly stewed carrots for his supper, and every now and then he rubbed his stomach gently, to help them digest. The tapping of the branches on the window and the falling of the rain made a soothing music. Upon the shelf above the chimney stood a polished red apple. The Padre was trying to decide whether he should eat the apple or smoke his pipe before crawling into bed for a good night's sleep.

"Rat-a-tat-tat-tat," suddenly sounded the knocker on his door.

"My Goodness Gracious," he exclaimed, pushing his feet into his red slippers. "Who can be out on a night like this? It must be someone in real trouble."

"Who is there?" he called, putting his sensitive nose to the keyhole. He could learn more through his nose than many people can learn through their ears and eyes.

"It is Antonio, the stable-boy from the General's."

"Come in, come in," invited the Padre, seating himself again, and taking out his pipe.

The door opened and a dripping figure stepped inside. Very politely he waited on the door-mat, his cap in his hand.

"Your Honor will please to excuse me for coming so late," he said. "But it was only tonight that the General said he would send me away in disgrace. My Grandmother told me that Your Honor is the Godfather of all Spanish boys who do not have real fathers, so you will please to excuse my coming."

The Padre was reaching up for the red apple. "She told you the truth, Antonio. You sit here and eat this apple, while I put tobacco in my pipe." With a skillful movement of his left hind foot the Padre kicked dry branches upon the fire.

"And don't be in any hurry, Antonio. Take all the time you need. Tell me the very worst. Whatever the trouble, we can put it right."

"It is about the white horse," Antonio began, "the fat, white one, that the General rides in parades, at the head of his soldiers. He can't walk. It is his left front hoof." The boy gulped it out in a single breath.

"They say that it is my fault, that I made him fall when I rode him for exercise. But it's not true. I always go slowly, and turn corners at a walk."

"Let's go and see," said the Padre, going to the closet for his rubber coat. "And here's a cape for you to put around your shoulders."

Once at the General's, the Padre and Antonio hung their wet things in the harness room and unhooked the door of the box stall where the white horse lived. He was a superb animal, but he stood with one front foot off the floor.

"Excuse me, Your Excellency," said the Padre, "but can you tell me the cause of Your Excellency's lameness?"

The great beast pricked up his ears. "The cause of it!" he snorted. "Why a three-day-old colt would know that much, and yet these stupid doctors and professors have been pestering me for two weeks. A wire nail has gone into the tender center of my foot. It has no head. You cannot see it. The idiots, and they pretend to know so much."

"I thought as much," murmured the Padre, sympathetically. "And will Your Excellency co-operate with us, if we try to get the nail out?"

"Won't I, though!" The horse snorted again. "Why, I haven't been able to touch this foot to the ground for sixteen days."

"This is a case for the Rat Family, and for no one else," said the Padre to himself. He trotted over to a hole in the stable floor. His voice, as he leaned over the opening, was a soft whine through his nose. "Is the lady of the house at home?"

A gray muzzle appeared. "I am only a poor widow, Don Porko; my husband was caught in a trap last harvest time. But if my children and a poor soul like me can be of any help to you, you are more than welcome to our best."

"Indeed you can, Mrs. Furrynose," said the Padre with enthusiasm. "We animals are going to do what none of the veterinary professors knew how to do. Listen carefully. Of all the rats in this town which one has the strongest teeth?" Other heads had joined Mother Furrynose at the opening, and now they all answered in a single unanimous squeak, "Uncle Israel, down at the flour-mill."

"Good," said the Padre. "And now, Mrs. Furrynose, I want you to listen once more. Will you send your oldest boy for Uncle Israel right away? Tell him that Padre Porko needs all the husky boy and girl rats in this town at the General's stable in half-an-hour."

Before the Padre had finished his request, a sleek rat was out of the hole and running toward the door. "You can count on us, Chief," he called.

Hardly ten minutes had passed when a peculiar noise was heard outside the stable. It was like the wind blowing the dry leaves in October. It was a rustling, a bustling, a scratching, a scraping, a marching of countless feet. Uncle Israel entered at the head of his tribe. He was an old-fashioned Quaker rat, gray and gaunt, and the size of a half-grown kitten. When he smiled he showed his remarkable teeth, sharp as razors and the color of ivory. He motioned to his brown-coated army and they lined up in rows around the wall, watching him and the Padre with shoe-button eyes.

"I'm not so strong as I used to be," apologized Uncle Israel, "except for my teeth. I don't want to boast, but none of these young rats can hold on to things as hard as I can. As soon as I got your message I brought my relatives. We will do anything you say, Padre." The rows of heads nodded in agreement.

"Thank you for coming, Uncle Israel," said the Padre. "In a minute I'll explain what our work is going to be. First we must tell the General's horse our plan."

He stood by the shoulder of the white horse and spoke in his most persuasive way. "Your Excellency, we are ready for the operation that will cure your foot. But we must be sure of your co-operation. It may hurt, I'm afraid, especially at first."

"It can't hurt more than my hoof aches right now. Go ahead," said the horse.

"We must uncover the end of the nail so that Uncle Israel can grip it in his beautiful teeth. Please bend back your foot."

The General's horse rested his foot on the straw, with the

under side showing, and Uncle Israel, placing one paw on either edge of the tender V, began to gnaw, his teeth cutting in like a machine. Presently he sat up, squeaking excitedly. "I have it. It's right there. It's like a piece of wire. But I can get a good hold on it. What next, Padre?"

"Antonio," ordered the Padre, "bring the halters that hang in the harness room, and tie the ropes one to the other. And you, Uncle Israel, slip your head through this loop in the leather. We will run the long rope out across the stable floor so that everyone can find a hold. Take your time, Uncle Israel; everything depends upon your teeth. When you are ready for us to pull, wiggle your tail."

Things worked like clock-work. Uncle Israel held on. Three hundred young rats strained and pulled on the rope. The General's horse winced with the pain. The Padre walked up and down like a captain in a battle. But the nail in the foot of the white horse did not budge.

Padre Porko had an idea. "Widow Furrynose, what would give you the most pleasure in the world?"

The lady replied quickly. "To bury that deceitful black cat up at the miller's." Everybody sat up and clapped his paws.

"Well, young people," said the Padre, "think that you are pulling the hearse to the graveyard, and that the miller's black cat is in it. Wouldn't you manage to get that hearse to the graveyard? Pull like that."

The floor of the barn seemed alive. It was a rippling, gray-brown carpet of straining small bodies. The teeth of Uncle Israel were locked in a death grip. Padre Porko walked back and forth, singing, "Horrible cat, get her buried, haul the hearse."

And, inch by inch, a long, thin, villainous nail came out of the horse's foot.

Then what a racket! Everyone was squirming, and squeaking, and jumping and rolling over, and tickling and nipping tails, and telling how strong he was. The white horse and Antonio admired Uncle Israel's teeth. And all of his nephews and nieces and grandchildren were so proud of him that they kissed him on both whiskers. Padre Porko kept repeating, "I'm proud of you. Great work! I always say that we animals can do anything, if we will work together."

But it was the General's horse who brought the evening to its perfect close. He whinnied into the Padre's ear, "Please translate to Antonio that if he will unlock the oat box I'm sure our friends would enjoy a light lunch. The General himself would be the first to propose it. He will be very thankful when he visits the stable tomorrow and finds me trotting on four legs."

Mrs. Furrynose and Uncle Israel had the young people sit in circles of ten, while Antonio passed the refreshments, pouring a little pile of oats in the center of each circle. Over three hundred guests were served but their table manners were excellent. No one snatched or grabbed, or gobbled his food. Everyone said, "If you please," and "Thank you," and "Excuse me for talking when my mouth is full."

When the crunching was at its height, Uncle Israel made a speech. "Padre Porko, Your Excellency, and friends, relatives and neighbors, this is a proud and happy night for me. In all my life my teeth never did such good work before. They helped this noble white horse, and they enabled us rats to aid the Padre in one of his kind acts. But, also, tonight, my teeth brought me to the attention of a lovely lady, Madame Furrynose, and I am delighted to say that she will not be a widow much longer. One

and all, you are invited to the wedding, which will be held next Sunday afternoon in the flour-mill, while the miller is at church. And the Padre Porko has promised to send word to all dogs and cats of the town that none of our guests are to be caught while going, coming or at the party." A hurricane of cheers and clapping followed the speech.

The pink nose of the white horse pushed through the window of his stall, and the merrymakers looked up. "May I, too, offer a wedding present to these worthy friends? Every night I will leave a handful of grain in the corner of my manger. They will find it there for their midnight lunch. A wedded pair with such polite manners can be trusted not to disturb the repose of a hard-working old horse."

The morning sun crept along the stable wall until it shone directly upon the sleeping Antonio. He sat up and rubbed his eyes. How did it happen that he was not in his bed, but in the box stall of the General's horse? And the horse was stamping with the foot that had been lame. Queerer still, the grain box was open and half the oats were gone. And what was the meaning of the four halter ropes tied together?

These are questions which Antonio never could answer. But when he told this story to his children, he was no longer a stable boy. He was the head trainer of all the General's racing horses.

The Lobster Quadrille

LEWIS CARROLL

"Will you walk a little faster?" said a whiting to a snail,
"There's a porpoise close behind us, and he's treading on my tail.
See how eagerly the lobsters and the turtles all advance!
They are waiting on the shingle—will you come and join the
   dance?

Drawn after John Tenniel

Will you, won't you, will you, won't you, will you join the
   dance?
Will you, won't you, will you, won't you, won't you join the
   dance?

"You can really have no notion how delightful it will be
When they take us up and throw us, with the lobsters, out to
sea!"
But the snail replied, "Too far, too far!" and gave a look
askance—
Said he thanked the whiting kindly, but he would not join the
dance.
Would not, could not, would not, could not, would not join
the dance.
Would not, could not, would not, could not, would not join
the dance.

"What matters it how far we go?" his scaly friend replied.
"There is another shore, you know, upon the other side.
The further off from England the nearer is to France——
Then turn not pale, beloved snail, but come and join the dance.
Will you, won't you, will you, won't you, will you join the
dance?
Will you, won't you, will you, won't you, won't you join the
dance?"

From *Alice's Adventures in Wonderland.*

Aesop's Fables

Beyond his name, we know very little about Aesop. Legend has it that he was a slave in ancient Greece who was freed by his master because of the clever stories he told. He surely was not the first to teach little moral lessons in tales about talking beasts, but it is Aesop's name that has been attached to most of the famous fables that have come down to us. Here are a few of the best known.

The Town Mouse and the Country Mouse

A TOWN MOUSE once went on a visit to his cousin the Country Mouse whose home was in the fields. His country cousin made him heartily welcome and offered him all the best food he could find—beans, peas, and crusts of bread. The Town Mouse picked a little here and there, but it was clear that he did not enjoy the simple country fare.

"Cousin," he finally said, "I don't understand how you put up with such dull food. But of course you can't expect anything better in the country. Come home with me, and when you have lived in town for a week, you will never want to come back here."

The two set out for the city that very evening and arrived late at night. "You must be tired and hungry after your long journey," said the Town Mouse, and took his guest at once into a grand dining room where they found the remains of a fine feast—all kinds of meats, cheeses, cakes, jellies and other dainties. The dazzled Country Mouse was just trying to decide which tempting morsel to eat first, when the door opened, and in came a servant with a light. Both mice scampered off and hid until he left the room. When all was quiet again, they went back to their supper. But hardly had the Country Mouse swallowed his first mouthful, than he heard a terrific growling and barking and two huge dogs bounded into the room. Half frightened to death, he ran down from the table and into a hole where he saw the Town Mouse disappearing.

"Good-bye, Cousin," said the Country Mouse.

"What, going so soon?" said the other.

"Yes," he replied, "I seem to have lost my appetite."

A crust of bread in peace is better than a feast in fear.

The Crow and the Pitcher

A thirsty Crow flew around looking in vain for some water until she finally found a pitcher which had some in it. The water was so far down at the bottom, however, that she could not reach it with her beak. Again and again she tried, but was not able to catch a drop. The poor bird thought she would surely die of thirst, right there within sight of the water.

Suddenly she hit upon a plan. Gathering up some pebbles, she began to drop them into the water, one by one. With each pebble, the water rose higher and higher, until at last it reached the brim of the pitcher. Then the clever Crow was able to quench her thirst.

Necessity is the mother of invention.

The Fox and the Grapes

One hot summer day a Fox was strolling through an orchard when he spied a tempting bunch of grapes hanging over a high branch. "Just the thing to quench my thirst," said he. Drawing back a few steps, he took a run and a jump, but he just missed the grapes. He went back, took a running start once more, and jumped, but with no greater success this time. He looked up at the grapes, his mouth watering. Again and again, he tried to jump high enough to reach them, until at last, exhausted, he had to give up.

Then he walked away with his nose in the air, saying, "I didn't really want them, I'm sure they are sour."

It is easy to scorn what you can't get.

Belling the Cat

One day the mice held a general council to consider what they might do to protect themselves against their common enemy, the Cat. Some said one thing and some said another, but at last a Young Mouse stood up and announced that he had a plan which he thought would solve the problem.

"You will all agree," said he, "that our chief danger lies in the unexpected and sly manner in which our enemy comes upon us. Now, if we could receive some warning of her approach, we could easily hide from her. I propose, therefore, that a small bell be obtained and attached by a ribbon to the neck of the Cat. In this way we could always know when she was coming and be able to make our escape."

This proposal was met with great applause, until an Old Mouse arose and said, "This is all very fine, but who among us is so brave? Who will bell the Cat?" The mice looked at one another in silence and nobody volunteered.

It is easier to suggest a plan than to carry it out.

The Grasshopper and the Ant

JEAN DE LA FONTAINE

ALL summer long the grasshopper had been singing gayly. When the cold winter winds began to blow, he found himself without the tiniest morsel of food. So he went to his neighbor, the ant, who had been busily storing away grain during the summer.

"Kind friend, I am starving!" cried the grasshopper. "Please lend me some grain," he begged, "so that I may live until the spring comes. I will pay you back before August. I promise on my solemn oath as a grasshopper, that I will pay you back double the amount you lend me."

But the ant isn't a lending creature—that's one of her little faults. "What were you doing when it was warm?" she asked the pleading grasshopper.

"Night and day, for everyone who came around, I sang, if you please."

"You sang? Well, then I'm not a bit troubled about you. Now you may dance."

The Turtle and the Ducks

There was a Turtle that lived for many years in a pond with some Ducks. They were the best of friends and enjoyed the pond together in great peace and happiness. But at length there came a season so dry that there was no water at all left in the pond. The Ducks decided that it was not possible to stay here any longer and that they would have to move on to a new home. So they went sadly to the Turtle to bid him farewell.

"Friend Turtle," they said, "we are compelled to move on, and are very grieved to have to leave you behind in this condition. But we have a long journey to make and you cannot follow us because, alas, you cannot fly."

The Turtle bemoaned his fate at being left behind and begged and begged the Ducks to carry him along with them. The Ducks replied:

"It may be possible to take you along with us and save you. But only on one condition—if you follow our advice and keep a strict and perfect silence. If you promise not to speak a single word on the way, we will agree to carry you. But if we should meet with someone who will talk to us, then it is ten to one that you will start talking too. If you do, remember what we now tell you. This will mean your destruction."

"No," answered the Turtle, "don't be afraid. I will do exactly as you say."

That being settled, the Ducks brought a stick and said to the Turtle, "Just take the middle of this stick in your mouth and

From an East Indian Bidpai Fable.

hold fast to it. And remember not to say a single word until we come to the end of our journey."

Then the Ducks took up the stick by each end and raised him up in the air. Then they flew along in triumph carrying the turtle between them.

It was not long before they were flying over a village and all the people and children came running out to see the strange sight. They began to point up to the sky and shout:

"Oh, look at the Turtle hanging on to a stick! Look at the Turtle being carried between the Ducks! Did you ever see anything so ridiculous?"

The Turtle grew very angry at all this rude shouting and started to tell them that it was no business of theirs if he chose to be carried by his friends. Of course as soon as he opened his mouth to speak, he let go the stick, and fell to the ground.

As the Ducks flew on, they could hear the people below saying as they picked up the poor Turtle, "What a pity that this fellow couldn't keep his mouth shut. He just had to talk and that's why he lost his life."

Animals: Mostly Real

Michael Who Missed His Train

DOROTHY BRYAN

One morning the expressman delivered a large box to the mother of Mary and David. The children wondered what was in it.

It humped! It heaved! It sniffed!

A shiny eye peered out between the slats that were nailed across the side. Then there was a bark!

"It's a dog!" shouted Mary and David.

"Yes, it's Michael from Boston," said their mother. "But we already have Patsy, and we really cannot keep more than one dog on this small place, so Michael will have to go back to Boston as soon as he has had a little rest."

When Michael was taken out of the box, he proved to be a very friendly Sealyham terrier with big feet, big brown eyes, and a fine, strong tail for wagging.

He did not have the big brown spot over his right eye that Patsy had but he had small spots on his ears.

Mary and David and Patsy decided that they did not want Michael to go back to Boston. So they all met out under the dogwood tree to plan what to do about it.

"Mother loves Patsy and wants *her* to stay," David said. "Do you suppose it is because Patsy does tricks?"

They all turned and looked at Patricia.

She sat up and waved her paws.

"Patsy sits up," said Mary. "Why don't you sit up, Michael?"

Michael tried very hard, but when he had lifted his big front paws off the ground he leaned way toward one side, then way toward the other side, then w-a-y, w-a-y back, and over he rolled!

But Michael tried again and again until he could sit up, too—though he did not look very steady.

What to do? Michael was so willing—so loving—so anxious to make himself wanted.

Michael chased balls and sticks.

But he chased the cat next door, and *that* did not help!

They all ran indoors to Mother. "Sit up," Mary ordered.

Patsy sat up very straight, lightly waving her paws.

Michael tried once and fell over; tried twice and fell over; tried the third time, and sat up! His chest stuck way out; his paws dangled way down; he wobbled and he tottered—but he did *not* tumble over.

"That is very smart," admired Mother. "But one beggar is bad enough around this house. What would we do with two? Michael must go back to Boston."

Michael stretched himself tenderly on Mother's feet whenever she sat down.

But he stretched himself tenderly on the best silk cushion when he was lonesome for Mother's feet and that did not help!

When Patsy was eating her dinner, Michael just sat and watched politely, and no matter how s-l-o-w-l-y Patsy mincey-moused her dinner he would not steal a crumb.

But he brought home a large soup bone that belonged to somebody else and that did not help!

Michael taught himself to sing softly—woo! woo!! woo!!!

But he taught Patsy to sing, too, and whenever those two were left alone on the front seat of the automobile they w-o-o! w-o-o!! w-o-o-ed!!! together, louder and louder until everybody came running to see what the trouble was.

And that certainly did not help!

Whenever Michael did anything wrong, he put himself in the corner behind the door and tried not to do it again.

But somehow he was apt to forget to be a good dog, and that did not help at all!

So Mother said, "Michael means well, but he *must* go back to Boston."

Mary, David, Patsy, and Michael all met out under the weeping-willow tree. Patsy sat close beside Mary and kissed the tip of Michael's nose. "What shall we try now?" asked David.

"We will have to try a brand new surprise trick," answered Mary. "We must all put on our thinking caps."

So Mary made them each a newspaper hat, and they sat thinking—and thinking—and thinking—and thinking.

Then strange sounds began to come out from under the weeping-willow tree—whistlings and tootlings and thumpings and excited yippings. And a whole barrel of ginger snaps was used up as rewarding tid-bits.

After a long, long time Mary, David, Patsy, and Michael went tramping in to Mother.

David kept whistling the first few bars of "Yankee Doodle," over and over.

They all came to a stop in front of Mother's chair.

Patsy and Michael listened carefully. Everything was very quiet. Then—"Ta-Ra-Ra-Ra-Ra-Ra Boom!" said David.

At the word "Boom!" Patsy and Michael fell on their sides and lay just as still as still.

"Di-Yay!" cried Mary.

Patsy and Michael jumped to their feet as though they had been pulled by one string.

"They died for their country," explained David.

"And came alive again for you," added Mary.

"That is very clever," applauded Mother. "But Michael must really go back to Boston!!"

Mournful Michael!

So Michael was put into his box again and the slats were nailed across the side.

Mary and David counted out enough dog biscuits to last during the whole trip to Boston.

Crunch! Scrunch! Munch-munch!! went Michael—and all his meals for his trip to Boston were eaten up before he had even started. Michael was very loving and very sad at leaving—but, somehow, he was *always* hungry.

When the last biscuit crumb was licked up all was still.

The box humped! It heaved! It sniffed!

A sorrowful eye peered out between the slats nailed across the side.

Then there was a moan!

"I will get out the car and take Michael to his train," Mother said hastily.

"Oh, please! Won't you let us carry him down ourselves?" begged Mary. "He isn't heavy."

"And it isn't far," added David.

"Well, all right," said Mother. "Be careful. Good-bye, Michael. I am sorry to see you leave, but we really cannot keep more than one dog on this small place, so you must go back to Boston." She patted Michael's nose through the slats and went quickly into the house.

"Let's give him some soft leaves for a bed on his way to Boston," Mary suggested.

So they put down the box and gathered oak leaves and pushed them between the slats.

Michael scratched round and round and made himself a cosy nest.

Slowly, slowly they moved on.

"He likes to toss pine cones," David said. "Let's find a nice big one for Michael to play with on his way to Boston."

So they put down the box and Patsy found a big pine cone that they squeezed in between the slats.

Michael nosed it and nibbled it but he could not toss it very well. There was not enough room. So he buried it under the oak leaves.

Slowly, slowly they trudged on.

"Do you want to change hands?" Mary asked. "My right arm is getting tired."

"All right," answered David. "So is my left arm."

So they put down the box and changed sides. They both patted Michael between the bars on the way around the box.

Slowly, slowly they tramped on.

Mary and David had just changed hands again when—

Toot! Toot!

"It's the train!" cried Mary.

"And we haven't Michael's ticket or anything," shouted David. They started to run.

The box kept bumping their legs.

Michael rolled from side to side, barking and scratching.

Patsy ran, too.

Just as they rushed around the last curve in the path, Toot! Toot—Toot!! the train gave a warning whistle and Puff—*puff—puff*, it pulled out of the station.

They put down the box.

"Michael has missed his train!" cried David.

"So he has," said Mary.

Mary and David pulled Michael out of the box and put him down beside Patsy. Slowly, slowly they trudged back to Mother, who was waiting at home, feeling rather lonely.

"Michael has missed his train," cried Mary and David.

There was a pause. They waited anxiously.

"What! Michael has missed his train," said Mother. "Well, then, of course—

"Michael *cannot* go back to Boston."

A Kitten

ELEANOR FARJEON

He's nothing much but fur
And two round eyes of blue,
He has a giant purr
And a midget mew.

He darts and pats the air,
He starts and cocks his ear,
When there is nothing there
For him to see and hear.

He runs around in rings,
But why we cannot tell;
With sideways leaps he springs
At things invisible—

Then half-way through a leap
His startled eyeballs close,
And he drops off to sleep
With one paw on his nose.

" 'Look, look, Mother!' Bambi exclaimed. 'There's a flower flying.'
" 'That's not a flower,' said his mother, 'that's a butterfly.' "

—Bambi

FROM

Bambi

FELIX SALTEN

When it was first published John Galsworthy said about Bambi: "I hardly know any story of animals that can stand beside this life study of a forest deer. Felix Salten is a poet. He feels nature deeply, and he loves animals. . . . it is a little masterpiece." In this and the stories of Mr. Salten that follow you will see what made him say that. Here is Bambi as a very young deer, just beginning to learn about life and nature.

Bambi Discovers the Meadow

IN EARLY SUMMER the trees stood still under the blue sky, held their limbs outstretched and received the direct rays of the sun. On the shrubs and bushes in the undergrowth, the flowers unfolded their red, white and yellow stars. On some the seed pods had begun to appear again. They perched innumerable on the fine tips of the branches, tender and firm and resolute, and seemed like small, clenched fists. Out of the earth came whole troops of flowers, like motley stars, so that the soil of the twilit forest floor shone with a silent, ardent, colorful gladness. Everything smelled of fresh leaves, of blossoms, of moist clods and green wood. When morning broke, or when the sun went down, the whole woods resounded with a thousand voices, and from morning till night, the bees hummed, the wasps droned, and filled the fragrant stillness with their murmur.

These were the earliest days of Bambi's life. He walked behind his mother on a narrow track that ran through the midst of the bushes. How pleasant it was to walk there. The thick foliage stroked his flanks softly and bent supplely aside. The track appeared to be barred and obstructed in a dozen places and yet they advanced with the greatest ease. There were tracks like this everywhere, running criss-cross through the whole woods. His mother knew them all, and if Bambi sometimes stopped before a bush as if it were an impenetrable green wall, she always found where the path went through, without hesitation or searching.

Bambi questioned her. He loved to ask his mother questions. It was the pleasantest thing for him to ask a question and then to hear what answer his mother would give. Bambi was never surprised that question after question should come into his mind continually and without effort. He found it perfectly natural, and it delighted him very much. It was very delightful, too, to wait expectantly till the answer came. If it turned out the way he wanted, he was satisfied. Sometimes, of course, he did not understand, but that was pleasant also because he was kept busy picturing what he had not understood, in his own way. Sometimes he felt very sure that his mother was not giving him a complete answer, was intentionally not telling him all she knew. And, at first, that was very pleasant, too. For then there would remain in him such a lively curiosity, such suspicion, mysteriously and joyously flashing through him, such anticipation, that he would become anxious and happy at the same time, and grow silent.

Once he asked, "Whom does this trail belong to, Mother?" His mother answered, "To us."

Bambi asked again, "To you and me?"

"Yes."

"To us two?"

"Yes."

"Only to us two?"

"No," said his mother, "to us deer."

"What are deer?" Bambi asked, and laughed.

His mother looked at him from head to foot and laughed too. "You are a deer and I am a deer. We're both deer," she said. "Do you understand?"

Bambi sprang into the air for joy. "Yes, I understand," he said. "I'm a little deer and you're a big deer, aren't you?"

His mother nodded and said, "Now you see."

But Bambi grew serious again. "Are there other deer besides you and me?" he asked.

"Certainly," his mother said. "Many of them."

"Where are they?" cried Bambi.

"Here, everywhere."

"But I don't see them."

"You will soon," she said.

"When?" Bambi stood still, wild with curiosity.

"Soon." The mother walked on quietly. Bambi followed her. He kept silent for he was wondering what "soon" might mean. He came to the conclusion that "soon" was certainly not "now." But he wasn't sure at what time "soon" stopped being "soon" and began to be a "long while." Suddenly he asked, "Who made this trail?"

"We," his mother answered.

Bambi was astonished. "We? You and I?"

The mother said, "We, we . . . we deer."

Bambi asked, "Which deer?"

"All of us," his mother said sharply.

They walked on. Bambi was in high spirits and felt like leaping off the path, but he stayed close to his mother. Something rustled in front of them, close to the ground. The fern fronds and wood-lettuce concealed something that advanced in violent motion. A threadlike, little cry shrilled out piteously; then all was still. Only the leaves and the blades of grass shivered back into place. A ferret had caught a mouse. He came slinking by, slid sideways, and prepared to enjoy his meal.

"What was that?" asked Bambi excitedly.

"Nothing," his mother soothed him.

"But," Bambi trembled, "but I saw it."

"Yes, yes," said his mother. "Don't be frightened. The ferret has killed a mouse." But Bambi was dreadfully frightened. A vast, unknown horror clutched at his heart. It was long before he could speak again. Then he asked, "Why did he kill the mouse?"

"Because," his mother hesitated. "Let us walk faster," she said as though something had just occurred to her and as though she had forgotten the question. She began to hurry. Bambi sprang after her.

A long pause ensued. They walked on quietly again. Finally Bambi asked anxiously, "Shall we kill a mouse, too, sometime?"

"No," replied his mother.

"Never?" asked Bambi.

"Never," came the answer.

"Why not?" asked Bambi, relieved.

"Because we never kill anything," said his mother simply.

Bambi grew happy again.

Loud cries were coming from a young ash tree which stood near their path. The mother went along without noticing them, but Bambi stopped inquisitively. Overhead two jays were quarreling about a nest they had plundered.

"Get away, you murderer!" cried one.

"Keep cool, you fool," the other answered, "I'm not afraid of you."

"Look for your own nests," the first one shouted, "or I'll break your head for you." He was beside himself with rage. "What vulgarity!" he chattered, "what vulgarity!"

The other jay had spied Bambi and fluttered down a few branches to shout at him. "What are you gawking at, you freak?" he screamed.

Bambi sprang away terrified. He reached his mother and

walked behind her again, frightened and obedient, thinking she
had not noticed his absence.

After a pause he asked, "Mother, what is vulgarity?"

"I don't know," said his mother.

Bambi thought a while; then he began again. "Why were they
both so angry with each other, Mother?" he asked.

"They were fighting over food," his mother answered.

"Will we fight over food, too, sometime?" Bambi asked.

"No," said his mother.

Bambi asked, "Why not?"

"Because there is enough for all of us," his mother replied.

Bambi wanted to know something else. "Mother," he began.
"What is it?"

"Will we be angry with each other sometime?" he asked.

"No, child," said his mother, "we don't do such things."

They walked along again. Presently it grew light ahead of
them. It grew very bright. The trail ended with the tangle of
vines and bushes. A few steps more and they would be in the
bright open space that spread out before them. Bambi wanted
to bound forward, but his mother had stopped.

"What is it?" he asked impatiently, already delighted.

"It's the meadow," his mother answered.

"What is a meadow?" asked Bambi insistently.

His mother cut him short. "You'll soon find out for yourself,"
she said. She had become very serious and watchful. She stood
motionless, holding her head high and listening intently. She
sucked in deep breathfuls of air and looked very severe.

"It's all right," she said at last, "we can go out."

Bambi leaped forward, but his mother barred the way.

"Wait till I call you," she said. Bambi obeyed at once and
stood still. "That's right," said his mother, to encourage him,
"and now listen to what I am saying to you." Bambi heard how
seriously his mother spoke and felt terribly excited.

"Walking on the meadow is not so simple," his mother went
on. "It's a difficult and dangerous business. Don't ask me why.
You'll find that out later on. Now do exactly as I tell you to.
Will you?"

"Yes," Bambi promised.

"Good," said his mother, "I'm going out alone first. Stay here and wait. And don't take your eyes off me for a minute. If you see me run back here, then turn round and run as fast as you can. I'll catch up with you soon." She grew silent and seemed to be thinking. Then she went on earnestly, "Run anyway as fast as your legs will carry you. Run even if something should happen . . . even if you should see me fall to the ground. . . . Don't think of me, do you understand? No matter what you see or hear, start running right away and just as fast as you possibly can. Do you promise me to do that?"

"Yes," said Bambi softly. His mother spoke so seriously.

She went on speaking. "Out there if I should call you," she said, "there must be no looking around and no questions, but you must get behind me instantly. Understand that. Run without pausing or stopping to think. If I begin to run, that means for you to run too, and no stopping until we are back here again. You won't forget, will you?"

"No," said Bambi in a troubled voice.

"Now I'm going ahead," said his mother, and seemed to become calmer.

She walked out. Bambi, who never took his eyes off her, saw how she moved forward with slow, cautious steps. He stood there full of expectancy, full of fear and curiosity. He saw how his mother listened in all directions, saw her shrink together, and shrank together himself, ready to leap back into the thickets. Then his mother grew calm again. She stretched herself. Then she looked around satisfied and called, "Come!"

Bambi bounded out. Joy seized him with such tremendous force that he forgot his worries in a flash. Through the thicket he could see only the green tree-tops overhead. Once in a while he caught a glimpse of the blue sky.

Now he saw the whole heaven stretching far and wide and he rejoiced without knowing why. In the forest he had seen only a stray sunbeam now and then, or the tender, dappled light that played through the branches. Suddenly he was standing in the blinding hot sunlight whose boundless power was beaming upon him. He stood in the splendid warmth that made him shut his eyes but which opened his heart.

Bambi was as though bewitched. He was completely beside himself with pleasure. He was simply wild. He leaped into the air three, four, five times. He had to do it. He felt a terrible desire to leap and jump. He stretched his young limbs joyfully. His breath came deeply and easily. He drank in the air. The sweet smell of the meadow made him so wildly happy that he had to leap into the air.

Bambi was a child. If he had been a human child he would have shouted. But he was a young deer, and deer cannot shout, at least not the way human children do. So he rejoiced with his legs and with his whole body as he flung himself into the air. His mother stood by and was glad. She saw that Bambi was wild. She watched how he bounded into the air and fell again awkwardly, in one spot. She saw how he stared around him, dazed and bewildered, only to leap up over and over again. She understood that Bambi knew only the narrow deer tracks in the forest and how his brief life was used to the limits of the thicket. He did not move from one place because he did not understand how to run freely around the open meadow.

So she stretched out her forefeet and bent laughingly towards Bambi for a moment. Then she was off with one bound, racing around in a circle so that the tall grass stems swished.

Bambi was frightened and stood motionless. Was that a sign for him to run back to the thicket? His mother had said to him, "Don't worry about me no matter what you see or hear. Just run as fast as you can." He was going to turn around and run as she had commanded him to, but his mother came galloping up suddenly. She came up with a wonderful swishing sound and stopped two steps from him. She bent towards him, laughing as she had at first and cried, "Catch me." And in a flash she was gone.

Bambi was puzzled. What did she mean? Then she came back again running so fast that it made him giddy. She pushed his flank with her nose and said quickly, "Try to catch me," and fled away.

Bambi started after her. He took a few steps. Then his steps became short bounds. He felt as if he were flying without any effort on his part. There was a space under his hoofs, space under his bounding feet, space and still more space. Bambi was beside himself with joy.

The swishing grass sounded wonderful to his ears. It was marvelously soft and as fine as silk where it brushed against him. He ran round in a circle. He turned and flew off in a new circle, turned around again and kept running.

His mother was standing still, getting her breath again. She kept following Bambi with her eyes. He was wild.

Suddenly the race was over. He stopped and came up to his mother, lifting his hoofs elegantly. He looked joyfully at her. Then they strolled contentedly side by side.

Since he had been in the open, Bambi had felt the sky and the sun and the green meadow with his whole body. He took one blinding, giddy glance at the sun, and he felt its rays as they lay warmly on his back.

Presently he began to enjoy the meadow with his eyes also. Its wonders amazed him at every step he took. You could not see the tiniest speck of earth the way you could in the forest. Blade after blade of grass covered every inch of the ground. It tossed and waved luxuriantly. It bent softly aside under every footstep, only to rise up unharmed again. The broad green meadow was starred with white daisies, with the thick, round red and purple clover blossoms and bright, golden dandelion heads.

"Look, look, Mother!" Bambi exclaimed. "There's a flower flying."

"That's not a flower," said his mother, "that's a butterfly."

Bambi stared at the butterfly, entranced. It had darted lightly from a blade of grass and was fluttering about in its giddy way. Then Bambi saw that there were many butterflies flying in the air above the meadow. They seemed to be in a hurry and yet moved slowly, fluttering up and down in a sort of game that delighted him. They really did look like gay flying flowers that would not stay on their stems but had unfastened themselves in order to dance a little. They looked, too, like flowers that come to rest at sundown but have no fixed places and have to hunt for them, dropping down and vanishing as if they really had settled somewhere, yet always flying up again, a little way at first, then higher and higher, and always searching farther and farther because all the good places have already been taken.

Bambi gazed at them all. He would have loved to see one close by. He wanted to see one face to face but he was not able to. They sailed in and out continually. The air was aflutter with them.

When he looked down at the ground again he was delighted with the thousands of living things he saw stirring under his hoofs. They ran and jumped in all directions. He would see a wild swarm of them, and the next moment they had disappeared in the grass again.

"Who are they, Mother?" he asked.

"Those are ants," his mother answered.

"Look," cried Bambi, "see that piece of grass jumping. Look how high it can jump!"

"That's not grass," his mother explained, "that's a nice grasshopper."

"Why does he jump that way?" asked Bambi.

"Because we're walking here," his mother answered, "he's afraid we'll step on him."

"O," said Bambi, turning to the grasshopper who was sitting on a daisy; "O," he said again politely, "you don't have to be afraid; we won't hurt you."

"I'm not afraid," the grasshopper replied in a quavering voice; "I was only frightened for a moment when I was talking to my wife."

"Excuse us for disturbing you," said Bambi shyly.

"Not at all," the grasshopper quavered. "Since it's you, it's perfectly all right. But you never know who's coming and you have to be careful."

"This is the first time in my life that I've ever been on the meadow," Bambi explained; "my mother brought me. . . ."

The grasshopper was sitting with his head lowered as though he were going to butt. He put on a serious face and murmured, "That doesn't interest me at all. I haven't time to stand here gossiping with you. I have to be looking for my wife. Hopp!" And he gave a jump.

"Hopp!" said Bambi in surprise at the high jump with which the grasshopper vanished.

Bambi ran to his mother. "Mother, I spoke to him," he cried.

"To whom?" his mother asked.

"To the grasshopper," Bambi said, "I spoke to him. He was very nice to me. And I like him so much. He's so wonderful and green and you can see through his sides. They look like leaves, but you can't see through a leaf."

"Those are his wings," said his mother.

"O," Bambi went on, "and his face is so serious and wise. But he was very nice to me anyhow. And how he can jump! 'Hopp!' he said, and he jumped so high I couldn't see him any more."

They walked on. The conversation with the grasshopper had excited Bambi and tired him a little, for it was the first time he had ever spoken to a stranger. He felt hungry and pressed close to his mother to be nursed.

Then he stood quietly and gazed dreamily into space for a little while with a sort of joyous ecstasy that came over him every time he was nursed by his mother. He noticed a bright flower moving in the tangled grasses. Bambi looked more closely at it. No, it wasn't a flower, but a butterfly. Bambi crept closer.

The butterfly hung heavily to a grass stem and fanned its wings slowly.

"Please sit still," Bambi said.

"Why should I sit still? I'm a butterfly," the insect answered in astonishment.

"O, please sit still, just for a minute," Bambi pleaded, "I've wanted so much to see you close to. Please."

"Well," said the butterfly, "for your sake I will, but not for long."

Bambi stood in front of him. "How beautiful you are!" he cried fascinated; "how wonderfully beautiful, like a flower!"

"What?" cried the butterfly, fanning his wings, "did you say like a flower? In my circle it's generally supposed that we're handsomer than flowers."

Bambi was embarrassed. "O, yes," he stammered, "much handsomer, excuse me, I only meant. . . ."

"Whatever you meant is all one to me," the butterfly replied.

He arched his thin body affectedly and played with his delicate feelers.

Bambi looked at him enchanted. "How elegant you are!" he said. "How elegant and fine! And how splendid and white your wings are!"

The butterfly spread his wings wide apart, then raised them till they folded together like an upright sail.

"O," cried Bambi, "I know that you are handsomer than the flowers. Besides, you can fly and the flowers can't because they grow on stems, that's why."

The butterfly spread his wings. "It's enough," he said, "that I can fly." He soared so lightly that Bambi could hardly see him or follow his flight. His wings moved gently and gracefully. Then he fluttered into the sunny air.

"I only sat still that long on your account," he said balancing in the air in front of Bambi. "Now I'm going."

That was how Bambi found the meadow.

A Snow-White Rabbit

FELIX SALTEN

He came as a gift on Easter Sunday, concealed in a gaily colored egg of cardboard. When the egg was opened he appeared: a tiny snow-white rabbit with coat as smooth as the finest silk velvet. How timid he was, how lonely and defenseless, as if he sensed already the difficult fate that was in store for him!

He was so small that he easily fitted into the palm of a hand and there he sat, humble and forlorn. His long ears, which dropped down his back, were a delicate pink. His eyes glowed like garnets, then again they looked dark blue, so that it was impossible to tell what color they really were. His pretty pointed nose moved constantly, while his little mouth drew back to meet it. At times this gave him an ironical look, and someone said this look seemed to express contempt of death. But it is hard to believe that a baby rabbit could be contemptuous of death. His mustache hairs were like thin silver wires which bristled and quaked around his mouth. Now everyone knows that real heroes sometimes tremble. But this poor rabbit hardly resembled a hero. He was just a frightened little waif.

The waif soon caused his master grave concern, for in the house lived a stately Persian tomcat and two dogs. One of the dogs, named Puck, was a dainty toy terrier. He was wise, peace loving and as gracious as a cavalier; the other dog, Lumpi, was a Maltese of rather doubtful line. He made up for his lack of racial purity by a soulful glance and an air of extreme sentimentality. Neither of these dogs was big nor wild, yet it was impossible to guess just how they would behave toward the rabbit.

Rustan the tomcat, however, was a definite menace. For he

was an untamed beast of prey and led a free and self-willed existence. He was known far and wide in the neighboring gardens. He came and went as he pleased. He indulged in nightly love affairs, fought bloody battles with his rivals and brought back open wounds to be nursed. In the garden at home two blackbirds fell victim to him and he tore a squirrel to bits.

The little rabbit could neither fly nor climb trees; what chance had he against such a foe?

First the master put him into a small cage which was placed on the lawn. Here the rabbit was safe from attack but the dogs were curious and pressed close to the bars of the cage while the tomcat kept pacing around it. Surrounded on all sides, the rabbit's fear and bewilderment increased so at the end of an hour his master decided to open the cage door. The rabbit now could have the freedom of the whole garden, but for a while he made no use of his freedom. He crouched in the farthest corner of the open cage and moved his little muzzle up and down as if he were mumbling to himself. Perhaps he was pondering his future. Strangely enough, as soon as he was free the other animals lost interest in him. The dogs romped around the garden as usual and the tomcat stretched out in the sun and slept.

Suddenly the rabbit leaped forth. Perhaps the grass smell lured him, or perhaps it was the fragrance of the flowers and the bright sunshine which gave him courage. At any rate he accomplished his heroic feat with all the daring and assurance of a lion. He hopped out on the lawn and immediately began to search for delicacies. The tomcat jumped up, stared at him in amazement, then retreated to a near-by woodpile whence he watched the actions of this strange guest. But the rabbit paid no attention to him and with an attitude which seemed to say, "What are cats to me?" darted here and there in the grass looking for stalks, weeds and the tastiest leaves. It was only when the dogs ran up and sniffed him that he showed some sign of fear. He lay flat on the ground and waited, apparently resigned to his fate. But the dogs did not harm him. They touched him with cautious paws; then, satisfied with their examination, left him in peace.

The rabbit grew swiftly. Every morning a plate of oat kernels and a little bowl of milk were placed in front of the house for him. After a few days he began to appear at the door regularly and if his meal was delayed longer than pleased him, he simply leaped down the kitchen steps to demand his due.

Then he began to assert his independence in other ways. At first the master would lock him in a shed at night to protect him from the rain and cold. But the rabbit did not want to be protected and at twilight he would crawl into the bushes. When the master tried to catch him he darted away and a strenuous rabbit-hunt would be on. Sometimes this chase continued for hours. One night, however, the master searched for him in vain. The rabbit had discovered a new retreat in the corner of the woodpile and from then on he always returned there to sleep. He had chosen this place himself and insisted upon being independent, so his master let him have his way. There was nothing else to do.

Now the rabbit was full grown. His pelt was as soft as ermine and as white as freshly fallen snow. He was completely free of fear or worry. The garden was his domain and he enjoyed there a life of ease and plenty. But as a rich man rarely has enough, the rabbit too was not satisfied with the abundance which was his. So he dug holes under the hedge and ventured into the neighbor's garden where he scented finer and rarer delicacies.

He always came home, however. But not because he was satisfied; he was never satisfied. He returned rather out of a sense of duty, which was very much to his credit. In the strange garden there was always the danger that he might meet big, vicious dogs. Then, too, the neighbor did not relish the idea of finding his roses, dahlias and other flowers gnawed and chewed. So very soon all exits were blocked for the rabbit and he was obliged to keep within his own frontiers. He submitted to this restraint with extreme good grace. In fact as time went on he proved himself to be a very obliging and talented creature who loved human beings and provided them with many happy surprises.

He was very deft in all his movements. When he sat up and looked around with a spruce turn of his head, he seemed particularly wise and superior. When the summer's heat plagued him, he lay in the shadows with his long hind legs spread to the sides, his breast and head held high. From this position he would gaze before him as if thinking profoundly.

The tomcat never deigned to play with him, so he attached himself more and more to the dogs. Sometimes when they were sitting together the rabbit would jump up suddenly, poke one of the dogs in the side and rush away. Catch me! Then both dogs pursued him, but the rabbit ran like mad. They could never catch him. Never. Occasionally he doubled back. He didn't need to, of course, for he was so fast that the dogs could not even reach him on a straight line. But he liked to tease them and let them feel how superior he was. Purposely he would slow his pace and when they were quite close—bang!—a ninety-degree turn and he whizzed away in a wide arc while the dogs stood by, dumfounded.

Later on he found still other ways to plague them. He let them come quite near, ran between them, then all of a sudden —hops!—with a high leap he bounded over them, sweeping through the air like a big white ball of wool. Apparently he liked this game very much, for he repeated the leap again and again. The dogs were less amused by it. Exhausted, they threw themselves on the grass and panted. But the rabbit was not tired. He came over, sat opposite them and laughed. This put the dogs in a very bad mood, for after all they didn't want the rabbit to make fools of them.

And at this point the difference in their characters became apparent. Lumpi, the Maltese, grew angry during the race and growled and snapped at the rabbit. But as he bit only into thin air, he grumbled even more, forgetting that his ability to run suffered from the use of his voice. Puck, the peaceful terrier, made

believe for a while that he was playing along in the game but
soon made an about-face, lay down and looked on quietly.
Finally both dogs refused to play. But this did them no good.
They had to! The rabbit would not let them rest. He poked them
in the ribs, bumped their heads, hunted them up and woke them
from their sleep. They were absolutely the slaves of his caprice.
Puck suffered most, for in him the rabbit recognized a passive
resistance. He threw himself against Puck and pinched his flank.
It was not a bite, only a pinch, but Puck yelped loudly. A tuft of
his black fur was missing.

Now the chase became reversed. The rabbit pursued the dogs.
They ran as hard as they could but he always caught them. With
a leap he would bounce onto the back of the nearest dog, upset
him and roll over on top of him. White silk and white curls,
when it was the Maltese; white silk and black curls when it was
the terrier. Puck finally rebelled. The idea of being hounded by a
rabbit was too much for him. In fact, he was so afraid of the
rabbit that he no longer dared go into the garden. He stayed in
the house, and when it was absolutely necessary to go outside,
took flight before the rabbit spied him.

The rabbit was a terrifying object to Puck only. To the tomcat he was still something to be regarded with cool astonishment

and to the Maltese he became a fighting and playing companion.

Strangely enough he began to assume some of the characteristics of a dog. When visitors rang, the dogs stormed to the gate, barking loudly. The rabbit stormed with them; in fact, he led them. Of course he did not bark, which after all could hardly be expected of him, but otherwise he behaved just like a dog. He let himself be petted and followed at the visitors' heels step by step. He went into the house every day, slipped in and out of all the rooms and lay for hours on the stairs. When someone came into the garden and called him he hopped up immediately and waited to be caressed.

But one day the call, "Bunny! Bunny!" echoed without response. The rabbit no longer heard it, for he was gone. Yes, the snow-white rabbit was gone.

The master searched for him with sadness and regret, for he had come to love this brave and independent little creature and knew that it had small chance of surviving in a world which shows no pity to the defenseless.

But the rabbit knew nothing of this. He knew only a desire to be free and that this freedom lay in the strange world beyond the frontiers of his garden. So in the night he made a hole beneath the fence again and ventured forth. And this time he did not return.

Zinnia and Her Babies

MARGERY BIANCO

Some time ago, in writing about cats, I spoke of Zinnia, the little black cat who has such a liking for dogs. I told how she will sit staring pensively at some dog which may happen to be in the room, and then all at once jump up, walk over to him, and begin washing his face and smoothing his hair, just like a nursemaid, holding his head between her two paws if he tries to move. And what a terrible time she had trying to straighten out the big long-haired collie! Much as she likes dogs, their occasional untidiness gets very much upon Zinnia's mind, and sooner or later she decides that something must be done about it.

I think Zinnia made up her mind long ago that all this so-called "cat and dog" business was just nonsense. Dogs are just like cats, if you treat them the right way, and a little good sound cat training would do them all the good in the world. Zinnia's owners are always afraid that she will one day, in her fearlessness, happen upon the wrong dog, and then she may get unpleasantly surprised. But so far all the dogs she has met have either returned her friendliness, or been far too surprised by it to think of attacking her.

The only other creatures that Zinnia seems to like better than dogs are—not human beings, for she is quite indifferent to petting or attention; and not even other cats, whom she just tolerates, but kittens. Anybody's kittens, though naturally she prefers her own. She is a born mother, and the voice of a kitten mewing will always bring her on a trot to see what the trouble is. Quite likely she may decide that the kittens are fretful because they are not in what she considers a good and comfortable place for them. In that case she will probably pick them up one by one and carry them off somewhere else, without bothering to consult their own mother at all.

One summer I remember Zinnia was bringing up a family of her own, four babies of a few weeks old, and she had them in the barn. There was a good deal of painting and other work going on about the house at that time, and Zinnia's mistress thought that the barn was the safest place for the kittens to stay in, at least until they were a little older, when there would be less danger of their tumbling into paint pots, or getting stepped upon by accident. So the barn door was kept closed, and Zinnia's own food and saucers of milk were carried out to her there twice a day.

Zinnia, however, had her own ideas. The barn was big and airy; the kittens had their own box lined with hay, and plenty of space to crawl safely about in. But that didn't satisfy her. It was sunny June weather; kittens should be out in the garden, enjoying the fresh air.

And every morning there they were, all four of them, packed into an old wheelbarrow by the woodshed, where they whimpered and blinked at the sunlight, looking, poor mites, anything but comfortable on the bare earthy boards. And there Zinnia would leave them, while she went off on some hunting excursion of her own.

For a long while no one could discover how Zinnia managed to bring those kittens out. Every evening, and often during the day as well, they were carried back to their own bed, and the barn door closed and bolted, with Zinnia and her babies inside. But it made no difference. Every morning, there they were back again in the wheelbarrow.

But at last we found out Zinnia's secret.

High up in the barn wall, near the rafters, was a window with one small pane missing. Because of the slope of the ground, the barn was so built as to be two stories high at the back instead of one, so that from the outside this window was even higher from the ground, some fourteen feet or more. One morning Zinnia's mistress, passing near the barn, heard a queer scraping sound, like the noise a squirrel makes scrambling down a tree trunk, and looked up to see Zinnia, who had just squeezed through the broken window with a kitten in her mouth and was letting herself down cautiously, backward, inch by inch, clinging with her claws to the smooth side of the barn.

The kitten safely landed on the ground, and dragged over to the wheelbarrow, Zinnia turned right around and went back for the next, by the same route.

Seeing that she was so determined about it, it seemed useless to shut the kittens up any longer, so after that the barn door was left ajar and Zinnia was free to carry her babies in and out in a less dangerous way. It was just like obstinate little Zinnia,

however, that having once got her own way in the matter she didn't seem to care any longer whether the kittens were indoors or out, but left them most of the time to crawl about by themselves on the barn floor, where they certainly seemed happier than when they were being dragged to and fro so ruthlessly every day.

All but one, the smallest of the four. Nearly always, if there happens to be one kitten in a litter smaller and weaker than the rest, the mother cat will choose it as her special favorite, and so it was with Zinnia. This particular kitten, a tiny maltese with a white chin, Zinnia took extra pains with. It was slower in learning to crawl and eat, due, everyone thought, to having been carried about so persistently by its mother, and perhaps getting a few bumps here and there sliding down the barn wall. Every day, long after she had left the other kittens to their own devices, Zinnia would still drag this weakly one out into the sunshine, whether or no, and leave it there for several hours in the wheelbarrow, and either her devotion, or the warm sunshine, had its good effect, for the little malty grew up in time just as strong as her brothers and sisters, though always a bit smaller.

But the queerest thing that Zinnia ever did was in regard to another sort of kitten altogether.

It happened one year that there was a new baby in the house— a real two-legged baby this time. Zinnia, of course, knew about the baby; cats know all about everything. But she had never shown any great curiosity about it, possibly because she was busy herself, just then, bringing up a family of her own tucked away in a basket on the porch.

It was pleasant spring weather and the baby, who was just a few weeks old, was put out every morning to take her nap in a wicker cradle on the lawn. Usually she slept soundly, but one morning she happened to be a little restless and fretful. Now the crying of a young baby does sometimes sound rather like the mewing of a kitten, especially if the baby is sleepy, and just complaining to itself, as this one was.

Zinnia was seated on the doorstep, washing her face, and when she heard this peculiar sort of noise she pricked her ears up and strolled over to see what it was all about. Standing up with her front paws on the edge of the cradle she peered in, and it evidently didn't take her long to make up her mind just why the baby was crying. "What that child needs," thought Zinnia, "is a mouse!"

So off she trotted down the garden, and round to the barn,

to reappear a moment or so later with a nice fat mouse dangling from her mouth. Straight over to the cradle she went, and dropped the mouse in, with a little crooning mew, just to draw the baby's attention to it.

Now the baby's mother had watched all this, and she thought at first that Zinnia had just made a very funny mistake, and had dropped the mouse there by accident. So she picked it up by its tail and took it over to Zinnia's own babies in their basket. But Zinnia would have none of this. She fished that dead mouse right out again and carried it over to the baby's cradle a second time, dropping it in with a little thump, as though to say: "You may think you know a lot about babies, but I've had more experience than you and, believe me or not, what that child needs is a *mouse!*"

Zinnia is a grandmother now, many times over. Most of her various babies are grown up and have families of their own though each summer there are new ones to take their place.

Zinnia herself is growing middle-aged. Her little pointed face, with its pale-green slanting eyes, is a shade more pointed than it used to be; her black fur, always a little reddish in the light, is taking on more and more of a rusty tone, the color of an old iron kettle that has been lying out in the sun. But she is as keen a mouser as ever, and her sense of responsibility is, if anything, more marked as time goes by. When I visited her last, only a short time ago, we had a very characteristic example of it.

A grown-up daughter of Zinnia's, Topsy, had died quite suddenly after only a couple of days' illness, leaving two pretty little kittens, about ten days older than Zinnia's own kittens. Luckily they were nearly big enough to lap for themselves, and meantime could be fed warm milk with a medicine dropper, but they missed their mother sadly, and the warmth and comfort of her body curled up beside them in the basket. Everyone was worried about poor Topsy's kittens and how they would get along without her, but before twenty-four hours had passed, Zinnia, as usual, had come to the rescue. She heard the little orphans mewing, took one look at them, and without more ado seized first one and then the other and dragged them up two flights of stairs to the attic, where she settled them comfortably in the box with her own three babies.

There will be no neglected kittens in any house where Zinnia lives, as long as she is there to look after them.

My Friend Toto

CHERRY KEARTON

SOME four years ago I was in Central Africa for the purpose of photographing wild animals in their natural surroundings—lions, elephants, leopards, rhinoceroses, hippopotami, and many other beasts, besides birds and even insects. I have always loved animals, and I have never felt any desire to hunt and shoot them. Instead I have devoted my life to watching them in their own "homes," and obtaining records with my cameras of what I see.

For this purpose I have traveled all over the world: throughout Africa, north, south, east and west, in India, Ceylon, Burma, Borneo, Canada and America. But always Central Africa has appealed to me more than any other country. And out of all Central Africa there are few places so fascinating as the lower slopes of the "Mountains of the Moon." They stand directly between Lake Albert on the north and Lake George on the south, while the immense Lake Victoria Nyanza lies some two hundred miles to the east. As one stands on these slopes the mountains tower over one to a height of nearly seventeen thousand feet, snow-tipped and wonderful. Around one is the jungle, wild and often impassable. Stretches of open country break through the tropical forests here and there, dotted with stunted trees; but for the most part, on the slopes of the mountains, there is nothing but close-growing vegetation, with trees sixty feet in height intertwined with creepers, where, except on the few paths laboriously cut by the natives, nothing but an elephant can force its way.

At the time of which I write, I was marching, with an expedition consisting of some twenty native "boys" or porters, through the Congo Free State, planning to go afterwards across British East Africa to Mombasa on the coast. Sometimes, when game was comparatively scarce, we would march each day for a week; at other times, when it was more plentiful, we would pitch our camp on a comparatively open spot and stay until I had exposed many hundreds of feet of cinematograph film and numerous photographic plates.

We had halted near the foot of the "Mountains of the Moon," which were clothed in everlasting mist; my tent was pitched, the baggage and boxes were safely piled, the porters were resting, and I had just returned from a short prospecting journey with my cameras, when I saw coming toward me an Englishman. It was an out of the way place to meet anyone but a native, but this man I knew was encamped a few miles away, shooting elephants. Our paths had crossed three weeks before, and I was not surprised to see him again.

As he came nearer I could see that he carried what looked like a bundle of some sort under his arm.

"Hallo!" I shouted. "What have you got there?"

"A chimp," he said, and he laughed. "The King of the Chimps, perhaps; or their Prime Minister. Too young for that, though. More likely an infant prodigy, with a great future before him."

I looked at the little fellow as I sat smoking. He certainly was a young chimpanzee, probably not more than one year old. He peered at me out of a pair of most intelligent eyes.

"He's a fine little chap," I said, and I put out a finger. The chimp at once extended his hand and took my finger gravely.

"He's a perfect gentleman, too," said the hunter. "Aren't you, Toto?"

"I can see he's quite a gentleman," I said.

The hunter let him loose. The chimp at once climbed on to my knee, looking up into my face with an expression which seemed to denote a real desire to make friends.

"He's quite taken with you, Kearton," said the elephant hunter.

"What are you going to do with him?" I asked.

The hunter laughed.

"Well," he said, "I'll tell you. We are off today to the coast. We're traveling light, and I may not come back. I brought him along to see whether you would care to keep him."

I looked again at Toto, smiling at him. The little fellow almost smiled back at me, looking just like a little Irishman. I can say without vanity—although as a matter of fact it is a thing over which I always rejoice—that most animals soon make friends with me. This one, I could see, would be no exception.

"He's a jolly good chimp," said the elephant hunter, "and far and away the most intelligent I ever came across."

I patted Toto on the head, and he proceeded to curl up against my chest, holding on to my sleeve while one arm crept round my neck.

Should I take him? I wondered. He might prove a tremendous nuisance. On an expedition such as mine the amount of extra baggage that can be carried was necessarily limited, and very few luxuries were possible. To carry a chimpanzee in such circumstances seemed absurd. Yet—well, I liked Toto at first sight; I was practically alone, since the native boys hardly counted as far as companionship went—and the idea of having a good-natured pet to play with appealed to me.

"All right," I said at last. "I'll take him."

I need not attempt to describe Toto. Whether or not he was handsome may best be judged from the picture that follows. Certainly he had features which would not count for beauty in a man: a large mouth, a very flat nose, and protruding ears. Yet in spite of that, there was something very pleasing about him: something pathetic that called for sympathy, and at the same time something roguish that showed him a real companion, always game for anything "sporting" and always ready to share a joke.

He stood about two feet high. He had very long arms and big hands. He was surprisingly strong, active and quite untiring.

When the elephant hunter left me, I put Toto down on the end of my bed and went outside to call Mahomed, the native boy who acted as my cook, valet and gunbearer. I wanted Mahomed to build a sort of kennel in which Toto could sleep at night, something light enough to be carried on the march and yet strong enough to keep him secure. But when we returned to the tent we found that Toto had his own ideas on the subject.

Chimpanzees build nests for themselves in the treetops: roomy, flat nests made of intertwined twigs and padded with dry grass. Toto seemed to have made up his mind already that he had come to my tent in order to stay there, and he was proceeding to build for himself a nest—on my bed. He had collected material from all round the tent; anything that resembled a stick, including my miniature telescope, had been carried into the heap.

I laughed at the sight. "He's determined to save you the trouble," I said to Mahomed. "But we'll have to do better for him than that. Go and get him some dry grass and make him a bed in your quarters."

When I began to clear my bed, Toto seemed to want to keep the things he had found, so I gave him the telescope to play with while I put the others away. He sat on the ground, and for an hour I heard no more of him except for the clicking of the telescope as he pulled it to and fro.

At last Mahomed returned, and Toto followed him quietly enough. A few minutes later I went out to see that he was comfortable. I found him curled on a bed of grass, looking at the native boys as they rolled themselves in their blankets. For some minutes he watched them with great interest. Then he realized that this strange method of covering oneself must somehow be superior to building a nest and sleeping on grass. If it were better for the boys, no doubt it would also be better for him. So he got up, quietly walked toward them, snatched one of the blankets and trotted away with it.

Naturally there was a great uproar then in the camp. The boy whose blanket had been taken was furious. Unfortunately, he made up his mind to get it back, and Toto was determined that he shouldn't. He grunted furiously as the boy chased him, and directly the boy's outstretched hand touched the trailing blanket Toto turned suddenly and bit him. A monkey's bite makes a wound which is uncommonly painful, and the boy did not risk letting it happen again. He retreated very sulkily and persuaded a friend to let him share a blanket for the night, while Toto departed with his booty and sat down on his bed, uttering victorious shouts.

The next night the same thing happened. But this time Toto got the worst of it. He was treated roughly by the porters, who, though they loved him, loved their blankets more. They lay in wait for Toto and gave him a warm reception. Repulsed and very unhappy, he walked over in the dark to my tent, grunted with irritation, and crawled on to my bed. There he sat jabbering, telling me no doubt exactly what he thought of those porters.

We did not know each other's language, but a sympathetic voice always means much to an animal, and after I had talked to him for a while he seemed pacified. It was late then, and I lay down, wanting to get to sleep. To my astonishment Toto crept in beside me. And before morning he had got the best half of my bed!

He was an affectionate little fellow. He put one arm round my neck and the other under his head, and lay there just like a child.

The next night I made him a little bed to himself in my tent, and ever afterwards he slept near me. He was happy there and as good as gold, but I knew that he regarded it as only the second best thing, for if ever I sat too long at the camp fire in the evening I always found that he had crept quietly into my bed and was lying there when I came, looking up knowingly, as if to say, "May'nt I stay, just this once?"

It did not take us more than a week, as may be imagined, to fall in love with each other. He wanted to go with me wherever I went. Sometimes this could not be allowed. On the first occasion, I thought I could trick him. After telling Mahomed to look after him, I crept out of the back of the camp, thinking that I had evaded him. But Toto soon smelt a rat. He seemed to guess which way I had gone, and slipping loose from the boy, he bolted and, taking a short cut, was close behind me before I had gone a hundred yards.

I stopped, talked to him seriously and firmly, and turned to lead him back to the camp. But Toto in those days was inclined to be "spoilt," and the idea of going back in disgrace did not appeal to him at all. He stamped and screamed, beat his hands against his head, and finally began to bang his head against the ground. Poor Toto! It was his first lesson in discipline, and he didn't like it.

Before Toto had been found by the elephant hunter, he had lived with his father and his mother, his brothers and sisters, uncles and aunts and cousins, in the trees of the forest. There were, so to speak, two quite different worlds in the forest: the world of the treetops, where the birds and the monkeys lived, and where it was bright and sunny and warm, and the world of the ground below, where lived the animals that could not climb, and where everything was dark and mysterious because the leaves overhead were so thick that the sun could hardly ever be seen. The monkeys of the upper world did not often go down to the ground, for there was danger from bigger animals and from snakes; but they looked down often enough, and there they saw the mother elephants with their babies, and heard them trumpeting whenever the children rambled out of sight; they saw the okapi, with his zebra-like stripes, stealing warily along, alert against attack; and the few pigmy black men who crept through the forest with bow and arrows in search of something for dinner. Now and then, too, in clearer places near a river, a hippo would lumber along, or a small herd of buffalo would pass on its way to drink.

And there, up aloft, Toto would have sat, watching and wondering, with all his small brain busy, while parrots and other birds in all their varied colors shrieked from the branches beside him and white-collared eagles hovered overhead.

That, probably, was the life of Toto before he came into the hands of my friend, the elephant hunter. I do not know how he was found. But I think that his mother must have been killed by one of the deadly poisoned arrows of the natives, and then Toto, not knowing or understanding what had happened, must have climbed down to the ground, missing the food that his mother would regularly have provided. And so he would have been found at the foot of a tree, a forlorn little object, who would certainly have been killed swiftly enough if the hunter had not come to his rescue. Poor little Toto! He was not to see his home again, nor swing as he used to do from branch to branch of those African trees; and yet I think that he has been happy, following me into very strange places, and finding at any rate a friend who loved him.

I had many miles to travel on that journey through Africa and much work to do. The moment the expedition halted I had to get out my cameras, and as soon as the tents were pitched and I had seen that all was in order I would take two of the native boys as carriers and start out to see what animals I could find. Sometimes I went more or less at random, ready to unslip my cinematograph camera whenever anything attracted my attention, and at other times I would make for a particular place, which I had seen in the distance through my glasses and chosen because it seemed a likely piece of country in which to find hippopotami, for instance, or a particular kind of bird.

But now, wherever I went, Toto came with me, shambling along with that curious four-legged walk which apes use when there are no trees on which to swing and they have to travel on the ground. After the first few days, I tried the experiment of giving him something to carry, at first something of little value which could not easily be broken, but later, when I saw how careful he could be, something more precious. He seemed to realize then that he was helping me, and he would clutch the box of film or whatever I had given him tightly to his chest and hop along just a pace behind me, looking up every now and again with a quaint expression of pleasure and pride.

He was also helpful in other ways. His eyesight was far sharper than that of a man, and he proved himself an excellent scout. My own eyes are accustomed to the jungle, and I do not often need field glasses to find the animals which I then stalk until I am near enough to use the camera. But Toto's eyes were far surer than mine, and often he would give me warning and show me the direction to take.

Once, while we were out together, Toto and I were resting under a little bush near some rocks. Before sitting down I had, as I thought, made sure that there was nothing within sight that I wanted to photograph, so that I could rest without fear of missing valuable opportunities. Suddenly Toto stood upright, thumping his chest excitedly, and turning to me with a little grunt, as if to say, "Be careful! Be careful!" But I could see nothing. I examined every inch of the grass in front of us, but nothing was visible. I took my glasses and studied the ground ahead more thoroughly. Then, fully one hundred and fifty yards away, I saw four tiny dark specks just showing above the grass. They were the tips of the horns of a pair of deer.

In the jungle Toto was always on the alert. Probably he had learnt caution from the dangers of life in his world of the tree-tops, when often a young monkey who strayed carelessly on the ground would disappear forever. Toto was suspicious of every-thing that he did not know for certain to be friendly. In particular, he was always terrified of snakes; and rightly so, for snakes must have ended the days of many of his young cousins at home.

It is no unusual thing in Central Africa to find on the ground the dried outer skin of a snake: for snakes shed a thin skin at regular seasons and glide away in all the glory of a freshly grown covering, while the discarded coat lies where it fell on the ground. But Toto did not know that, and to him a snake skin must contain a snake. I remember that once we came upon the thrown-off skin of a big puff adder. Toto very nearly trod on it. Then he bounded into the air, his hair quite literally standing on end. As time went on, Toto learned many things, but this, the snake which was no snake, was a mystery of Nature which was always beyond his understanding.

On another day, as we were going back to camp in the evening, Toto had wandered some ten yards in front of me, when suddenly a small snake slid out from behind a stone, passed right in front of Toto, and dropped into a crack between two rocks. Toto yelled with terror, then ran back to me, and stood, with his teeth chattering, holding his hand as if to show where he had been bitten. I examined it carefully, but could not see the tiny mark that would have been made by the snake's fangs. I made sure of this, and then told Toto that he was only frightened and that the snake had not touched him. He did not believe me. He had been so scared by the sudden sight of the snake that he was certain that he was hurt and probably imagined he was going to die. Knowing that this was not so, I tried to coax him to come back with me to camp. He would not come. I walked ahead, expecting him to follow. After a few paces, I looked back and saw the little fellow stretched out on the ground, convinced that he was too ill to move, and looking at me with piteous entreaty not to leave him. So I picked him up and carried him to my tent, where at last the sight of a bunch of bananas distracted his thoughts until he forgot his terror; and half an hour later he was sitting on my bed, playing as contentedly as ever.

But it must not be thought that Toto was a coward. He was very far from that. Of snakes he was always afraid. I never saw a chimpanzee that was not. And I don't think he had any particular friendship for crocodiles. Nor have I. But there was little else that he feared.

He did not walk into danger, and he always grunted his usual warning when we approached any animal that I had not seen, but I have never seen him scared into flight from a single animal, although on one occasion, at least, I, at any rate, would dearly have liked to have taken to my heels.

This was when we were together one day at a considerable distance from the camp. I was looking for a suitable place to hide the camera and myself, so that I could take pictures of vultures, hyena and jackal.

A few yards away was a river, and a little dip in the ground near its bank was filled with water, either from a hidden channel joining it to the river or else from a spring. Round this pool were the tracks where many animals had come to drink, and it was there that I expected to get my photographs. A few thick bushes, making a little clump about ten yards across, stood close to the pool, and I planned to hide amongst them with my camera. I walked toward the spot, happily enough, thinking of the good pictures that I could obtain without great difficulty.

Suddenly something touched my arm. It was Toto. He stood beside me, gazing first at the clump of bushes and then at me. At first he merely stared, as if uncertain whether an alarm should be given or not; then he seemed to make up his mind, and he pulled harder at my sleeve as if to draw me away, giving several of his deep-throated, warning grunts.

I stopped. I knew by that time that Toto did not give the alarm unnecessarily. Undoubtedly there was something hidden among those bushes. Whether it was any animal dangerous to man I did not know, but it happened that I was entirely un-armed, and I decided to make certain what lay ahead of me before going any closer. So I turned away, getting to a greater distance from the bushes, while I worked round to the other side, where I hoped to find a gap into which I could look. Toto kept close at my side, stopping after every few yards and standing upright to look behind him.

At last we reached the opposite side of the clump, and turning, I began to approach it again, rather more warily than I had done before. Suddenly I saw the leaves of the nearest bush move, and I stopped. Something was moving into the open from behind that bush . . . something yellow . . . a lion!

Several times I have photographed lions in Africa, but I would not go toward one without a weapon, although I should only use it in the direst emergency. But now I had nothing more effective than my camera tripod, and I quickly decided to retreat. In fact, I must confess that my main desire at that moment was to put five hundred yards between that lion and myself as quickly as possible.

But to have run would have been to invite pursuit. A man-eating lion will always attack if he thinks he has an easy victim. If I had turned to run, that lion would have been across my body, tearing at my flesh, before I had gone twenty yards.

I knew that my only chance was to face him squarely, and edge quietly backward as best I could. At first I stood perfectly still, staring. It was a painful ordeal. I have no idea for how long I stood there, perhaps for a minute, or a minute and a half; but to me it seemed almost a matter of hours.

Slowly the lion moved, taking a few steps backward. Then he turned and snarled, showing his fangs as if deciding that I was unworthy of royal attention. Slowly, I began to retreat. Toto all the time had stood firmly beside me, watching as I watched and waiting till I gave the word to move. Gradually we retreated together until we were nearly a hundred yards from that clump of bushes. Then at last I turned and hurried away, glancing back every now and again to make certain that there was no pursuit.

That night when I found Toto in my bed I did not turn him out.

This adventure was the second turning-point in Toto's life. When my friend the elephant hunter brought him to me and I agreed to take him, I gave but little thought to the future. At the moment I was busy in Africa and there I should remain for some months. I knew, vaguely, that the day would come when I should turn toward the coast and eventually go back to England, and if I gave the matter a thought I must have assumed that then Toto would be left behind. Without having troubled to consider the matter, I suppose that I intended to leave him in a forest where he might join a passing family of chimpanzees, and soon forget that he had ever known any other life than that of the treetops. A chimp's memory is long lived, but I hoped this little fellow, whom then I hardly knew, would soon forget and be happy, playing monkey games among the branches.

But now everything seemed changed. For one thing, we had had adventure together. We had risked our lives, and, without a doubt, now it was Toto that had saved mine. By every unwritten law of the African wilds, whether of white man, of native, or of beast, that should have prevented me from deserting him.

No, it was out of the question to keep Toto for a few weeks or months as a plaything and then to leave him to take his chance of whether he first found friends or enemies. But it was equally out of the question to restore him to his own family. For one thing, we were now fully two hundred miles from the spot where he had been found. But the more important objection was that Toto's family would not have received him at all in the way in which the Prodigal Son was received by his father. On the contrary, since apes know by instinct when one of their number has been in contact with human beings, they would have regarded him at the best as a stranger, while it is more than possible that, considering him a traitor to his race, they would have killed him.

To take Toto back was therefore unthinkable. Besides, I must confess that I no longer wanted him to leave me.

If he was not to go, only one thing was possible. He must come with me on my travels, out of Central Africa, through British East Africa, and so by way of Nairobi to the coast, then across the sea to Marseilles and eventually to England.

I considered this plan very carefully. The first part of the journey presented no great difficulties. We had already traveled over a hundred miles together, and I had grown accustomed to carrying Toto pickaback for mile after mile. At first he had clung desperately, clasping his hands under my chin until I was nearly throttled; but gradually I had shown him how to balance with his legs at my waist and hold me tightly by the shoulders. Then we were both comfortable enough, and sometimes I would even forget all about him till he would suddenly lay his head on my shoulder and try softly to kiss my cheek.

Thinking the matter over, I had little doubt that Toto could safely be brought through the jungle and as far as Nairobi. But there we should have left the wild and open country behind us. Toto, of course, had never seen a house nor walked on a pavement. He had never seen a white woman, and the only men he had ever met were the elephant hunter, the native boys of my expedition, and myself. In the wilds, his pranks were amusing, but what would happen in a town? What would other people, the people I was to stay with, say of him, and would they even tolerate him at all?

But if he was indeed to come with me to London, he must begin to get used to civilization some time, and the sooner the better. And as far as that went, he was already a very well-behaved little fellow. He was learning daily what might be done and what was forbidden. He was even learning manners and many becoming little habits.

For instance, he had learned to wash.

This began one day when he sat outside the tent and watched one of the boys cleaning his teeth. The native did not use a brush as we do, but a little wooden stick with a frayed and fibrous end, which did its work exceedingly well. Toto picked this up when the boy laid it down and, like the perfect imitator that he was, put it into his own mouth, drawing it to and fro as the boy had done.

Doing this seemed to give him great satisfaction, and for several days he did it every morning. Then he began to realize that I did something a little different, and he decided upon an experiment. One morning I noticed him fumbling in my valise, and a minute later I saw that he had taken my toothbrush.

Now, though I had every desire that Toto should be well brought up, and should learn in time to wash behind his ears and clean his teeth three times a day, I preferred to keep a toothbrush, at any rate, to myself. So I chased him round the tent, took the brush away, and then gave him a new one, just as it was bought, in a little paper bag.

He put it at once into his mouth, and soon became entangled with the paper. In a few minutes, however, he got rid of this and settled down to the new experience.

He found the method of the white man considerably more difficult than that of the native. He had, as may be seen from his picture, a fairly large mouth; but that, instead of making the matter easier, rather added to his difficulties, because he was uncertain into which part of his mouth the brush should be put. First of all he brushed his tongue, and it tickled. Then he tried to eat it.

"Steady, old fellow," I said. "Watch what I do," and taking my own brush I held it up to attract his attention. Toto imitated me at once, holding the brush so that it scraped his nose and made him sneeze.

I laughed at that, and Toto, who always hated to be laughed at, flew into a temper, flung the brush on the floor, and stamped on it. But as soon as I tried to pick it up, he snatched it and began again, this time with greater success.

The next thing that interested him was my bath. He sat watching me at my morning tub, and then directly I got out he got in. He did not mind the water, but it puzzled him. At first he could not distinguish between wetting and drying. As soon as he was in the bath he picked up the towel and started to use it. Naturally the towel immediately got wet and he made little progress. He would rub his face with the sopping material, and then, feeling very damp and uncomfortable, would look up at me to make sure that I was not laughing at him. I think he knew that he was doing it wrong, without being able to decide what was the matter.

So I gave him a lesson, performing each operation very slowly while he watched me with an expression of extraordinary seriousness. He wanted to learn. There were many things in this strange way of life that he had come into which puzzled him, but he was determined to master them one by one. Now he saw me take first the soap and then the sponge; and then get out and stand beside the bath to dry myself. When I had finished he began, and so well had he learnt the lesson that he did it perfectly—almost. He made a lather with the soap and began on his face, spluttering uncomfortably, and then, with a piece of originality, he reached for his brush and cleaned his teeth. He was very methodical, and he seemed to think it right that everything to do with the face should be settled in one operation. Then he washed his hands, and next his feet, holding the sponge so that the water trickled on to them, exactly as I had done. But then he thought he had finished.

"Go on, Toto," I said. "Don't forget your body."

But he would not do any more. He became accustomed to follow me into the bath every morning directly I left it, but he would never wash anything besides his face, hands and feet, and then he would clamber out and dry himself.

Afterwards he would take a brush and a mirror and complete his toilet.

He was also learning to behave properly at mealtimes. When in the early morning I would call to the boy to get my tea, Toto would slip out of his bed, stand at the entrance to the tent and give a shout in imitation of mine. Then when the boy appeared, Toto would come too, holding his cup in one hand and the saucer in the other. He would stand patiently beside me till I was ready to pour out, and then he would hold up the cup for me to fill it.

He was fond of sugar, and if he did not think I had given him enough he would slip his hand up to the sugar basin, look imploringly at me, and wait until I gave him the word to help himself.

More than anything else he liked bananas, and however many I gave him he always wanted more. Sometimes he would help himself, and eventually I had to keep them in a locked box. But one day Toto watched me as I took the keys from my pocket, unlocked the case, tore off two bananas and gave them to him. A little later we were playing together by the fire when I felt a hand at my pocket. I went on with the game, pretending not to notice. Toto put his hand stealthily into my trouser pocket and drew out the keys. Wondering what he would do, I went outside the tent, and after waiting a minute to make him think I had gone away I looked silently in at the doorway. Toto was sitting in front of the banana box, trying one key after another in the lock until he found the right one. Then he took out a banana and began to gobble it up as fast as he could.

When I came in suddenly and caught him in the act, I think he was surprised that I only laughed and let him finish the fruit. But then Toto did not share my remembrance of a very small boy, many years ago, who stole the key of his mother's larder in search of strawberry jam . . .

Chimpanzees are not accustomed to regular mealtimes. They sit and nibble all day, taking a leaf from one branch and fruit from another. I gave Toto, from the first, four good meals a day, but it was a long time before he accustomed himself to the routine and felt satisfied. At first he would enjoy a meal with me and then slip out and invite himself to dinner with the porters, taking very good care that no one had a bigger helping of their mealie food than he did. But gradually he came to prefer eating only with me, and to feel that there were advantages in not running away directly our meal was finished. He would sit on a chair watching and imitating nearly everything I did. Sometimes he would read the newspaper, if it was mail day and one was within reach. He would prop himself up against the back of the chair and wrestle with the problem of unfolding the big sheet without overbalancing, until he could hold it outstretched in front of him exactly like a man in a West End Club.

One day he watched me in silence for a long while as I sat smoking. Then he came toward me and reached up to touch my pipe.

"It's an evil habit, Toto," I said, laughing. "You'd better keep off it."

But soon I found that he was serious. He wanted to smoke. So I gave him an old pipe, wondering what he would do with it. He went back to his chair, put the stem between his teeth, and leant back luxuriously, closing his eyes. For a time he seemed content, and for some days after that wherever he went he carried the pipe as if it was his most precious possession. Then he realized that I used to put brown grass into the bowl of mine and set fire to it, and he wanted to do the same with his. I let him try. The matches proved a difficulty, but at last he learnt to strike them and to light the top of the tobacco. But he did not realize the secret of the art of smoking and he was puzzled when the flame in his pipe died directly, while mine continued to send forth clouds of smoke.

It was constantly a problem for him, and often I felt that he was longing for me to show him how it was done. I tried to do so, but my drawing in of breath must have looked to him merely a matter of making faces; so that I roared with laughter when he began to imitate my expression.

Still, he played every evening with the pipe. Many months later, it chanced that he drew in his breath through his mouth while the pipe was between his teeth. He gasped. He choked. He coughed. But the secret was found, and from that night he exhausted his half-ounce of tobacco every week.

It was while Toto was playing with his pipe one evening, long before this discovery, that I finally made up my mind to take him home with me.

Pushing back my chair, I got up.

"Toto, old fellow," I said, "you shall come to London."

Toto looked up at once. Then he tucked the pipe into a fold of skin between his ear and his shoulder where he liked to keep it, climbed off the chair, and ran toward me, so that I felt that he approved of my decision and was eager to start.

Waukewa's Eagle

JAMES BUCKHAM

O NE DAY, when the Indian boy Waukewa was hunting along the mountain-side, he found a young eagle with a broken wing, lying at the base of a cliff. The bird had fallen from an aery on a ledge high above, and being too young to fly, had fluttered down the cliff and injured itself so severely that it was likely to die. When Waukewa saw it he was about to drive one of his sharp arrows through its body, for the passion of the hunter was strong in him, and the eagle plunders many a fine fish from the Indian's drying-frame. But a gentler impulse came to him as he saw the young bird quivering with pain and fright at his feet, and he slowly unbent his bow, put the arrow in his quiver, and stooped over the panting eaglet. For fully a minute the wild eyes of the wounded bird and the eyes of the Indian boy, growing gentler and softer as he gazed, looked into one another. Then the struggling and panting of the young eagle ceased; the wild, frightened look passed out of its eyes, and it suffered Waukewa to pass his hand gently over its ruffled and draggled feathers. The fierce instinct to fight, to defend its threatened life, yielded to the charm of the tenderness and pity expressed in the boy's eyes; and from that moment Waukewa and the eagle were friends.

Waukewa went slowly home to his father's lodge, bearing the wounded eaglet in his arms. He carried it so gently that the broken wing gave no twinge of pain, and the bird lay perfectly still, never offering to strike with its sharp beak the hands that clasped it.

Warming some water over the fire at the lodge, Waukewa bathed the broken wing of the eagle, and bound it up with soft strips of skin. Then he made a nest of ferns and grass inside the lodge, and laid the bird in it. The boy's mother looked on with shining eyes. Her heart was very tender. From girlhood she had loved all the creatures of the woods, and it pleased her to see some of her own gentle spirit waking in the boy.

When Waukewa's father returned from hunting, he would have caught up the young eagle and wrung its neck. But the boy pleaded with him so eagerly, stooping over the captive and defending it with his small hands, that the stern warrior laughed and called him his "little squaw-heart." "Keep it, then," he said, "and nurse it until it is well. But then you must let it go, for we will not raise up a thief in the lodges." So Waukewa promised that when the eagle's wing was healed and grown so that it could fly, he would carry it forth and give it its freedom.

It was a month—or, as the Indians say, a moon—before the young eagle's wing had fully mended and the bird was old enough and strong enough to fly. And in the meantime Waukewa cared for it and fed it daily, and the friendship between the boy and the bird grew very strong.

But at last the time came when the willing captive must be freed. So Waukewa carried it far away from the Indian lodges, where none of the young braves might see it hovering over and be tempted to shoot their arrows at it, and there he let it go. The young eagle rose toward the sky in great circles, rejoicing in its freedom and its strange, new power of flight. But when Waukewa began to move away from the spot, it came swooping down again; and all day long it followed him through the woods as he hunted. At dusk, when Waukewa shaped his course for the Indian lodges, the eagle would have accompanied him. But the boy suddenly slipped into a hollow tree and hid, and after a long time the eagle stopped sweeping about in search of him and flew slowly and sadly away.

Summer passed, and then winter; and spring came again, with its flowers and birds and swarming fish in the lakes and streams. Then it was that all the Indians, old and young, braves and squaws, pushed their light canoes out from shore and with spear and hook waged pleasant war against the salmon and the red-spotted trout. After winter's long imprisonment, it was such joy to toss in the sunshine and the warm wind and catch savory fish to take the place of dried meats and corn!

Above the great falls of the Apahoqui the salmon sported in the cool, swinging current, darting under the lee of the rocks and leaping full length in the clear spring air. Nowhere else were such salmon to be speared as those which lay among the riffles at the head of the Apahoqui rapids. But only the most daring braves ventured to seek them there, for the current was strong, and should a light canoe once pass the danger-point and get caught in the rush of the rapids, nothing could save it from going over the roaring falls.

Very early in the morning of a clear April day, just as the sun was rising splendidly over the mountains, Waukewa launched his canoe a half-mile above the rapids of the Apahoqui, and floated downward, spear in hand, among the salmon-riffles. He was the only one of the Indian lads who dared fish above the falls. But he had been there often, and never yet had his watchful eye and his strong paddle suffered the current to carry his canoe beyond

the danger-point. This morning he was alone on the river, having risen long before daylight to be first at the sport.

The riffles were full of salmon, big, lusty fellows, who glided about the canoe on every side in an endless silver stream.

Waukewa plunged his spear right and left, and tossed one glittering victim after another into the bark canoe. So absorbed in the sport was he that for once he did not notice when the canoe began to glide more swiftly among the rocks. But suddenly he looked up, caught his paddle, and dipped it wildly in the swirling water. The canoe swung sidewise, shivered, held its own against the torrent, and then slowly, inch by inch, began to creep upstream toward the shore. But suddenly there was a loud, cruel snap, and the paddle parted in the boy's hands, broken just above the blade! Waukewa gave a cry of despairing agony. Then he bent to the gunwale of his canoe and with the shattered blade fought desperately against the current. But it was useless. The racing torrent swept him downward; the hungry falls roared tauntingly in his ears.

Then the Indian boy knelt calmly upright in the canoe, facing the mist of the falls, and folded his arms. His young face was stern and lofty. He had lived like a brave hitherto—now he would die like one.

Faster and faster sped the doomed canoe toward the great cataract. The black rocks glided away on either side like phantoms. The roar of the terrible waters became like thunder in the boy's ears. But still he gazed calmly and sternly ahead, facing his fate as a brave Indian should. At last he began to chant the death-song, which he had learned from the older braves. In a few moments all would be over. But he would come before the Great Spirit with a fearless hymn upon his lips.

Suddenly a shadow fell across the canoe. Waukewa lifted his eyes and saw a great eagle hovering over, with dangling legs, and a spread of wings that blotted out the sun. Once more the eyes of the Indian boy and the eagle met; and now it was the eagle who was master!

With a glad cry the Indian boy stood up in his canoe, and the eagle hovered lower. Now the canoe tossed up on that great swelling wave that climbs to the cataract's edge, and the boy lifted his hands and caught the legs of the eagle. The next moment he looked down into the awful gulf of waters from its very verge. The canoe was snatched from beneath him and plunged down the black wall of the cataract; but he and the struggling eagle were floating outward and downwards through the cloud of mist. The cataract roared terribly, like a wild beast robbed of its prey. The spray beat and blinded, the air rushed upward as they fell. But the eagle struggled on with his burden. He fought his way out of the mist and the flying spray. His great wings threshed the air with a whistling sound. Down, down they sank, the boy and the eagle, but ever farther from the precipice of water and the boiling whirlpool below. At length, with a fluttering plunge, the eagle dropped on a sand-bar below the whirlpool, and he and the Indian boy lay there a minute, breathless and exhausted. Then the eagle slowly lifted himself, took the air under his free wings, and soared away, while the Indian boy knelt on the sand, with shining eyes following the great bird till he faded into the gray of the cliffs.

FROM

Black Beauty

ANNA SEWELL

This is an old-fashioned story, much more sentimental than most modern ones, yet many children today still vote Black Beauty *their favorite book. It tells the whole life story of a spirited riding horse who suffers abuse and mistreatment and, through no fault of his own, passes from one owner to another until at last he is put up for sale as a common work-horse. Here he is, being offered for sale at a county fair, and waiting to see what the future may hold for him.*

A Horse Fair

No DOUBT a horse fair is a very amusing place to those who have nothing to lose; at any rate, there is plenty to see.

Long strings of young horses out of the country, fresh from the marshes; and droves of shaggy little Welsh ponies, no higher than Merrylegs; and hundreds of cart horses of all sorts, some of them with their long tails braided up and tied with scarlet cord; and a good many like myself, handsome and high-bred, but fallen into the middle class through some accident or blemish, unsoundness of wind, or some other complaint.

There were some splendid animals quite in their prime, and fit for anything. They were throwing out their legs and showing off their paces in high style, as they were trotted out with a leading rein, the groom running by their side. But round in the background there were a number of poor things, sadly broken down with hard work, with their knees knuckling over and their hind legs swinging out at every step; and there were some very dejected-looking old horses, with the underlip hanging down and the ears lying back heavily, as if there were no more pleasure in life, and no more hope. There were some so thin you might see all their ribs, and some with old sores on their backs and hips. These were sad sights for a horse to look upon, who knows not but that he may come to the same state.

There was a great deal of bargaining, of running up and beating down; and, if a horse may speak his mind, so far as he understands, I should say there were more lies told and more trickery at that horse fair than a clever man could give an account of. I was put with two or three other strong, useful-looking horses, and a good many people came to look at us. The gentlemen always turned from me when they saw my broken knees, though the man who had me swore it was only a slip in the stall.

The first thing was to pull my mouth open, then to look at my eyes, then feel all the way down my legs and give me a hard feel of the skin and flesh, and then try my paces. It was wonderful what a difference there was in the way these things were done. Some did it in a rough, offhand way, as if one was only a piece of wood; while others would move their hands gently over one's body, with a pat now and then, as much as to say, "By your leave." Of course I judged a good deal of the buyers by their manners to myself.

There was one man that made me think that if he would buy me I should be happy. He was not a gentleman, nor yet one of the loud, flashy sort that called themselves so. He was rather a small man, but well made, and quick in all his motions. I knew in a moment, by the way he handled me, that he was used to horses. He spoke gently, and his gray eye had a kindly, cheery look in it. It may seem strange to say—but it is true all the same —that the clean, fresh smell there was about him made me take to him. There was no smell of old beer and tobacco, which I hated, but a fresh smell, as if he had come out of a hayloft. He offered twenty-three pounds for me; but that was refused, and he walked away. I looked after him, but he was gone, and a very hard-looking, loud-voiced man came. I was dreadfully afraid he would have me, but he walked off.

One or two more came who did not mean business. Then the hard-faced man came back again and offered twenty-three pounds. A very close bargain was being driven, for my salesman began to think he should not get all he asked, and must come down; but just then the gray-eyed man came back again. I could not help reaching out my head toward him. He stroked my face kindly.

"Well, old chap," he said, "I think we should suit each other. I'll give twenty-four for him."

"Say twenty-five, and you shall have him."

"Twenty-four ten," said my friend, in a very decided tone, "and not another sixpence—yes, or no?"

"Done," said the salesman, "and you may depend upon it there's a monstrous deal of quality in that horse, and if you want him for cab work he is a bargain."

The money was paid on the spot, and my new master took my halter and led me out of the fair to an inn, where he had a saddle and bridle ready. He gave me a good feed of oats, and stood by while I ate it, talking to himself and talking to me. Half an hour after we were on our way to London, through pleasant lanes and country roads, until we came into the great London thoroughfare, on which we traveled steadily, till in the twilight we reached the great city.

The gas lamps were already lighted; there were streets to the right, and streets to the left, and streets crossing each other, for mile upon mile. I thought we should never come to the end of them. At last we came to a long cab stand, when my rider called out in a cheery voice, "Good night, Governor!"

"Halloo!" cried a voice. "Have you got a good one?"

"I think so," replied the owner.

"I wish you luck with him."

"Thank ye, Governor," and he rode on. We soon turned up one of the side streets, and about halfway up that we turned into a very narrow street with rather poor-looking houses on one side, and what seemed to be coach houses and stables on the other.

My owner pulled up at one of the houses and whistled. The door flew open and a young woman, followed by a little girl and boy, ran out. There was a very lively greeting as my rider dismounted. "Now then, Harry, my boy, open the gates, and mother will bring us the lantern."

The next minute they were all standing round me in a small stable yard.

"Is he gentle, Father?"

"Yes, Dolly, as gentle as your own kitten; come and pat him." At once the little hand was patting about over my shoulder without fear. How good it felt!

"Let me get him a bran mash while you rub him down," said the mother.

"Do, Polly, it's just what he wants; and I know you've got a beautiful mash ready for me."

"Sausage dumpling and apple turnover!" shouted the boy, which set them all laughing. I was led into a comfortable, clean-smelling stall with plenty of dry straw, and after a capital supper I lay down, thinking I was going to be happy.

A London Cab Horse

My new master's name was Jeremiah Barker, but as everyone called him Jerry, I shall do the same. Polly, his wife, was just as good a match as a man could have. She was a plump, trim, tidy little woman, with smooth, dark hair, dark eyes, and a merry little mouth. The boy was nearly twelve years old, a tall, frank, good-tempered lad; and little Dorothy (Dolly they called her) was her mother over again at eight years old. They were all wonderfully fond of each other; I never knew such a happy, merry family before or since.

Jerry had a cab of his own, and two horses, which he drove and attended to himself. His other horse was a tall, white, rather large-boned animal, called Captain. He was old now, but when he was young he must have been splendid. He had still a proud way of holding his head and arching his neck; in fact, he was a high-bred, fine-mannered, noble old horse, every inch of him. He told me that in his early youth he went to the Crimean War; he belonged to an officer in the cavalry, and used to lead the regiment. I will tell more of that hereafter.

The next morning, when I was well groomed, Polly and Dolly came into the yard to see me and make friends. Harry had been helping his father since the early morning, and had stated his opinion that I should turn out "a regular brick." Polly brought me a slice of apple, and Dolly a piece of bread, and made as much of me as if I had been the "Black Beauty" of olden time. It was a great treat to be petted again and talked to in a gentle voice, and I let them see as well as I could that I wished to be friendly. Polly thought I was very handsome, and too good for a cab, if it was not for the broken knees.

"There's no one to tell us whose fault that was," said Jerry, "and as long as I don't know I shall give him the benefit of the doubt; for a firmer, neater stepper I never rode. We'll call him 'Jack,' after the Colonel—shall we, Polly?"

"Do," she said, "for I like the name."

Captain went out in the cab all morning. Harry came in after school to feed me and give me water. In the afternoon I was put into the cab. Jerry took as much pains to see if the collar and bridle fitted comfortably as if he had been John Manly over again. When the crupper was let out a hole or two, it all fitted well. There was no checkrein, no curb, nothing but a plain ring snaffle. What a blessing that was!

After driving through the side street we came to the large cab stand where Jerry had said "Good night." On one side of this wide street were high houses with wonderful shop fronts, and on the other was an old church and churchyard surrounded by iron palisades.

Alongside these iron rails a number of cabs were drawn up, waiting for passengers. Bits of hay were lying about on the ground. Some of the men were standing together talking; some were sitting on their boxes reading the newspapers; and one or two were feeding their horses with bits of hay, and giving them a drink of water. We pulled up in the rank at the back of the last cab. Two or three men came round and began to look at me and pass their remarks.

"Very good for a funeral," said one.

"Too smart-looking," said another, shaking his head in a very wise way, "you'll find out something wrong one of these fine mornings, or my name isn't Jones."

"Well," said Jerry pleasantly, "I suppose I need not find it out till it finds me out, eh? And if so, I'll keep up my spirits a little longer."

Then there came up a broad-faced man, dressed in a great gray coat with gray capes and great white buttons, a gray hat, and a blue comforter tied loosely round his neck. His hair was gray, too; but he was a jolly-looking fellow, and the other men made way for him. He looked me all over, as if he had been going to buy me, and then straightening himself with a grunt, he said, "He's the right sort for you, Jerry; I don't care what you gave for him, he'll be worth it." Thus my character was established on the stand.

This man's name was Grant, but he was called "Gray Grant," or "Governor Grant." He had been the longest on that stand of any of the men, and he took it upon himself to settle matters and stop disputes. He was generally a good-humored, sensible man; but if his temper was a little out, as it was sometimes when he had drunk too much, nobody liked to come too near his fist, for he could deal a very heavy blow.

The first week of my life as a cab horse was trying. I had never been used to London, and the noise, the hurry, the crowds of horses, carts and carriages, that I had to make my way through, made me feel anxious and harassed. But I soon found that I could trust my driver, and then I made myself easy, and got used to it.

Jerry was as good a driver as I had ever known, and what was better, he took as much thought for his horses as he did for himself. He soon found out that I was willing to work and he never laid the whip on me, unless it was gently drawing the end of it over my back, when I was to go on. Generally I knew this quite well by the way in which he took up the reins; and I believe his whip was more frequently stuck up by his side than in his hand.

In a short time my master and I understood each other as well as horse and man can do. In the stable he did all that he could for our comfort. The stalls were the old-fashioned style, too much on the slope; but he had two movable bars fixed across the back of our stalls, so that at night, when we were resting, he just took off our halters and put up the bars, and thus we could turn and stand whichever way we pleased. This is a great comfort.

Jerry kept us very clean, and gave us as much change of food as he could, and always plenty of it. Not only that, but he always gave us plenty of fresh, clean water, which he allowed to stand by us both night and day, except, of course, when we came in warm.

Some people say that a horse ought not to drink all he likes; but I know if we are allowed to drink when we want it we drink only a little at a time, and it does us a great deal more good than swallowing down half a bucketful at a time, because we have been left without it till we are thirsty and miserable. Some grooms will go home to their beers, and leave us for hours with our dry hay and oats and nothing to moisten them. Then of course we gulp down too much at once, which helps to spoil our breathing and sometimes chills our stomachs. But the best thing that we had here was our Sundays for rest!

We worked so hard in the week that I do not think we could have kept up to it but for that day; besides, we had time to enjoy each other's company. It was on these days that I learned my companion's history.

Jerry Barker

I never knew a better man than my new master. He was kind and good, and as strong for the right as John Manly; and so good-tempered and merry, that very few people could pick a quarrel with him. He was very fond of making little songs, and singing them to himself. One he was very fond of was this:

> Come, father and mother,
> And sister and brother,
> Come all of you, turn to
> And help one another.

And so they did. Harry was as clever at stable work as a much older boy, and always wanted to do what he could. Then Polly and Dolly used to come in the morning to help with the cab—to brush and beat the cushions, and rub the glass, while Jerry was giving us a cleaning in the yard, and Harry was rubbing the harness. There used to be a deal of laughing and fun between them, and it put Captain and me in much better spirits than if we had heard scolding and hard words. They were always up early in the morning, for Jerry would say:

> *If you in the morning*
> *Throw minutes away,*
> *You can't pick them up*
> *In the course of the day;*
> *You may hurry and scurry,*
> *And flurry and worry,*
> *You've lost them forever,*
> *Forever and aye.*

He could not bear any careless loitering and waste of time; and nothing was so near making him angry as to find people, who were always late, wanting a cab horse to be driven hard, to make up for their idleness.

One day two wild-looking young men came out of a tavern close by the stand and called Jerry.

"Here, cabby! look sharp, we are rather late. Put on the steam, will you, and take us to the Victoria in time for the one o'clock train? You shall have a shilling extra."

"I will take you at the regular pace, gentlemen; shillings don't pay for putting on steam like that."

Larry's cab was standing next to ours; he flung open the door and said, "I'm your man, gentlemen! take my cab; my horse will get you there all right," and as he shut them in with a wink toward Jerry, said, "It's against his conscience to go beyond a jog trot." Then slashing his jaded horse, he set off as hard as he could.

Jerry patted me on the neck. "No, Jack, a shilling would not pay for that sort of thing—would it, old boy?"

Although Jerry was set against hard driving to please careless people, he always went a good, fair pace, and was not against putting on the steam, as he said, if only he knew why. I remember one morning as we were on the stand waiting for a fare, that a young man, carrying a heavy portmanteau, trod on a piece of orange peel and fell down with great force.

Jerry was the first to run and lift him up. He seemed much stunned, and as they led him into a shop he walked as if he were in great pain. Jerry, of course, came back to the stand, but in about ten minutes one of the shopmen called him, so we drew up to the pavement.

"Can you take me to the Southeastern Railway?" said the young man. "This unlucky fall has made me late, I fear; but it is of great importance that I should not lose the twelve o'clock train. I should be most thankful if you could get me there in time, and will gladly pay you an extra fare."

"I'll do my very best," said Jerry heartily, "if you think you are well enough, sir," for he looked dreadfully white and ill.

"I must go," he said earnestly, "please open the door, and let us lose no time."

The next minute Jerry was on the box, with a cheery chirrup to me and a twitch of the rein that I well understood.

"Now, then, Jack, my boy," said he, "spin along; we'll show them how we can get over the ground, if we only know why."

It is always difficult to drive fast in the city in the middle of the day, when the streets are full of traffic, but we did what could be done; and when a good driver and a good horse, who understand each other, are of one mind, it is wonderful what they can do. I had a very good mouth—that is, I could be guided by the slightest touch of the rein.

That is a great thing in London, among carriages, omnibuses, carts, vans, trucks, cabs, and great wagons creeping along at a walking pace; some going one way, some another, some going slowly, others wanting to pass them; omnibuses stopping short every few minutes to take up a passenger, obliging the horse that is coming to pull up too, or to pass, and get before them. Perhaps you try to pass, but just then something else comes dashing in through the narrow opening, and you have to keep in behind the omnibus again. Presently you think you see a chance and manage to get to the front, getting so near the wheels on each side that half an inch nearer and they would scrape. Well—you get along for a bit, but soon find yourself in a long train of carts and carriages all obliged to go at a walk. Perhaps

you come to a regular block up, and have to stand still for minutes together, till something clears out into a side street or the policeman interferes. You have to be ready for any chance—to dash forward if there be an opening, and be quick as a rat dog to see if there be room and if there be time, lest you get your own wheels locked or smashed, or the shaft of some other vehicle run into your chest or shoulder. All this is what you have to be ready for. If you want to get through London fast in the middle of the day, it needs a deal of practice.

Jerry and I were used to it, and no one could beat us at getting through when we were set upon it. I was quick and bold and could trust my driver; Jerry was quick and patient at the same time, and could trust his horse, which was a great thing, too. He seldom used the whip; I knew by his voice, and his click, click, when he wanted to get on fast, and by the rein where I was to go; so there was no need for whipping. But I must go back to my story.

The streets were very full that day, but we got on pretty well as far as the bottom of Cheapside, where there was a block for three or four minutes. The young man put his head out and said, "I think I had better get out and walk; I shall never get there if this goes on."

"I'll do all that can be done, sir," said Jerry. "I think we shall be in time; this block up cannot last much longer, and your luggage is very heavy for you to carry, sir."

Just then the cart in front of us began to move on, and then we had a good turn. In and out—in and out we went, as fast as horseflesh could do it, and for a wonder had a good clear time on London Bridge, for there was a whole train of cabs and carriages, all going our way at a quick trot—perhaps wanting to catch that very train. At any rate, we whirled into the station, with many more, just as the great clock pointed to eight minutes to twelve o'clock.

"Thank God! we are in time," said the young man, "and thank you, too, my friend, and your good horse. You have saved me more than money can ever pay for; take this extra half crown."

"No, sir, no, thank you all the same. I am glad we hit the time, sir; but don't stay now, sir, the bell is ringing. Here, porter! take this gentleman's luggage—Dover line—twelve o'clock train —that's it," and without waiting for another word, Jerry wheeled me round to make room for other cabs that were dashing up at the last minute, and drew up on one side till the crush was passed.

"So glad!" he said, "so glad! poor young fellow! I wonder what it was that made him so anxious?"

Jerry often talked to himself quite loud enough for me to hear, when we were not moving.

On Jerry's return to the rank, there was a good deal of laughing and chaffing at him for driving hard to the train for an extra fare, as they said, all against his principles, and they wanted to know how much he had pocketed.

"A good deal more than I generally get," said he, nodding slyly, "what he gave me will keep me in little comforts for several days."

"Gammon!" said one.

"He's a humbug," said another, "preaching to us, and then doing the same himself."

"Look here, mates," said Jerry, "the gentleman offered me half a crown extra, but I didn't take it. 'Twas pay enough for me to see how glad he was to catch that train; and if Jack and I choose to have a quick run now and then, to please ourselves, that's our business, not yours."

"Well," said Larry, "*you'll* never be a rich man."

"Most likely not," said Jerry, "but I don't know that I shall be the less happy for that. I have heard the Commandments read a great many times, and I never noticed that any of them said 'Thou shalt be rich'; and there are a good many curious things said in the New Testament about rich men, that I think would make me feel rather queer if I was one of them."

"If you ever do get rich," said Governor Gray, looking over his shoulder across the top of his cab, "you'll deserve it, Jerry, and you won't find a curse come with your wealth. As for you, Larry, you'll die poor; you spend too much in whipcord."

"Well," said Larry, "what is a fellow to do if his horse won't go without it?"

"You never take the trouble to see if he will go without it; your whip is always going as if you had the St. Vitus's dance in your arm; and if it does not wear you out it wears your horse out. You know you are always changing your horses, and why? because you never give them any peace or encouragement."

"Well, I have not had good luck," said Larry, "that's what it is."

"And you never will," said the Governor. "Good Luck is rather particular with whom she rides, and prefers those who have common sense and a good heart; at least, that is my experience." Governor Gray turned round again to his newspaper, and the other men went to their cabs.

Jerry's New Year

Christmas and the New Year are very merry times for some people; but for cabmen and cabmen's horses it is no holiday, though it may be a harvest. There are so many parties, balls, and places of amusement open, that the work is hard and often late. Sometimes driver and horse have to wait for hours in the rain or frost, shivering with cold, while the merry people within are dancing away to the music. I wonder if the beautiful ladies ever think of the weary cabman waiting on his box, and his patient beast standing till his legs get stiff with cold.

I had now most of the evening work, as I was well accustomed to standing, and Jerry was also more afraid of Hotspur's taking cold. We had a great deal of late work in the Christmas week, and Jerry's cough was bad; but, however late we were, Polly sat up for him, and came out with a lantern to meet him, looking anxious and troubled.

On the evening of the New Year we had to take two gentlemen to a house in one of the West End squares. We set them down at nine o'clock, and were told to come again at eleven. "But," said one of them, "as it is a card party you may have to wait a few minutes, but don't be late."

As the clock struck eleven we were at the door, for Jerry was always punctual. The clock chimed the quarter, one, two, three, and then struck twelve, but the door did not open.

The wind had been very changeable, with squalls of rain during the day, but now it came on sharp, driving sleet, which seemed to come all the way round; it was very cold, and there was no shelter. Jerry got off his box and came and pulled one of my cloths a little more over my neck; then he took a turn or two up and down, stamping his feet; then he began to beat his arms, but that set him off coughing; so he opened the cab door and sat at the bottom with his feet on the pavement, and was a little sheltered. Still the clock chimed the quarters, and no one came. At half-past twelve he rang the bell and asked the servant if he would be wanted that night.

"Oh, yes, you'll be wanted safe enough," said the man, "you must not go, it will soon be over." And again Jerry sat down, but his voice was so hoarse I could hardly hear him.

At a quarter-past one the door opened and the two gentlemen came out. They got into the cab without a word and told Jerry where to drive; it was nearly two miles. My legs were numb with cold, and I thought I should have stumbled. When the men got out they never said they were sorry to have kept us waiting so long, but were angry at the charge. However, as Jerry never charged more than was his due, he never took less, and they had to pay for the two hours and a quarter waiting; but it was hard-earned money to Jerry.

At last he got home. He could hardly speak, and his cough was dreadful. Polly asked no questions, but opened the door and held the lantern for him.

"Can't I do something?" she said.

"Yes; get Jack something warm, and then boil me some gruel."

This was said in a hoarse whisper. He could hardly get his breath, but he gave me a rubdown, as usual, and even went up into the hayloft for an extra bundle of straw for my bed. Polly brought me a warm mash that made me comfortable, and then they locked the door.

It was late the next morning before anyone came, and then it was only Harry. He cleaned us and fed us, and swept out the stalls; then he put the straw back again as if it was Sunday. He was very still, and neither whistled nor sang. At noon he came again and gave us our food and water. This time Dolly came with him; she was crying, and I could gather from what they said that Jerry was dangerously ill, and the doctor said it was a bad case. So two days passed, and there was great trouble indoors. We only saw Harry, and sometimes Dolly. I think she came for company, for Polly was always with Jerry, and he had to be kept very quiet.

On the third day, while Harry was in the stable, a tap came at the door, and Governor Grant came in.

"I wouldn't go to the house, my boy," he said, "but I want to know how your father is."

"He is very bad," said Harry, "he can't be much worse. They

call it 'bronchitis'; the doctor thinks it will turn one way or another tonight."

"That's bad, very bad," said Grant, shaking his head, "I know two men who died of that last week. It takes 'em off in no time; but while there's life there's hope, so you must keep up your spirits."

"Yes," said Harry, quickly, "and the doctor said that father had a better chance than most men, because he didn't drink. He said yesterday the fever was so high, that if father had been a drinking man it would have burned him up like a piece of paper; but he thinks he will get over it. Don't you think he will, Mr. Grant?"

The Governor looked puzzled. "If there's any rule that good men should get over these things, I am sure he will, my boy; he's the best man I know. I'll look in early tomorrow."

Early next morning he was there.

"Well?" said he.

"Father is better," said Harry. "Mother thinks he will get over it."

"Thank God!" said the Governor, "and now you must keep him warm, and keep his mind easy, and that brings me to the horses. You see, Jack will be all the better for the rest of a week or two in a warm stable, and you can easily take him a turn up and down the street to stretch his legs; but this young one, if he does not get work, will soon be all up on end, as you may say, and will be rather too much for you; and when he does go out, there'll be an accident."

"It is like that now," said Harry. "I have kept him short of corn, but he's so full of spirit I don't know what to do with him."

"Just so," said Grant. "Now, look here, will you tell your mother that, if she is agreeable, I will come for him every day until something is arranged, and take him for a good spell of work, and whatever he earns, I'll bring your mother half of it, and that will help with the horses' feed. Your father is in a good club, I know, but that won't keep the horses, and they'll be eating their heads off all this time. I'll come at noon and hear what she says." Without waiting for Harry's thanks, he was gone.

At noon I think he went and saw Polly, for he and Harry came to the stable together, harnessed Hotspur, and took him out. For a week or more he came for Hotspur, and when Harry thanked him or said anything about his kindness, he laughed it off, saying it was all good luck for him, for his horses were wanting a little rest which they would not otherwise have had.

Jerry grew better steadily, but the doctor said that he must never go back to the cab work again if he wished to live to be an old man. The children had many consultations together about what Father and Mother would do, and how they could help to earn money.

One afternoon Hotspur was brought in very wet and dirty.

"The streets are nothing but slush," said the Governor, "it will give you a good warming, my boy, to get him clean and dry."

"All right, Governor," said Harry, "I shall not leave him till he is; you know I have been trained by my father."

"I wish all the boys had been trained like you," said the Governor.

While Harry was sponging off the mud from Hotspur's body and legs, Dolly came in, looking very full of something.

"Who lives at Fairstowe, Harry? Mother has got a letter from Fairstowe; she seemed so glad, and ran upstairs to father with it."

"Don't you know? Why, it is the name of Mrs. Fowler's place —Mother's old mistress, you know—the lady that Father met last summer, who sent you and me five shillings each."

"Oh! Mrs. Fowler; of course I know about her. I wonder what she is writing to Mother about."

"Mother wrote to her last week," said Harry. "You know she told Father if he ever gave up the cab work she would like to know. I wonder what she says; run in and see, Dolly."

Harry scrubbed away at Hotspur with a huish! huish! like any old hostler. In a few minutes Dolly came dancing into the stable.

"Oh! Harry, there never was anything so beautiful; Mrs. Fowler says we are all to go and live near her. There is a cottage now empty that will just suit us, with a garden and a hen house and apple trees, and everything! and her coachman is going away in the spring, and then she will want Father in his place; and there are good families round, where you can get a place in the garden, or the stable, or as a page boy. There's a good school for me, too, and Mother is laughing and crying by turns, and Father does look so happy!"

"That's uncommon jolly," said Harry, "and just the right thing, I should say; it will suit Father and Mother both. But I don't intend to be a page boy with tight clothes and rows of tight buttons. I'll be a groom or a gardener."

It was quickly settled that as soon as Jerry was well enough, they should remove to the country, and that the cab and horses should be sold as soon as possible.

This was heavy news for me, for I was not young now, and could not look for any improvement in my condition. Since I left Birtwick I had never been so happy as with my master Jerry; but three years of cab work, even under the best conditions, will tell on one's strength, and I felt that I was not the horse that I had been.

Grant said at once that he would take Hotspur; and there were men on the stand who would have bought me, but Jerry said I should not go back to cab work again with just anybody, so the Governor promised to find a place for me where I should be comfortable.

The day came for going away. Jerry had not been allowed to go out yet, and I never saw him after that New Year's eve. Polly and the children came to bid me good-by.

"Poor old Jack! dear old Jack! I wish we could take you with us," she said, and then laying her hand on my mane, she put her face close to my neck and kissed me. Dolly was crying and kissed me, too. Harry stroked me a great deal, but said nothing, only he seemed very sad, and so I was led away to my new place.

"Rikki-tikki-tavi"

RUDYARD KIPLING

THIS is the story of the great war that Rikki-tikki-tavi fought single-handed, through the bathrooms of the big bungalow in Segowlee cantonment. Darzee, the tailor-bird, helped him, and Chuchundra, the musk-rat, who never comes out into the middle of the floor, but always creeps round by the wall, gave him advice; but Rikki-tikki did the real fighting.

He was a mongoose, rather like a little cat in his fur and his tail, but quite like a weasel in his head and his habits. His eyes and the end of his restless nose were pink; he could scratch himself anywhere he pleased, with any leg, front or back, that he chose to use; he could fluff up his tail till it looked like a bottle-brush, and his war-cry, as he scuttled through the long grass, was: "Rikk-tikk-tikki-tikki-tchk!"

One day, a high summer flood washed him out of the burrow where he lived with his father and mother, and carried him, kicking and clucking, down a roadside ditch. He found a little wisp of grass floating there, and clung to it till he lost his senses. When he revived, he was lying in the hot sun on the middle of a garden path, very draggled indeed, and a small boy was saying: "Here's a dead mongoose. Let's have a funeral."

"No," said his mother; "let's take him in and dry him. Perhaps he isn't really dead."

They took him into the house, and a big man picked him up between his finger and thumb, and said he was not dead but half choked; so they wrapped him in cotton-wool, and warmed him, and he opened his eyes and sneezed.

"Now," said the big man (he was an Englishman who had just moved into the bungalow); "don't frighten him, and we'll see what he'll do."

It is the hardest thing in the world to frighten a mongoose, because he is eaten up from nose to tail with curiosity. The motto of all the mongoose family is, "Run and find out"; and Rikki-tikki was a true mongoose. He looked at the cotton-wool, decided that it was not good to eat, ran all round the table, sat up and put his fur in order, scratched himself, and jumped on the small boy's shoulder.

"Don't be frightened, Teddy," said his father. "That's his way of making friends."

"Ouch! He's tickling under my chin," said Teddy.

Rikki-tikki looked down between the boy's collar and neck, snuffed at his ear, and climbed down to the floor, where he sat rubbing his nose.

"Good gracious," said Teddy's mother, "and that's a wild creature! I suppose he's so tame because we've been kind to him."

"All mongooses are like that," said her husband. "If Teddy doesn't pick him up by the tail, or try to put him in a cage, he'll run in and out of the house all day long. Let's give him something to eat."

They gave him a little piece of raw meat. Rikki-tikki liked it immensely, and when it was finished he went out into the veranda and sat in the sunshine and fluffed up his fur to make it dry to the roots. Then he felt better.

"There are more things to find out about in this house," he said to himself, "than all my family could find out in all their lives. I shall certainly stay and find out."

He spent all that day roaming over the house. He nearly drowned himself in the bath-tubs, put his nose into the ink on a writing-table, and burnt it on the end of the big man's cigar, for he climbed up in the big man's lap to see how writing was done. At nightfall he ran into Teddy's nursery to watch how kerosene-lamps were lighted, and when Teddy went to bed Rikki-tikki climbed up too; but he was a restless companion, because he had to get up and attend to every noise all through the night, and find out what made it. Teddy's mother and father came in, the last thing, to look at their boy, and Rikki-tikki was awake on the pillow. "I don't like that," said Teddy's mother; "he may bite the child." "He'll do no such thing," said the father. "Teddy's safer with that little beast than if he had a bloodhound to watch him. If a snake came into the nursery now—"

But Teddy's mother wouldn't think of anything so awful.

Early in the morning Rikki-tikki came to early breakfast in the veranda riding on Teddy's shoulder, and they gave him banana and some boiled egg; and he sat on all their laps one after the other, because every well-brought-up mongoose always hopes to be a house-mongoose some day and have rooms to run about in, and Rikki-tikki's mother (she used to live in the General's house at Segowlee) had carefully told Rikki what to do if ever he came across white men.

Then Rikki-tikki went out into the garden to see what was to be seen. It was a large garden, only half cultivated, with bushes as big as summer-houses of Marshal Niel roses, lime and orange trees, clumps of bamboos, and thickets of high grass. Rikki-tikki licked his lips. "This is a splendid hunting-ground," he said, and his tail grew bottle-brushy at the thought of it, and he scuttled up and down the garden, snuffing here and there till he heard very sorrowful voices in a thorn-bush.

It was Darzee, the tailor-bird, and his wife. They had made a beautiful nest by pulling two big leaves together and stitching them up the edges with fibres, and had filled the hollow with cotton and downy fluff. The nest swayed to and fro, as they sat on the rim and cried.

"What is the matter?" asked Rikki-tikki.

"We are very miserable," said Darzee. "One of our babies fell out of the nest yesterday, and Nag ate him."

"H'm!" said Rikki-tikki, "that is very sad—but I am a stranger here. Who is Nag?"

Darzee and his wife only cowered down in the nest without answering, for from the thick grass at the foot of the bush there came a low hiss—a horrid cold sound that made Rikki-tikki jump back two clear feet. Then inch by inch out of the grass rose up the head and spread hood of Nag, the big black cobra, and he was five feet long from tongue to tail. When he had lifted one-third of himself clear of the ground, he stayed balancing to and fro exactly as a dandelion-tuft balances in the wind, and he looked at Rikki-tikki with the wicked snake's eyes that never change their expression, whatever the snake may be thinking of.

"Who is Nag?" said he. "I am Nag. The great god Brahm put his mark upon all our people when the first cobra spread his hood to keep the sun off Brahm as he slept. Look, and be afraid!"

He spread out his hood more than ever, and Rikki-tikki saw the spectacle-mark on the back of it that looks exactly like the eye part of a hook-and-eye fastening. He was afraid for the minute; but it is impossible for a mongoose to stay frightened for any length of time, and though Rikki-tikki had never met a live cobra before, his mother had fed him on dead ones, and he knew that all a grown mongoose's business in life was to fight and eat snakes. Nag knew that too, and at the bottom of his cold heart he was afraid.

"Well," said Rikki-tikki, and his tail began to fluff up again, "marks or no marks, do you think it is right for you to eat fledglings out of a nest?"

Nag was thinking to himself, and watching the least little movement in the grass behind Rikki-tikki. He knew that mongooses in the garden meant death sooner or later for him and his family, but he wanted to get Rikki-tikki off his guard. So he dropped his head a little, and put it on one side.

"Let us talk," he said. "You eat eggs. Why should not I eat birds?"

"Behind you! Look behind you!" said Darzee.

Rikki-tikki knew better than to waste time in staring. He jumped up in the air as high as he could go, and just under him whizzed by the head of Nagaina, Nag's wicked wife. She had crept up behind him as he was talking, to make an end of him; and he heard her savage hiss as the stroke missed. He came down almost across her back, and if he had been an old mongoose he would have known that then was the time to break her back with one bite; but he was afraid of the terrible lashing return-stroke of the cobra. He bit, indeed, but did not bite long enough, and he jumped clear of the whisking tail, leaving Nagaina torn and angry.

"Wicked, wicked Darzee!" said Nag, lashing up as high as he could reach toward the nest in the thorn-bush, but Darzee had built it out of reach of snakes, and it only swayed to and fro.

Rikki-tikki felt his eyes growing red and hot (when a mongoose's eyes grow red, he is angry), and he sat back on his tail and hind legs like a little kangaroo, and looked all around him, and chattered with rage. But Nag and Nagaina had disappeared into the grass. When a snake misses its stroke, it never says anything or gives any sign of what it means to do next. Rikki-tikki did not care to follow them, for he did not feel sure that he could manage two snakes at once. So he trotted off to the gravel path near the house, and sat down to think. It was a serious matter for him.

If you read the old books of natural history, you will find they say that when the mongoose fights the snake and happens to get bitten, he runs off and eats some herb that cures him. That is not true. The victory is only a matter of quickness of eye and quickness of foot—snake's blow against mongoose's jump—and as no eye can follow the motion of a snake's head when it strikes, that makes things much more wonderful than any magic herb. Rikki-tikki knew he was a young mongoose, and it made him all the more pleased to think that he had managed to escape a blow from behind. It gave him confidence in himself, and when Teddy came running down the path, Rikki-tikki was ready to be petted.

But just as Teddy was stooping, something flinched a little in the dust, and a tiny voice said: "Be careful. I am death!" It was Karait, the dusty brown snakeling that lies for choice on the dusty earth; and his bite is as dangerous as the cobra's. But he is so small that nobody thinks of him, and so he does the more harm to people.

Rikki-tikki's eyes grew red again, and he danced up to Karait with the peculiar rocking, swaying motion that he had inherited from his family. It looks very funny, but it is so perfectly balanced a gait that you can fly off from it at any angle you please; and in dealing with snakes this is an advantage. If Rikki-tikki had only known, he was doing a much more dangerous thing than fighting Nag, for Karait is so small, and can turn so quickly, that unless Rikki bit him close to the back of the head, he would get the return-stroke in his eye or lip. But Rikki did not know: his eyes were all red, and he rocked back and forth, looking for a good place to hold. Karait struck out. Rikki jumped sideways and tried to run in, but the wicked little dusty gray head lashed within a fraction of his shoulder, and he had to jump over the body, and the head followed his heels close.

Teddy shouted to the house: "Oh, look here! Our mongoose is killing a snake"; and Rikki-tikki heard a scream from Teddy's mother. His father ran out with a stick, but by the time he came up, Karait had lunged out once too far, and Rikki-tikki had sprung, jumped on the snake's back, dropped his head far between his fore-legs, bitten as high up the back as he could get hold, and rolled away. That bite paralysed Karait, and Rikki-tikki was just going to eat him up from the tail, after the custom of his family at dinner, when he remembered that a full meal makes a slow mongoose, and if he wanted all his strength and quickness ready, he must keep himself thin.

He went away for a dust-bath under the castor-oil bushes, while Teddy's father beat the dead Karait. "What is the use of that?" thought Rikki-tikki. "I have settled it all"; and then Teddy's mother picked him up from the dust and hugged him, crying that he had saved Teddy from death, and Teddy's father said that he was a providence, and Teddy looked on with big scared eyes. Rikki-tikki was rather amused at all the fuss, which, of course, he did not understand. Teddy's mother might just as well have petted Teddy for playing in the dust. Rikki was thoroughly enjoying himself.

That night, at dinner, walking to and fro among the wine-glasses on the table, he could have stuffed himself three times over with nice things; but he remembered Nag and Nagaina, and though it was very pleasant to be patted and petted by Teddy's mother, and to sit on Teddy's shoulder, his eyes would get red from time to time, and he would go off into his long war-cry of "Rikk-tikk-tikki-tikki-tchk!"

Teddy carried him off to bed, and insisted on Rikki-tikki sleeping under his chin. Rikki-tikki was too well bred to bite or scratch, but as soon as Teddy was asleep he went off for his nightly walk round the house, and in the dark he ran up against Chuchundra, the musk-rat, creeping round by the wall. Chuchundra is a broken-hearted little beast. He whimpers and cheeps all the night, trying to make up his mind to run into the middle of the room, but he never gets there.

"Don't kill me," said Chuchundra, almost weeping. "Rikki-tikki, don't kill me."

"Do you think a snake-killer kills musk-rats?" said Rikki-tikki scornfully.

"Those who kill snakes get killed by snakes," said Chuchundra, more sorrowfully than ever. "And how am I to be sure that Nag won't mistake me for you some dark night?"

"There's not the least danger," said Rikki-tikki; "but Nag is in the garden, and I know you don't go there."

"My cousin Chua, the rat, told me—" said Chuchundra, and then he stopped.

"Told you what?"

"H'sh! Nag is everywhere, Rikki-tikki. You should have talked to Chua in the garden."

"I didn't—so you must tell me. Quick, Chuchundra; or I'll bite you!"

Chuchundra sat down and cried till the tears rolled off his whiskers. "I am a very poor man," he sobbed. "I never had spirit enough to run out into the middle of the room. H'sh! I mustn't tell you anything. Can't you hear, Rikki-tikki?"

Rikki-tikki listened. The house was as still as still, but he thought he could just catch the faintest "scratch-scratch" in the world—a noise as faint as that of a wasp walking on a window-pane—the dry scratch of a snake's scales on brickwork.

"That's Nag or Nagaina," he said to himself; "and he is crawling into the bathroom sluice. You're right, Chuchundra; I should have talked to Chua."

He stole off to Teddy's bathroom, but there was nothing there, and then to Teddy's mother's bathroom. At the bottom of the smooth plaster wall there was a brick pulled out to make a sluice for the bath-water, and as Rikki-tikki stole in by the masonry curb where the bath is put, he heard Nag and Nagaina whispering together outside in the moonlight.

"When the house is emptied of people," said Nagaina to her husband, "he will have to go away, and then the garden will be our own again. Go in quietly, and remember that the big man who killed Karait is the first one to bite. Then come out and tell me, and we will hunt for Rikki-tikki together."

"But are you sure that there is anything to be gained by killing the people?" said Nag.

"Everything. When there were no people in the bungalow, did we have any mongoose in the garden? So long as the bungalow is empty, we are king and queen of the garden; and remember that as soon as our eggs in the melon-bed hatch (as they may to-morrow), our children will need room and quiet."

"I had not thought of that," said Nag. "I will go, but there is no need that we should hunt for Rikki-tikki afterward. I will kill the big man and his wife, and the child if I can, and come away quietly. Then the bungalow will be empty, and Rikki-tikki will go."

Rikki-tikki tingled all over with rage and hatred at this, and then Nag's head came through the sluice, and his five feet of cold body followed it. Angry as he was, Rikki-tikki was very frightened as he saw the size of the big cobra. Nag coiled himself up, raised his head, and looked into the bathroom in the dark, and Rikki could see his eyes glitter.

"Now, if I kill him here, Nagaina will know; and if I fight him on the open floor, the odds are in his favour. What am I to do?" said Rikki-tikki-tavi.

Nag waved to and fro, and then Rikki-tikki heard him drinking from the biggest water-jar that was used to fill the bath. "That is good," said the snake. "Now, when Karait was killed, the big man had a stick. He may have that stick still, but when he comes in to bathe in the morning he will not have a stick. I shall wait here till he comes. Nagaina—do you hear me?—I shall wait here in the cool till daytime."

There was no answer from outside, so Rikki-tikki knew Nagaina had gone away. Nag coiled himself down, coil by coil, round the bulge at the bottom of the water-jar, and Rikki-tikki stayed still as death. After an hour he began to move, muscle by muscle, toward the jar. Nag was asleep, and Rikki-tikki looked at his big back, wondering which would be the best place for a good hold. "If I don't break his back at the first jump," said Rikki, "he can still fight; and if he fights—O Rikki!" He looked at the thickness of the neck below the hood, but that was too much for him; and a bite near the tail would only make Nag savage.

"It must be the head," he said at last; "the head above the hood; and when I am once there, I must not let go."

Then he jumped. The head was lying a little clear of the water-jar, under the curve of it; and, as his teeth met, Rikki braced his back against the bulge of the red earthenware to hold down the head. This gave him just one second's purchase, and he made the most of it. Then he was battered to and fro as a rat is shaken by a dog—to and fro on the floor, up and down, and round in great circles; but his eyes were red, and he held on as the body cart-whipped over the floor, upsetting the tin dipper and the soap-dish and the flesh-brush, and banged against the tin side of the bath. As he held he closed his jaws tighter and tighter, for he made sure he would be banged to death, and, for the honour of his family, he preferred to be found with his teeth locked. He was dizzy, aching, and felt shaken to pieces when something went off like a thunderclap just behind him; a hot wind knocked him senseless, and red fire singed his fur. The big

man had been wakened by the noise, and had fired both barrels of a shot-gun into Nag just behind the hood.

Rikki-tikki held on with his eyes shut, for now he was quite sure he was dead; but the head did not move, and the big man picked him up and said: "It's the mongoose again, Alice; the little chap has saved our lives now." Then Teddy's mother came in with a very white face, and saw what was left of Nag, and Rikki-tikki dragged himself to Teddy's bedroom and spent half the rest of the night shaking himself tenderly to find out whether he really was broken into forty pieces, as he fancied.

When morning came he was very stiff, but well pleased with his doings. "Now I have Nagaina to settle with, and she will be worse than five Nags, and there's no knowing when the eggs she spoke of will hatch. Goodness! I must go and see Darzee," he said.

Without waiting for breakfast, Rikki-tikki ran to the thorn-bush where Darzee was singing a song of triumph at the top of his voice. The news of Nag's death was all over the garden, for the sweeper had thrown the body on the rubbish-heap.

"Oh, you stupid tuft of feathers!" said Rikki-tikki angrily. "Is this the time to sing?"

"Nag is dead—is dead—is dead!" sang Darzee. "The valiant Rikki-tikki caught him by the head and held fast. The big man brought the bang-stick, and Nag fell in two pieces! He will never eat my babies again."

"All that's true enough; but where's Nagaina?" said Rikki-tikki, looking carefully round him.

"Nagaina came to the bathroom sluice and called for Nag," Darzee went on; "and Nag came out on the end of a stick—the sweeper picked him up on the end of a stick and threw him upon the rubbish-heap. Let us sing about the great, the red-eyed Rikki-tikki!" and Darzee filled his throat and sang.

"If I could get up to your nest, I'd roll all your babies out!" said Rikki-tikki. "You don't know when to do the right thing at the right time. You're safe enough in your nest there, but it's war for me down here. Stop singing a minute, Darzee."

"For the great, the beautiful Rikki-tikki's sake I will stop," said Darzee. "What is it, O Killer of the terrible Nag?"

"Where is Nagaina, for the third time?"

"On the rubbish-heap by the stables, mourning for Nag. Great is Rikki-tikki with the white teeth."

"Bother my white teeth! Have you ever heard where she keeps her eggs?"

"In the melon-bed, on the end nearest the wall, where the sun strikes nearly all day. She hid them there weeks ago."

"And you never thought it worth while to tell me? The end nearest the wall, you said?"

"Rikki-tikki, you are not going to eat her eggs?"

"Not eat exactly; no. Darzee, if you have a grain of sense you will fly off to the stables and pretend that your wing is broken, and let Nagaina chase you away to this bush. I must get to the melon-bed, and if I went there now she'd see me."

Darzee was a feather-brained little fellow who could never hold more than one idea at a time in his head; and just because he knew that Nagaina's children were born in eggs like his own, he didn't think at first that it was fair to kill them. But his wife was a sensible bird, and she knew that cobra's eggs meant young cobras later on; so she flew off from the nest, and left Darzee to keep the babies warm, and continue his song about the death of Nag. Darzee was very like a man in some ways.

She fluttered in front of Nagaina by the rubbish-heap, and cried out, "Oh, my wing is broken! The boy in the house threw a stone at me and broke it." Then she fluttered more desperately than ever.

Nagaina lifted up her head and hissed, "You warned Rikki-tikki when I would have killed him. Indeed and truly, you've chosen a bad place to be lame in." And she moved toward Darzee's wife, slipping along over the dust.

"The boy broke it with a stone!" shrieked Darzee's wife.

"Well! It may be some consolation to you when you're dead to know that I shall settle accounts with the boy. My husband lies on the rubbish-heap this morning, but before night the boy in the house will lie very still. What is the use of running away? I am sure to catch you. Little fool, look at me!"

Darzee's wife knew better than to do that, for a bird who looks at a snake's eyes gets so frightened that she cannot move.

Darzee's wife fluttered on, piping sorrowfully, and never leaving the ground, and Nagaina quickened her pace.

Rikki-tikki heard them going up the path from the stables, and he raced for the end of the melon-patch near the wall. There, in the warm litter about the melons, very cunningly hidden, he found twenty-five eggs, about the size of a bantam's eggs, but with whitish skin instead of shell.

"I was not a day too soon," he said; for he could see the baby cobras curled up inside the skin, and he knew that the minute they were hatched they could each kill a man or a mongoose. He bit off the tops of the eggs as fast as he could, taking care to crush the young cobras, and turned over the litter from time to time to see whether he had missed any. At last there were only three eggs left, and Rikki-tikki began to chuckle to himself, when he heard Darzee's wife screaming:

"Rikki-tikki, I led Nagaina toward the house, and she has gone into the veranda, and—oh, come quickly—she means killing!"

Rikki-tikki smashed two eggs, and tumbled backward down the melon-bed with the third egg in his mouth, and scuttled to the veranda as hard as he could put foot to the ground. Teddy and his mother and father were there at early breakfast; but Rikki-tikki saw that they were not eating anything. They sat stone-still, and their faces were white. Nagaina was coiled up on the matting by Teddy's chair, within easy striking-distance of Teddy's bare leg, and she was swaying to and fro singing a song of triumph.

"Son of the big man that killed Nag," she hissed, "stay still. I am not ready yet. Wait a little. Keep very still, all you three. If you move I strike, and if you do not move I strike. Oh, foolish people, who killed my Nag!"

Teddy's eyes were fixed on his father, and all his father could do was to whisper, "Sit still, Teddy. You mustn't move. Teddy, keep still."

Then Rikki-tikki came up and cried: "Turn round, Nagaina; turn and fight!"

"All in good time," said she, without moving her eyes. "I will settle my account with you presently. Look at your friends,

Rikki-tikki. They are still and white; they are afraid. They dare not move, and if you come a step nearer I strike."

"Look at your eggs," said Rikki-tikki, "in the melon-bed near the wall. Go and look, Nagaina."

The big snake turned half round, and saw the egg on the veranda. "Ah-h! Give it to me," she said.

Rikki-tikki put his paws one on each side of the egg, and his eyes were blood-red. "What price for a snake's egg? For a young cobra? For a young king-cobra? For the last—the very last of the brood? The ants are eating all the others down by the melon-bed."

Nagaina spun clear round, forgetting everything for the sake of the one egg; and Rikki-tikki saw Teddy's father shoot out a big hand, catch Teddy by the shoulder, and drag him across the little table with the tea-cups, safe and out of reach of Nagaina.

"Tricked! Tricked! Tricked! Rikk-tck-tck!" chuckled Rikki-tikki. "The boy is safe, and it was I—I—I that caught Nag by the hood last night in the bathroom." Then he began to jump up and down, all four feet together, his head close to the floor. "He threw me to and fro, but he could not shake me off. He was dead before the big man blew him in two. I did it. Rikki-tikki-tck-tck! Come then, Nagaina. Come and fight with me. You shall not be a widow long."

Nagaina saw that she had lost her chance of killing Teddy, and the egg lay between Rikki-tikki's paws. "Give me the egg, Rikki-tikki. Give me the last of my eggs, and I will go away and never come back," she said, lowering her hood.

"Yes, you will go away, and you will never come back; for you will go to the rubbish-heap with Nag. Fight, widow! The big man has gone for his gun! Fight!"

Rikki-tikki was bounding all round Nagaina, keeping just out of reach of her stroke, his little eyes like hot coals. Nagaina gathered herself together, and flung out at him. Rikki-tikki jumped up and backward. Again and again and again she struck, and each time her head came with a whack on the matting of the veranda, and she gathered herself together like a watch-spring. Then Rikki-tikki danced in a circle to get behind her, and Nagaina spun round to keep her head to his head, so that the rustle of her tail on the matting sounded like dry leaves blown along by the wind.

He had forgotten the egg. It still lay on the veranda, and Nagaina came nearer and nearer to it, till at last, while Rikki-tikki was drawing breath, she caught it in her mouth, turned to the veranda steps, and flew like an arrow down the path, with Rikki-tikki behind her. When the cobra runs for her life, she goes like a whip-lash flicked across a horse's neck.

Rikki-tikki knew that he must catch her, or all the trouble would begin again. She headed straight for the long grass by the thorn-bush, and as he was running Rikki-tikki heard Darzee still singing his foolish little song of triumph. But Darzee's wife was wiser. She flew off her nest as Nagaina came along, and flapped her wings about Nagaina's head. If Darzee had helped they might have turned her; but Nagaina only lowered her hood and went on. Still, the instant's delay brought Rikki-tikki up to her, and as she plunged into the rathole where she and Nag used to live, his little white teeth were clenched on her tail, and he went down with her—and very few mongooses, however wise and old they may be, care to follow a cobra into its hole. It was dark in the hole; and Rikki-tikki never knew when it might open out and give Nagaina room to turn and strike at him. He held on savagely, and stuck out his feet to act as brakes on the dark slope of the hot, moist earth.

Then the grass by the mouth of the hole stopped waving, and Darzee said: "It is all over with Rikki-tikki! We must sing his death-song. Valiant Rikki-tikki is dead! For Nagaina will surely kill him underground."

So he sang a very mournful song that he made up on the spur of the minute, and just as he got to the most touching part the grass quivered again, and Rikki-tikki, covered with dirt, dragged himself out of the hole leg by leg, licking his whiskers. Darzee stopped with a little shout. Rikki-tikki shook some of the dust out of his fur and sneezed. "It is all over," he said. "The widow will never come out again." And the red ants that live between the grass stems heard him, and began to troop down one after another to see if he had spoken the truth.

Rikki-tikki curled himself up in the grass and slept where he was—slept and slept till it was late in the afternoon, for he had done a hard day's work.

"Now," he said, when he awoke, "I will go back to the house. Tell the Coppersmith, Darzee, and he will tell the garden that Nagaina is dead."

The Coppersmith is a bird who makes a noise exactly like the beating of a little hammer on a copper pot; and the reason he is always making it is because he is the town-crier to every Indian garden, and tells all the news to everybody who cares to listen. As Rikki-tikki went up the path, he heard his "attention" notes like a tiny dinner-gong; and then the steady "Ding-dong-tock! Nag is dead—dong! Nagaina is dead! Ding-dong-tock!" That set all the birds in the garden singing, and the frogs croaking; for Nag and Nagaina used to eat frogs as well as little birds.

When Rikki got to the house, Teddy and Teddy's mother (she

still looked very white, for she had been fainting) and Teddy's father came out and almost cried over him; and that night he ate all that was given him till he could eat no more, and went to bed on Teddy's shoulder, where Teddy's mother saw him when she came to look late at night.

"He saved our lives and Teddy's life," she said to her husband. "Just think, he saved all our lives!"

Rikki-tikki woke up with a jump, for all the mongooses are light sleepers.

"Oh, it's you," said he. "What are you bothering for? All the cobras are dead; and if they weren't, I'm here."

Rikki-tikki had a right to be proud of himself; but he did not grow too proud, and he kept that garden as a mongoose should keep it, with tooth and jump and spring and bite, till never a cobra dared show its head inside the walls.

Darzee's Chaunt

Sung in honour of Rikki-tikki-tavi

> Singer and tailor am I—
>   Doubled the joys that I know—
> Proud of my lilt through the sky,
>   Proud of the house that I sew—
> Over and under, so weave I my music—so weave I the house
> that I sew.

> Sing to your fledglings again,
>   Mother, oh lift up your head!
> Evil that plagued us is slain,
>   Death in the garden lies dead.
> Terror that hid in the roses is impotent—flung on the dunghill
> and dead!

> Who hath delivered us, who?
>   Tell me his nest and his name.
> Rikki, the valiant, the true,
>   Tikki, with eyeballs of flame,
> Rik-tikki-tikki, the ivory-fanged, the hunter with eyeballs of
> flame.

Give him the Thanks of the Birds,
   Bowing with tail-feathers spread!
Praise him with nightingale-words—
   Nay, I will praise him instead.
Hear! I will sing you the praise of the bottle-tailed Rikki, with
   eyeballs of red!

Here Rikki-tikki interrupted, and the rest of the song is lost.

How Kari Saved Our Lives in the Jungle

DHAN GOPAL MUKERJI

Wʜᴇɴ Kari grew to be five years old, he was almost as high as the ceiling. He was never trained for hunting. We never thought of killing anything except snakes and tigers, and these we killed when they came toward the village and injured men. So Kari never had the training of a hunting elephant. Just the same, he was very alert and steady in the face of danger, so when it was a question of going into the jungle on the back of an elephant, we generally took Kari with us. During such trips we did not put a cloth of gold on his back or silver bells on his sides. These bells are made in certain parts of India where silversmiths know how to melt and mix silver so that when the clapper strikes the sides of the bell there will be a sound like rushing water. The two bells are tied by a silver chain and slung over the elephant's back, one dangling on each side of him. We never put a *howdah* on the back of Kari. Very few Hindus put *howdahs* on elephants.

Do you know what a *howdah* is? It is a box with high sides inside of which there are chairs for travelers. The *howdahs* are generally for people who are not accustomed to elephants. They need the high sides so that when the elephant walks they will not fall from his back. They stay in their seats leaning on the edge of the box and see very little, especially children who are not tall enough to see over the sides. That is why Indian children prefer riding bareback on an elephant to taking a *howdah*.

One evening when my brother and I went out, we put a mattress on Kari's back and tied it very tightly with cords so that it would not slip, for it is not pleasant to slip and fall under an elephant's belly and be stepped on. But Kari was trained so that he would not have stepped on us even if we had slipped under him. We tightened the cords to the mattress, however, and lay down for the night. Though we had bells, we lifted them up and silenced the clappers, so that in walking through the jungle road they would not ring and frighten the animals, for the forest is

the dwelling place of silence, and silence being the voice of God, no man dares to disturb it. We lay on the back of Kari and looked up. In India, the stars are so close that you can almost pluck them, and the velvet blue of the sky is like a river of stillness running between banks of silver.

As we lay there, unable to go to sleep right away, we heard jungle sounds. The heavy tread of the elephant was like clouds brushing the crests of the forest. Once in a while you could see a tiger come out of the jungle, cross a road, and disappear in the distance; but Kari was so brave he never condescended to

notice the comings and goings of tigers. Once we heard the bark
of a fox very near us, and then he came out of the jungle. Kari
stopped and the fox passed across the road, then we moved on
again. In the moonlight which made the road look like a river
of silver, we saw squirrels leaping from branch to branch.

You know, perhaps, that elephants can sleep as they walk.
Presently Kari's walk slackened into a slow pace, and we felt
quite sure that he was dozing. Then we remembered nothing,
for we, too, fell asleep. I cannot tell how much time passed before we were startled out of our sleep by a terrible roar, a ghastly
trumpeting of the elephant, and a terrible lunge of his body. We
had to hold on to his back very tightly to avoid being thrown
off. In a few seconds both of us had turned over and were lying
on our faces, holding on to the cords that held the mattress to
Kari's back, while he broke into a run.

Trees bent and broke, branches fell, and we could hear the
monkeys stampeding from tree to tree, and flocks of birds, startled out of their sleep, falling upon us, their wings beating our
faces. We shouted to Kari to be calm, but he went on as if he
were mad. We heard boars snorting and running away, and
strange-looking horned creatures leaping and bounding off in all
directions. Then a tree in front of us fell, and the jungle throbbed
for a moment. It seemed as though a shiver ran through Kari's
body, and he stopped stock still. It was very difficult to tell
exactly what had happened until we got off Kari's back. I spoke
to him and he shook his head, then I spoke again and urged him
to put up his head. He obeyed and I climbed down by his trunk.
I felt it was very wet, however, and he shook me off with pain.

My brother spoke to me from above and said when I told
him how the trunk felt, "Now I know. You see, this is autumn
when bears eat Mohula in the moonlight under the thick shade
of the trees. As you know, Mohula intoxicates bears, and makes
them sleepy. Some bear had fallen asleep under the trees and
Kari, who was also asleep and consequently did not even smell
him with his trunk, must have come upon him without suspect-
ing his presence. Although all bears are brought up to respect
elephants, this one, no doubt, was so sleepy that he did not

know who was upon him and so I am sure he must have sprung
up in his surprise and scratched Kari's trunk."

If Kari had been wide awake he would have killed the bear,
but being sleepy, the shock and the surprise of the attack and
the pain in his trunk frightened him so that he ran out into the
jungle, mad with terror.

I put my hand on the trunk again. Yes, it was bleeding; I
could see in the moonlight that it was not perspiration because
my hand was dark red. I spoke to Kari again; this time he did
not shake his head so furiously. He was rather willing to listen,
and I told him I was very sorry about his trunk but could do
nothing here; I also told him to go back to the road. He shook
his head—that meant "No." Do you know why he did not want
to go back to that road? You shall learn at the end of this story.

I got upon his back again. "Since he won't go back to the
road," said my brother, "we must give him the master call so
that he can make a road through the jungle," and we gave him
the master call.

At this Kari lifted his bleeding trunk and smote down the first tree, and then he struck down the next tree. He came upon a third which his trunk could not pull down, so he turned around and walked away from it. After taking a few steps he stopped and slowly walked backwards and with one push of his back knocked this tree down.

At this we could hear the flocks of birds flying in the air and feel the stamping feet below as herds of animals ran in every direction. We heard the vibrant jabber of monkeys from treetops, and each time a new tree fell, there was more jabbering and more leaping away from tree to tree.

We clung to the elephant's back with our nails and teeth.

Soon we found ourselves on the road, three miles ahead of where Kari had been frightened by the bear.

Do you know why he did not go back to the same spot? Because no animal ever likes to return to the place where he lost his pride. For to be frightened is to lose one's pride.

The Rum Tum Tugger

T. S. ELIOT

The Rum Tum Tugger is a Curious Cat:
If you offer him pheasant he would rather have grouse.
If you put him in a house he would much prefer a flat,
If you put him in a flat then he'd rather have a house.
If you set him on a mouse then he only wants a rat,
If you set him on a rat then he'd rather chase a mouse.
Yes, the Rum Tum Tugger is a Curious Cat—
  And there isn't any call for me to shout it:
    For he will do
    As he do do
      And there's no doing anything about it!

The Rum Tum Tugger is a terrible bore:
When you let him in, then he wants to be out;
He's always on the wrong side of every door,
As soon as he's at home, then he'd like to get about.
He likes to lie in the bureau drawer,
But he makes such a fuss if he can't get out.
Yes, the Rum Tum Tugger is a Curious Cat—
  And it isn't any use for you to doubt it:
    For he will do
    As he do do
      And there's no doing anything about it!

The Rum Tum Tugger is a curious beast:
His disobliging ways are a matter of habit.
If you offer him fish then he always wants a feast;
When there isn't any fish then he won't eat rabbit.

If you offer him cream then he sniffs and sneers,
For he only likes what he finds for himself;
So you'll catch him in it right up to the ears,
If you put it away on the larder shelf.
The Rum Tum Tugger is artful and knowing,
The Rum Tum Tugger doesn't care for a cuddle;
But he'll leap on your lap in the middle of your sewing,
For there's nothing he enjoys like a horrible muddle.
Yes, the Rum Tum Tugger is a Curious Cat—
  And there isn't any need for me to spout it:
    For he will do
    As he do do
      And there's no doing anything about it!

Basta, a Holy Cat
of Bubastis

ARTHUR WEIGALL

O<small>NE</small> summer during a heat-wave, when the temperature in
the shade on my verandah in Luxor was a hundred and twenty-
five degrees Fahrenheit, I went down to cooler Lower Egypt to
pay a visit to an English friend of mine stationed at Zagazig, the
native city which stands beside the ruins of ancient Bubastis.

He was about to leave Egypt, and asked me whether I would
like to have his cat, a dignified, mystical-minded, long-legged,
small-headed, green-eyed female, whose orange-yellow hair,
marked with grayish-black stripes in tabby pattern, was so short
that she gave the impression of being naked—an impression, however, which did not in any way detract from her air of virginal
chastity.

Her name was Basta, and though her more recent ancestors
had lived wild amongst the ruins, she was so obviously a de-
scendant of the holy cats of ancient times, who were incarnations
of the goddess Basta, that I thought it only right to accept the
offer and take her up to Luxor to live with me. To be the expert
in charge of Egyptian antiquities, and not to have an ancient
Egyptian cat to give an air of mystery to my headquarters, had,
indeed, always seemed to me to be somewhat wanting in show-
manship on my part.

Thus it came about that on my departure I drove off to the
railroad-station with the usually dignified Basta bumping about
and uttering unearthly howls inside a cardboard hat-box, in the
side of which I had cut a small round hole for ventilation. The
people in the streets and on the station platform seemed to be

under the impression that the noises were digestive and that I was in dire need of a doctor; and it was a great relief to my embarrassment when the hot and panting train steamed in.

Fortunately I found myself alone in the compartment, and the hat-box on the seat at my side had begun to cause me less anxiety, when suddenly Basta was seized with a sort of religious frenzy. The box rocked about, and presently out through the air-hole came a long, snake-like paw which waved weirdly to and fro in space for a moment, and then was withdrawn, its place being taken by a pink nose which pushed itself outwards with such frantic force that the sides of the hole gave way, and out burst the entire sandy, sacred head.

She then began to choke, for the cardboard was pressing tightly around her neck; and to save her from strangulation I was obliged to tear the aperture open, whereupon she wriggled out, leapt in divine frenzy up the side of the carriage, and prostrated herself on the network of the baggage-rack, where her hysteria caused her to lose all control of herself, and if I say modestly that she was overcome with nausea I shall be telling but a part of the dreadful tale.

The rest of the journey was like a bad dream; but at the Cairo terminus where I had to change into the night express for Luxor I got the help of a native policeman who secured a large laundry basket from the sleeping-car department, and after a prolonged struggle, during which the train was shunted into a distant siding, we managed somehow to imprison the struggling Basta once more.

The perspiring policeman and I then carried the basket at a run along the tracks back to the station in the sweltering heat of the late afternoon, and I just managed to catch my train; but during this second part of my journey Basta traveled in the baggage-van, whence, in the hot and silent night, whenever we were at a standstill, her appalling incantations came drifting to my ears.

I opened the basket in an unfurnished spare room in my house, and like a flash Basta was up the bare wall and onto the curtain-pole above the window. There she remained all day in a sort of mystic trance; but at sunset the saucer of milk and plate of fish which I had provided for her at last enticed her down, and in the end she reconciled herself to her new surroundings, and indicated by her behaviour that she was willing to accept my house as her earthly temple.

With Pedro, my pariah dog, there was not the slightest trouble: he had no strong feelings about cats, and she on her part graciously deigned to acknowledge his status—as, I believe, is generally the case in native households. She sometimes condescended to visit my horse and donkey in their stalls; and for Laura, my camel, she quickly developed a real regard, often sleeping for hours in her stable—perhaps because at that time they were both unmarried girls and had their innocence and its hopes in common.

I was not worried as to how she would treat the chickens and pigeons, because her former owner at Zagazig had insisted upon her respecting his hen-coop and pigeon-cote; but I was a little anxious about the ducks, for she had not previously known any, and in ancient times her ancestors used to be trained to hunt wild geese and ducks and were fed with pâté de foie gras on holy days and anniversaries.

In a corner of the garden I had made a miniature duck-pond which was sunk rather deeply in the ground and down to which I had cut a narrow, steeply sloping passage or gangway. During the day, after the ducks had been up and down this slope several times, the surface used to become wet and slippery, and the ducks, having waddled down the first few inches, were forced to toboggan down the rest of it on their tails, with their two feet sticking out in front of them and their heads well up.

Basta was always fascinated by this slide and by the splash at the bottom, and used to sit and watch it all for hours, which made me think at first that she would one day spring at one of them; but she never did. Field-mice, and water-rats down by the Nile, were her only prey; and in connection with the former I may mention a curious occurrence.

One hot night I was sitting smoking my pipe on the verandah, when my attention was attracted by two mice which had crept into the patch of brilliant moonlight before my feet, and were boldly nibbling some crumbs left over from a cracker thrown to

Pedro earlier in the evening. I watched them silently for a while and did not notice that Basta had seen them and was preparing to spring, nor did I observe a large white owl sitting aloft amongst the overhanging roses and also preparing to pounce.

Suddenly, and precisely at the same moment, the owl shot down on the mice from above and Basta leapt at them from beside me. There was a collision and a wild scuffle; fur and feathers flew; I fell out of my chair; and then the owl made off screeching in one direction and the cat dashed away in the other; while the mice, practically clinging to one another, remained for a moment or so too terrified to move.

During the early days of her residence in Luxor, Basta often used to go down to the edge of the Nile to fish with her paw; but she never caught anything, and in the end she got a fright and gave it up.

I was sitting by the river one morning watching her trying to catch one of a little shoal of small fish which were sunning themselves in the shallow water, when there came swimming into view a twelve- or fourteen-inch fish which I recognized (by its whiskers and the absence of a dorsal fin) as the electric cat-fish pretty common in the Nile—a strange creature able to give you an electric shock like hitting your funnybone.

These fish obtain their food in a curious way: they hang round any shoal of small fry engaged in feeding, and then glide quietly into their midst and throw out this electric shock, whereupon the little fellows are all sick to the stomach, and the big fellow gets their disgorged dinners.

I was just waiting to see this happen with my own eyes—for it had always seemed a bit far-fetched—when Basta made a dart at the intruder with her paw, and got a shock. She uttered a yowl as though somebody had trodden on her, and leapt high in the air; and never again did she put her foot near the water. She was content after that with our daily offering of a fish brought from the market and fried for her like a burnt sacrifice.

My bedroom was on the ground floor of my house, and as I used to leave the long-windows open, Basta often wandered into the room in the night and jumped onto my bed, smelling faintly of Laura's stable. Pedro used also to come in occasionally, and when they met in the darkness there was generally a little quiet hissing and growling, though hardly enough to wake me up; but when there was a moon and the room was not quite dark they used sometimes to catch sight of themselves in the long mirror, and I would then be violently awakened either by Pedro's ferocious barking or by Basta's savage yowls.

Neither of them would ever do this in the daytime, because they knew then that what they saw was only their own reflection; but at night the illusion was more convincing, and they never ceased to be deceived by it.

Basta had a most unearthly voice, and when she was feeling emotional she would let out a wail which at first was like the crying of a phantom baby, and then became the tuneless song of a lunatic, and finally developed into the bloodcurdling howl of a soul in torment. And when she spat the percussion was like that of a spring-gun.

There were some wild cats, or, rather, domestic cats who, like Basta's own forebears, had taken to a wild life, living in a grove of trees beside the river just beyond my garden wall; and it was generally the proximity of one of these which started her off, but sometimes the outburst was caused by her own unfathomable thoughts as she went her mysterious ways in the darkness of the night.

I think she must have been clairvoyant, for she often seemed to be seeing things not visible to me. Sometimes, perhaps when she was cleaning fish or mouse from her face, she would pause with one foot off the ground and stare in front of her, and then back away with bristling hair or go forward with friendly little mewing noises; and sometimes she would leap off a chair or sofa, her tail lashing and her green eyes dilated. But it may have been worms.

Once I saw her standing absolutely rigid and tense on the lawn, staring at the rising moon; and then all of a sudden she did a sort of dance such as cats sometimes do when they are playing with other cats. But there was no other cat, and, anyway, Basta never played: she never forgot that she was a holy cat.

Her chaste hauteur was so great that she would not move out of the way when people were walking about, and many a time her demoniacal shriek, and perhaps a crash of breaking glass, informed the household that somebody had tripped over her. It was astonishing, however, how quickly she recovered her dignity and how well she maintained the pretense that whatever happened to her was at her own celestial wish and was not our doing.

If I called her she would pretend not to hear, but would come a few moments later when it could appear that she had thought

of doing so first; and if I lifted her off a chair she would jump back onto it and then descend with dignity as though of her own free will. But in this, of course, she was more like a woman than like a divinity.

The Egyptian cat is a domesticated species of the African wild-cat, and no doubt its strange behaviour and its weird voice were the cause of its being regarded as sacred in ancient times; but although the old gods and their worship have been forgotten these many centuries, the traditional sanctity of the race has survived. Modern Egyptians think it unlucky to hurt a cat, and in the native quarters of Cairo and other cities hundreds of cats are daily fed at the expense of benevolent citizens. They say that they do this because cats are so useful to mankind in killing off mice and other pests; but actually it is an unrecognized survival of the old beliefs.

In the days of the Pharaohs, when a cat died the men of the household shaved off their eyebrows and sat around wailing and rocking themselves to and fro in simulated anguish. The body was embalmed and buried with solemn rites in the local cats' cemetery, or was sent down to Bubastis to rest in the shadow of the temple of their patron goddess. I myself have dug up hundreds of mummified cats; and once, in fact, when I had a couple of dozen of the best specimens standing on my verandah waiting to be despatched to the Cairo Museum, Basta was most excited about it, and walked around sniffing at them all day. They certainly smelt awful.

Egyptian cats—living ones, I mean—were imported into ancient Greece and Italy by Phoenician traders, and became the part-ancestors of most of the European breeds; but Basta, who was of the pure Bubastis stock, was nevertheless quite unlike any cats at home. She was so lanky, her head was so small for her body, her yellow fur was so stiff and short and made her look so undressed, and she was so eminently uncanny.

On my lawn there was a square slab of stone which had once been the top of an altar dedicated to the sun-god, but was now used as a sort of low garden table; and sometimes when she had caught a mouse she used to deposit the chewed corpse upon this slab—nobody could think why, unless, as I always told people, she was really making an offering to the sun. It was most mysterious of her; but it led once to a very unfortunate episode.

A famous French antiquarian, who was paying a polite call, was sitting with me beside this sacred stone drinking afternoon tea and eating fresh dates, when Basta appeared on the scene with a small dead mouse in her mouth, which in her usual way she deposited upon the slab—only on this occasion she laid it on my guest's plate which was standing on the slab.

We were talking at the moment and did not see her do this, and anyhow the Frenchman was as blind as a bat; and, of course, as luck would have it, he immediately picked up the wet, mole-coloured mouse instead of a ripe brown date, and the thing had almost gone into his mouth before he saw what it was and, with a yell, flung it into the air.

It fell into his upturned sun-helmet which was lying on the grass beside him; but he did not see where it had gone, and jumping angrily to his feet in the momentary belief that I had played a school-boy joke on him, he snatched up his helmet and was in the act of putting it on his head when the mouse tumbled out onto the front of his shirt and slipped down inside his buttoned jacket.

At this he went more or less mad, danced about, shook himself, and finally trod on Basta who completed his frenzy by uttering a fiendish howl and digging her claws into his leg. The dead mouse, I am glad to say, fell onto the grass during the dance without passing through his roomy trousers as I had feared it might; and Basta, recovering her dignity, picked it up and walked off with it.

It is a remarkable fact that during the five or six years she spent with me she showed no desire to be anything but a spinster all her life, and when I arranged a marriage for her she displayed such dignified but violent antipathy towards the bridegroom that the match was a failure. In the end, however, she fell in love with one of the wild cats who lived amongst the trees beyond my wall, and nothing could prevent her going off to visit him from time to time, generally at dead of night.

He did not care a hoot about her sanctity, and she was feminine enough to enjoy the novelty of being roughly treated. I never actually saw him, for he did not venture into the garden, but I used to hear him knocking her about outside my gates; and when she came home scratched and bitten and muttering something about holy cats, it was plain that she was desperately happy. She licked her wounds, indeed, with deep and voluptuous satisfaction.

A dreadful change came over her. She had lost her precious dignity, and was restless and inclined to be savage; her digestion played embarrassing tricks on her; and once she mortally offended Laura by clawing her nose. There was a new glint in her green eyes as she watched the ducks sliding into the pond; the pigeons interested her for the first time; and for the first time, too, she ate the mice she had caught.

Then she began to disappear for a whole day or night at a time, and once when I went in search of her amongst the trees outside and found her sharpening her claws on a branch above my head, she put her ears back and hissed at me until I could see every one of her teeth and halfway down her pink throat. I tried by every method to keep her at home when she came back, but it was all in vain, and at last she left me forever.

Weeks afterwards I caught sight of her once again amongst the trees, and it was evident that she was soon to become a mother. She gave me a friendly little mew this time, but she would not let me touch her; and presently she slipped away into the undergrowth. I never knew what became of her.

"Buck had sprung in on the instant, and at the end of three hundred yards, amid a mad swirl of water, he overhauled Thornton."

—*The Call of the Wild*

Coaly-Bay, the Outlaw Horse

ERNEST THOMPSON SETON

Five years ago in the Bitterroot Mountains of Idaho there was a beautiful little foal. His coat was bright bay; his legs, mane, and tail were glossy black—coal black and bright bay—so they named him Coaly-Bay.

"Coaly-Bay" sounds like "Kolibey," which is an Arab title of nobility, and those who saw the handsome colt, and did not know how he came by the name, thought he must be of Arab blood. No doubt he was, in a faraway sense; just as all our best horses have Arab blood, and once in a while it seems to come out strong and show in every part of the creature, in his frame, his power, and his wild, free, roving spirit.

Coaly-Bay loved to race like the wind; he gloried in his speed and his tireless legs; when he was careering with the herd of colts, if they met a fence or ditch, it was as natural for Coaly-Bay to overleap it as it was for the others to sheer off. So he grew up strong of limb, restless of spirit, and rebellious at any thought of restraint. Even the kindly curb of the hay-yard or the stable was unwelcome, and he soon showed that he would rather stand out all night in a driving storm than be locked in a comfortable stall where he had no vestige of the liberty he loved so well.

He became very clever at dodging the horse wrangler whose job it was to bring the horse herd to the corral. The very sight of the man set Coaly-Bay going. He became what is known as a "Quit-the-bunch"—that is, a horse of such independent mind that he will go his own way the moment he does not like the way of the herd.

So each month the colt became more set on living free, and more cunning in the means he took to win his way. Far down in his soul, too, there must have been a streak of cruelty, for he stuck at nothing and spared no one that seemed to stand between him and his one desire.

When he was three years of age, just in the perfection of his young strength and beauty, his real troubles began, for now his owner undertook to break him to ride. He was as tricky and vicious as he was handsome, and the first day's experience was a terrible battle between the horse trainer and the beautiful colt.

But the man was skillful. He knew how to apply his power, and all the wild plunging, bucking, rearing, and rolling of the wild one had no desirable result. With all his strength the horse was hopelessly helpless in the hands of the skillful horseman, and Coaly-Bay was so far mastered at length that a good rider could use him. But each time the saddle went on, he made a new fight. After a few months of this the colt seemed to realize that it was useless to resist; it simply won for him lashings and spurrings, so he pretended to reform. For a week he was ridden each day, and not once did he buck, but on the last day he came home lame.

His owner turned him out to pasture. Three days later he seemed all right; he was caught and saddled. He did not buck, but within five minutes he went lame as before. Again he was turned out to pasture, and after a week, saddled, only to go lame again.

His owner did not know what to think, whether the horse really had a lame leg or was only shamming, but he took the first chance to get rid of him, and though Coaly-Bay was easily worth fifty dollars, he sold him for twenty-five. The new owner felt he had a bargain, but after being ridden half a mile Coaly-Bay went lame. The rider got off to examine the foot, whereupon Coaly-Bay broke away and galloped back to his old pasture. Here he was caught, and the new owner, being neither gentle nor sweet, applied spur without mercy, so that the next twenty miles was covered in less than two hours, and no sign of lameness appeared.

Now they were at the ranch of this new owner. Coaly-Bay was led from the door of the house to the pasture, limping all the way, and then turned out. He limped over to the other horses. On one side of the pasture was the garden of a neighbor. This man was very proud of his fine vegetables and had put a six-foot fence around the place. Yet the very night after Coaly-Bay arrived, certain of the horses got into the garden somehow and did a great deal of damage. But they leaped out before daylight and no one saw them.

The gardener was furious, but the ranchman stoutly maintained that it must have been some other horses, since his were behind a six-foot fence.

Next night it happened again. The ranchman went out very early and saw all his horses in the pasture, with Coaly-Bay behind them. His lameness seemed worse now instead of better. In a few days, however, the horse was seen walking all right, so the ranchman's son caught him and tried to ride him. But this seemed too good a chance to lose; all his old wickedness returned to the horse; the boy was bucked off at once and hurt. The ranchman himself now leaped into the saddle; Coaly-Bay bucked for ten minutes, but finding he could not throw the man, he tried to crush his leg against a post, but the rider guarded himself well. Coaly-Bay reared and threw himself backward; the rider slipped off, the horse fell, jarring heavily, and before he could rise the man was in the saddle again. The horse now ran away, plunging and bucking; he stopped short, but the rider did not go over his head, so Coaly-Bay turned, seized the man's boot in his teeth and but for heavy blows on the nose would have torn him dreadfully. It was quite clear now that Coaly-Bay was an "outlaw"— that is, an incurably vicious horse.

The saddle was jerked off, and he was driven, limping, into the pasture.

The raids on the garden continued, and the two men began to quarrel over them. But to prove that his horses were not guilty the ranchman asked the gardener to sit up with him and watch. That night as the moon was brightly shining they saw, not all the horses, but Coaly-Bay, walk straight up to the garden fence—no sign of a limp now—easily leap over it, and proceed to gobble the finest things he could find. After they had made sure of his identity, the men ran forward. Coaly-Bay cleared the fence like a deer, lightly raced over the pasture to mix with the horse herd, and when the men came near him he had—oh, such an awful limp.

"That settles it," said the rancher. "He's a fraud but he's a beauty, and good stuff, too."

"Yes, but it settles who took my garden truck," said the other.

"Wal, I suppose so," was the answer; "but look a here, neighbor, you haven't lost more'n ten dollars in truck. That horse is easily worth—a hundred. Give me twenty-five dollars, take the horse, an' call it square."

"Not much I will," said the gardener. "I'm out twenty-five dollars' worth of truck; the horse isn't worth a cent more. I'll take him and call it even."

And so the thing was settled. The ranchman said nothing about Coaly-Bay being vicious as well as cunning, but the gardener found out, the very first time he tried to ride him, that the horse was as bad as he was beautiful.

Next day a sign appeared on the gardener's gate:

FOR SALE:
First class horse
sound and gentle
$10.00

Now at this time a band of hunters came riding by, going to hunt bear. They had guns and everything needed for bear-hunting, except bait. It is usual to buy some worthless horse or cow, drive it into the mountains where the bears are, and kill it there. So, seeing the sign, the hunters called to the gardener: "Haven't you got a cheaper horse?"

The gardener replied: "Look at him there, ain't he a beauty? You won't find a cheaper horse if you travel a thousand miles."

"We are looking for an old bear bait, and five dollars is our limit," replied the hunter.

Horses were cheap and plentiful in that country: buyers were scarce. The gardener feared that Coaly-Bay would escape. "Wal, if that's the best you can do, he's yourn."

The hunter handed him five dollars, then said: "Now stranger, the bargain's settled. Will you tell me why you sell this fine horse for five dollars?"

"Mighty simple. He can't be rode. He's dead lame when he's going your way and sound as a dollar going his own; no fence in the country can hold him; he's a dangerous outlaw. He's wickeder nor old Nick."

"Well, he's an almighty handsome bear bait," and the hunters rode on.

Coaly-Bay was driven with the pack horses, and limped dreadfully on the trail. Once or twice he tried to go back, but he was easily turned by the men behind him. His limp grew worse, and toward night it was painful to see him.

The leading guide remarked: "That thar limp is no fake. He's got some deep-seated trouble."

Day after day the hunters rode farther into the mountains driving the horses along and hobbling them at night. Coaly-Bay went with the rest, limping along, tossing his head and his long splendid mane at every step. One of the hunters tried to ride him and nearly lost his life, for the horse seemed possessed of a demon as soon as the man was on his back.

The road grew harder as it rose. A very bad bog had to be crossed one day. Several horses were mired in it, and as the men rushed to the rescue, Coaly-Bay saw his chance of escape. He wheeled in a moment and turned himself from a limping, low-headed, sorry, bad-eyed creature into a high-spirited horse. Head and tail aloft now, shaking their black streamers in the wind, he gave a joyous neigh, and, without a trace of lameness, dashed for his home one hundred miles away, threading each narrow trail with perfect certainty, though he had seen it but once before, and in a few minutes he had steamed away from their sight.

The men were furious, but one of them, saying not a word, leaped on his horse—to do what? Follow that free-ranging racer? Sheer folly. Oh, no!—he knew a better plan. He knew the country. Two miles around by the trail, half a mile by the rough cutoff that he took, was Panther Gap. The runaway must pass through that, and Coaly-Bay raced down the trail to find the guide below awaiting him. Tossing his head with anger he wheeled on up the trail again, and within a few yards recovered his monotonous limp and evil expression. He was driven into camp, and there he vented his rage by kicking in the ribs of a harmless little pack horse.

This was bear country, and the hunters resolved to end his dangerous pranks and make him useful for once. They dared not catch him; it was not really safe to go near him, but two of the guides drove him to a distant glade where bears abounded.

"Guess this'll do," said the older man. "Well, here goes for a sure death or clean miss," said the other confidently, and waiting till the limper was out in the middle of the meadow, he gave a short, sharp whistle. Instantly Coaly-Bay was alert. He swung and faced his tormentors, his noble head erect, his nostrils flaring; a picture of horse beauty—yes, of horse perfection.

The rifle was leveled, the very brain its mark, just on the cross line of the eyes and ears, that meant sure, sudden, painless death.

The rifle cracked. The great horse wheeled and dashed away. It was sudden death or miss—and the marksman *missed*.

Away went the wild horse at his famous best, not for his eastern home, but down the unknown western trail, away and away; the pine woods hid him from view, and left behind was the rifleman vainly trying to force the empty cartridge from his gun.

Down that trail with an inborn certainty he went, and on through the limpid Clearwater, and on, responsive to some unknown guide that subtly called him from the farther west. And so he went till the dwindling pines gave place to scrubby cedars and these in turn were mixed with sage, and onward still till the faraway flat plains of Salmon River were about him, and ever on, tireless, as it seemed, he went, and crossed the canyon of the mighty Snake, and up again to the high, wild plains where the wire fence still is not, and on, beyond the Buffalo Hump, till moving specks on the far horizon caught his eager eyes, and coming on and near, they moved and rushed aside to wheel and face about. He lifted up his voice and called to them, the long shrill neigh of his kindred when they bugled to each other on the far Chaldean plain; and back their answer came. This way and that they wheeled and sped and caracoled, and Coaly-Bay drew nearer, called, and gave the countersigns his kindred know, till this they were assured—he was their kind, he was of the wild free blood that man had never tamed. And when the night came down on the purpling plain his place was in the herd as one who after many a long hard journey in the dark had found his home.

Long may he roam—this is my wish, and this—that I may see him once again in all the glory of his speed with his black mane on the wind, the spurgalls gone from his flanks, and in his eye the blazing light that grew in his faroff forebears' eyes as they spurned Arabian plains to leave behind the racing wild beast and the fleet gazelle—yes, too, the driving sandstorm that o'erwhelmed the rest, but strove in vain on the dusty wake of the desert's highest born.

Our Friend Tasso

FELIX SALTEN

It was not our doing that the dog's name was Tasso. He bore this proud, remarkably literary label when we bought him, though it is doubtful if he was named in honor of Torquato Tasso, the Renaissance bard.

We had just come home from a long journey, and among the many things we had seen that impressed us were those big beautiful dogs, to us an unfamiliar breed—as big, almost, as bears, and covered with thick rust-red or steel-gray curly hair. Their mighty heads, with bushy amber eyebrows, had an expression of human benevolence. Among other dogs, they sat in monumental calm and dignity. Self-possessed, they spurned every approach. They gazed indifferently ahead or they looked strangers up and down with a brief glance which seemed to say, If you please!

At once we had wanted to own such a dog. But the dealers demanded high prices, and the possible difficulties of our long return journey frightened us off. And then, a few days after we got home again, we encountered a peasant, with such a dog, on the road that leads along the shore of the lake. That was pure coincidence. . . . No, it was a dispensation of fate.

Where could the peasant have got the dog? we asked.

We learned that somewhere in the neighborhood a landowner had gone bankrupt, and sold off all his possessions. This dog, among other things, had fallen to the peasant and he was willing to pass him on to us—at a small profit.

Tasso seemed so thoroughly in accord with the transaction that he came along as if he had always been a member of our family. He didn't even turn his head to look down the road after the peasant.

The name Tasso seemed to us perfectly suited to the magnificent animal, who was strong, wise, majestic and gentle. He had the long rust-red curly hair with iron-gray streaks. All his huge body was thickly covered with it right down to the giant paws. With the stumpy tail and woolly torso he resembled a storybook teddy bear. Yet in the lines of his stance and the ease of his gait—in all of his movements—he possessed the indescribable grace of a noble line. Sometimes his face suggested Bismarck's, because of the bushy blond eyebrows and the deeply reflective gaze of the beautiful eyes. If he were called out of a sleep or a doze, he would lift his head quickly. Then he had the ruffled and confused look of a man who has been tousling his hair while reading absorbedly. Also in other ways Tasso reminded one of men. But always of worthy, interesting men.

When we brought him home to the farm, a critical situation developed. Our overseer owned a big black Newfoundland called Galto, an animal very quick with his jaws. We thought Galto and Tasso might be friends for all that. At any rate, we decided to try. When they first met, each was held by a chain. Galto growled fiercely and showed his teeth; the hairs on his back bristled. Tasso turned away as if he were saying, I prefer to ignore this sort of thing. They did not become friends, those two.

But things did not end there. It proved later that matters had been only temporarily postponed. In the meantime, we kept Tasso and Galto away from each other. When one was let out of doors, the other had to stay in. We hoped that this system would get us through the summer at least, but . . .

Anyway, Tasso was a fascinating house companion. He showed that in his first encounter with our little red cat. We had quite forgotten about Malvina when we took Tasso into the dining room with us our first evening at home. We were far into our meal when she came bounding in, full of playful spirit.

Tasso was startled and began to run around the room. But we were all too frightened to think of anything to do. The giant, however, recovered his composure first and sauntered over to the cat apologetically. Malvina leaped onto a chair to equalize the difference in their heights and played with him coquettishly and good-naturedly for the rest of the evening.

When we looked for the red kitten next morning, we found her lying with Tasso, asleep, snuggled tight against his woolly flank, and Tasso, already awake, didn't dare move.

A few weeks later we had another fright on the kitten's account. We came upon Tasso in the corridor, with the little cat hanging limp in his great jaws. At our stern command he put her carefully down on the floor. But she stood on all fours, quite alive, and miaowed up at Tasso as if she wanted to be carried again. The hound looked up at us: I haven't done anything to her! No, he had done nothing to hurt her. As a virtuous dog he had little or no understanding of the fact that cats sometimes become frolicsome in the night and sally forth in search of a playmate of their own kind. But when sleeping time came, he had no peace until she was with him. He would go to fetch his little bed companion and carry her willy-nilly in his mouth to their place.

In other ways, too, Tasso was a desirable inmate of the house. It never occurred to him to beg, either for the pleasure of being let out of doors or at table for a morsel. Nor did he ever fall on his food voraciously, but ate calmly, choosily, as refined as the aristocratic dog he really was. Now and then he would come, sit himself down and put his paw on the shoulder of one of us. That good heavy paw on the shoulder was like the confirmation of enduring friendship.

He was also a pleasant companion on our wanderings through the forest and the fields. There was never any need to watch over him, call him, scold him, nor, certainly, to punish him. It was enchanting to see him exercise his enormous strength in swift dashing and running, when he let his great energy work itself out in harmless and enthusiastic romping. One moment he would be far away and the next, swiftly back again. He invariably took care not to lose us for a moment. He loved to swim and was tireless at it. No wonder, for he was the finest specimen of otterhound.

Though Tasso never fought unless attacked, he was a dangerous fighter. Otterhounds' teeth are sharp and pointed and the strength of their jaws is annihilating. They bite with much greater speed than other dogs, such as bulls and terriers, who grab on tight with a single bite and don't let go.

We were convinced of the accuracy of these observations one day when we set out on a walk with Tasso around a near-by lake. In a house by the shore there lived a surly bulldog, the terror of everybody and everything that passed there. The bulldog promptly attacked Tasso. But he was out of luck. In an instant he lay on the ground, doomed. Tasso let him go only when we whistled. The vanquished was a pitiable sight as he slipped away, bloody, perplexed and humbled.

But we didn't whistle Tasso out of the battle with Galto, the overseer's Newfoundland. Though we made such an effort to keep these two apart, one day they managed to elude us. Their moment had come. We decided not to interfere, for we realized that this smoldering enmity had to be worked out to its logical end. There was no other way. Only then could there be peace.

This time it was again Tasso who was attacked. He stood there calmly, looking at the Newfoundland and wagging his short curly stump. That gentle wagging was so touching; it bespoke an earnest wish to be friendly, the last faint hope for a peaceful encounter. He kept up this exceptionally friendly wagging to the very instant of the attack.

The Newfoundland, on the other hand, advanced slowly on tense legs, provocative and threatening. Then fast as lightning he leaped for Tasso's flank. The battle that ensued was staggering, like elemental conflict. The womenfolk cried out and burst into frightened tears as the two big animals flung themselves on each other in fury. No one dared to step between them. No one was allowed to. There had to be a final decision.

Tasso and Galto rose on their hind legs, seized each other's shoulders with their forepaws like wrestlers. Their jaws slashed at each other amid a welter of growls, sharp yaps and deep angry barks. Bright red blood ran over Galto's ears. He dropped his attack and covered himself momentarily. Then he pressed toward Tasso's throat. But the other's power was irresistible and magnificent. In another moment Galto lay prone in the grass and summoned all his remaining strength to evade the fangs that flashed and tugged at him, shook him and sought his throat. When for the space of a short panting breath, Tasso let him loose, Galto made away in jerky bounds, his tail tucked under, his ears laid back, as if he were escaping from death—which in truth he was.

Tasso stood still, looked after him, then shook himself and came over to us, all friendliness and good temper again as if nothing had happened. By not pursuing his fleeing enemy but letting him make good his escape, Tasso proved that quarreling and fighting were not for him. He proved it again and again whenever he met the Newfoundland. For Galto fled precipitately every time he so much as saw Tasso. But Tasso only looked after him and turned away as if he were embarrassed.

We noticed that Tasso kept flapping his ears in a peculiar manner and we called a veterinary from near by—one we had never employed before. He did not seem overly wise, but looked honest and upright. He turned out to be too wise and far from upright. Promptly he satisfied himself that Tasso was laboring under lung-and-liver disease and had only two more months to live. He proposed to destroy Tasso at once and then, to console me for Tasso's loss, he would bring me a beautiful St. Bernard he was prepared to dispose of cheap.

We said we would wait out the two months until Tasso's natural end, whereupon the man handed me a little bottle of medicine from which I was to give Tasso drops. He answered the question how it happened that he had brought precisely the right medicine, with the cool assertion that he had been certain in advance what illness the dog had been suffering from. Then he accepted his fee as if he had honestly earned it and went away.

So we took Tasso to the city, to a first-class veterinary institute. In the train, and during his treatments he behaved every bit as well as he did at home. He had the instinctive tact to fit himself into every situation without grumbling or moodiness; he made no difficulties and was always affable. Inside of a few days he was cured of his ear trouble and in sound health again.

On the return journey, when we left the train to continue by road through the forest, he didn't ride with us, but leaped out of the wagon to celebrate an enthusiastic reunion with the forest, the mountains, the tumbling brooks. Then he bounded back onto the road, fell in before the horses and trotted sedately along as a kind of four-footed herald all the way back to the mountain farm.

Our life together resumed its pleasant course for some months until, finally, we had to be separated from him. Fortunately he made no difficulties, for had he opposed it or become melancholy, we couldn't have parted from him.

The problem was that we were going abroad for two or three years, and it was impossible to take Tasso along. Just at this time a relative of ours, a charming, sympathetic woman, came to visit us from her home two days' journey away. The first time they had met, friendship between her and Tasso had been instantaneous and her subsequent visits had been as much to see Tasso as to see us. So it was natural that we should give Tasso to her.

She held long conversations with Tasso and invited him to visit her. "I have everything you need there, my good friend," she would say; "you'll get as much food there as you want, a good mattress and a nice garden." Tasso sat in front of her, one of his paws on her shoulder, looking straight into her eyes and listening as if he understood every word. He went off with her, dutifully and understandingly, and that is how we parted. . . .

On our return from abroad two years later, we went to visit our relatives, and saw Tasso again. He received us magnificently. No human friend ever greeted us so openly, so completely without reservation, so devotedly, so exuberantly and jubilantly. "I'm glad you're here!" He sat with us all the time, his head on our knees or his paw on our shoulders, and he was filled with love and tenderness.

He had adapted himself perfectly to his new life and his new friends. In fact, he seemed much better off here than he had been with us. Every day his master walked the long distance from his house to his factory on foot so that Tasso might get exercise.

He had two companions in the animal world—a large lean Siamese tomcat of morose disposition, and a tiny black-and-white terrier as gay and irresponsible as Tasso was dignified and thoughtful. Our relatives cared for him properly and dealt with him almost as if he were an adult member of the family, which in fact he was. And in return, he had attached himself loyally to his new friends. But still he had not ceased to be our friend, also.

He had one single vice now, we were told. Probably it had always been slumbering in him and had awakened only now. As soon as he laid eyes on a white hen—on one or two or three or four—he rushed right in and choked every one of them to death. Then he laid them out in a row, sat down in front of the line and laughed, with mouth open, tongue out and crinkled eyes. He laughed so heartily it was impossible for anyone to be angry with him.

A few years later we visited our relatives and Tasso again. He was just as exuberantly delighted, just as tender, as before. His spirit was almost imperceptibly milder, attenuated. The beginning of old age had brought an expression of apprehension into his beautifully eloquent eyes. He no longer ran great distances, but was fully satisfied with a new responsibility: he was custodian of the garden gate.

On his collar hung the key. Whenever visitors came and the bell shrilled through the house, Tasso would rush to the gate and go close to the fence so that the visitors might detach the key from his collar, let themselves in and then replace the key on Tasso's neck. But he never gave the key to strangers; when he saw an unfamiliar face he barked so that others might come to unlock the gate if they chose; he wouldn't. There was one man at the place, a gardener, whom Tasso ignored. When that man rang and Tasso saw him, he made an about-face, let the man wait outside and didn't even call anybody by barking. There is no doubt he had a reason.

Tasso grew old and frail. His deep powerful voice left him and he saw weakly out of only one eye. So a quick and gentle end was prepared for him.

We mourned Tasso as a friend who warmed and brightened the lives of others with unstinted devotion. He deserves a posthumous tribute as only a good man does. He was beautiful, strong and good. His was a character reliable in love, slow to hate and eager to serve, filled with confidence in himself and others, and he was a joy in everything he did and was. His life was animated by purity, undemanding devotion and good sense. He had that ability to discriminate which made his friendship worth having, and he was truly a friend, not merely a devoted servant. He always gave more, much more than he received, in attentiveness and warmth of heart.

Words of praise like these must be said for Tasso, but they may also be said of many other dogs. The human beings of whom they can be said are, unhappily, very few and very rare.

FROM
Kildee House

RUTHERFORD MONTGOMERY

Animal Friends

JEROME KILDEE had built himself a house on the mountain-
side. It was an odd house because Jerome Kildee was an odd
man. He built his house under a giant redwood tree on Windy
Point. Since the days of Julius Caesar creatures had been building homes at the foot of the redwood or in its branches. At the
time Jerome built his house most folks did not build on knobs
high on a mountainside, even the round-topped, wooded mountains of the Pacific Coast Range.

What the neighbors said or what they thought was of no
concern to Jerome. The day he walked out on Windy Point, and
looked up at the giant redwood towering into the sky, and stood
savoring the deep silence, he knew he was going to stay. When
he turned from the great tree and looked down over the green
ridges, the smoky valley, into the gray-white haze of the Pacific,
he smiled. This was a land of silence, the place for a silent man.

The house Jerome built was not as wide as the redwood; to
have made it so wide would have been a waste of space, because
Jerome did not need that much room. He toted the biggest window he could buy to the cabin, and set it in the wall which
faced a panorama of ridges and valleys. The window was as
high as the wall; it was one wall as far across as the door. It had
been rolled out as a plate-glass window for a store.

The back wall was the redwood trunk. It made an odd house,
one wall curved inward, and finished with shaggy redwood bark.
Jerome rented a horse and packed Monterey stone up for a fire-

place. The fireplace was a thing of beauty. It filled one end of the room. The cream Monterey stone, traced through with threads of red, was carefully fitted and matched for grain; the hearth was wide, and the mantel was inlaid with chips of abalone shell. It was the last piece of stonework Jerome planned to make, and he made it a masterpiece. In a recess back of the last slab of stone he tucked away the tools of his trade and sealed them into the wall. Jerome Kildee, maker of fine monuments, was no more. There remained only Jerome Kildee, philosopher, a silent little man seeking to become a part of a silent mountain.

Jerome Kildee did not work. He owned the hundred acres of woods and hillside around him, but he did not clear any of it. He bought all of his food and he had stove and fireplace wood hauled up and stacked outside his door. Jerome hired the Eppys to haul the wood to the bottom of the hill, then up the hill with their tractor because there was only a winding footpath up from his mailbox. The Eppys laughed and made quite a bit of it. Jerome had hundreds of cords of oak and madroña close to his cabin. The farmer and his sons would have cut it and sawed it for a tenth of what Jerome paid for the wood and the hauling.

Jerome had no near neighbors, nor would he ever have any, because he had built in the exact center of his hundred acres. He had gone through life silent, unable to talk to people, expecting them to leave him to his own thoughts. He had never visited the Eppy family after they hauled his wood, although they lived at the foot of his hill on the north side. They put him down as a queer one. The nine Eppys, as they were known locally, were robust folks. The six sons were all over six feet tall. Emma Lou would someday be almost as tall as her brothers. The Cabot place, at the foot of the mountain on the other side of the hill, was certainly not a place where Jerome would care to go. It was a fine estate with landscaped gardens and a swimming pool. The Cabots had one son, Donald Roger, who had never given Jerome more than a brief look.

But Jerome Kildee found he was not without friends. He had a host of friends and he didn't have to talk to them to keep their friendship. In fact, his silence helped to keep them friendly. They were all interested in him, a new experience for Jerome, and he was interested in them. Jerome found that they were not unlike the people back where he had operated his monument shop. They were willing to take advantage of him, they were selfish, and some of them were thieves, like the trade rats who packed off anything they could carry, regardless of whether or not they could use it. He soon learned that none of the raccoons could be trusted inside the cabin. They unscrewed the caps off ketchup bottles as easily as he could do it; they unlatched cupboard doors or opened them if there was a knob on them. One old raccoon, who was the neighborhood grouch, lived in a hole in the trunk of his redwood tree. Old Grouch had refused to move when Jerome built his house. He considered the redwood tree his tree. He made it clear to Jerome that he was trespassing.

The pair of spotted skunks who set up housekeeping under his floor were folks of a different sort from the raccoons. They were not dull-witted stinkers of the sort Jerome had known in his boyhood, dumb fellows who for ages had been depending upon poison gas instead of their wits for protection. They carried guns but seldom used them. The little spotted skunks were as smart as the raccoons, and about as curious. They had a real sense of humor and were always playing pranks on the raccoons. With them around, Jerome always had to get down on his hands and knees and explore the chimney of his fireplace before he built a fire. The skunks liked the fireplace and would gladly have traded it for their nest under the floor. They were not big stinkers like the swamp skunks, so Jerome could always fish them out of the chimney with his broom.

Jerome would probably have been crowded out of his house by the assortment of mice that found his house and the fine bark wall of the redwood to their liking if it had not been for the spotted skunks. The skunks had large appetites, so they kept the mouse population on an even keel. Two big wood mice lived in a bark nest back of a knot in the tree trunk. They furnished dinners for the spotted skunks with a regularity which should have become monotonous. How they could go on having big families, nursing them to a size to go out into the world, only to have them gobbled up one at a time as they left the nest, was more than Jerome could understand.

There was another pair of mice who lived under his bed in a box of old letters, which they made good use of without snooping into the contents, or trying to figure out why Jerome had tied them in bundles. They chewed up all of the letters except those written in indelible pencil. This removed from Jerome's life any desire to brood over the past. The spotted skunks could not get into the box. The mice went in through a knothole in the end. But their families suffered the same fate as the wood mice. And they went on having big families.

Jerome's wooded acres harbored many black-tailed deer and many gray foxes and possums. The foxes never made friends, and

the possums ignored him because he never kept chickens. They had no bump of curiosity to draw them to his house. He saw them often and had a nodding acquaintance with them, so to speak. The black-tails visited his garbage pit regularly. The does often brought their fawns into his yard. But they did not bother much with him because he did not grow a garden or set out young fruit trees. He was about like any other dweller on the wooded mountain: he just lived there.

It was during the second year that Old Grouch turned the head of a dainty little miss. She was just sixteen months old, and like many another lass before her, she fell in love with a good-for-nothing. Old Grouch brought her to his nest in the redwood. It was high up on the tree where a burl formed a deep pocket. Old Grouch had learned that a redwood tree was a safe haven. When coon dogs chased him, followed by yelling humans, all he had to do was shinny up the giant tree. The hunters could not shake him out or climb the tree. Of course after Jerome came, the coon dogs and the hunters stayed away.

Old Grouch brought his bride home in January during the heavy rains. In April she presented him with a family. Like many another good-for-nothing, Old Grouch failed to provide for his family, though he did share the nest with them, taking the dry side and grabbing any of the food she rustled which suited his taste. Jerome couldn't climb the tree to look into the nest, but he heard the babies and listened to the family chitchat over them.

Old Grouch mildly irritated Jerome. He was smug and fat, always ready to march into the cabin and demand part of Jerome's fried egg or lamb chop, but never thanking his host for anything, and always staying outside unless there was food. Any friendly advance was always met with a snarl or a snapping of white fangs. He was a surly fellow, but Jerome admired the way he had with the ladies.

His wife was of a different sort. She was friendly and thankful to Jerome for bits of food he gave her. She visited the cabin while he was in it, and not just when it was mealtime. She would have taken over his larder if he had allowed it. Her willingness to shift Old Grouch's responsibility for the family to him gave Jerome a problem. He was forced to invent new catches for his cupboard doors, and to fashion latches for his pull drawers.

Outwitting the slim little bride was no easy matter. With feminine wile she made up to Jerome, letting him stroke her head and scratch around her ears, smiling coyly up at him as he sat in his padded chair, but raiding his cupboard as sure as he went for a walk. Jerome fixed inside catches for the doors worked by wires which went up through the inside of the cupboard and were pulled by strings dangling from the ceiling, well out of reach of a raccoon. The pull drawers became pop-out drawers worked by wires with dangling strings attached to them. Jerome's house was well decorated with strings hanging from the ceiling. A large button dangled at the end of each string like a black spider.

When Jerome wanted an egg for breakfast he pulled a string, and open popped a drawer exposing the egg carton. Then Jerome always had to take out two eggs because the minute the door popped open in popped Mrs. Grouch, and Jerome had to split fifty-fifty with her. He could have closed and barred the door, but then he would have had to sit by the big window eating his egg with Mrs. Grouch's furry bangs pressed against the plate glass, her bright eyes watching every bite he took, her little tongue dripping hungrily.

The rains lasted a long time that spring, keeping on until June. Mrs. Grouch stood the home her old man had provided for her as long as she could. The babies were growing and taking up more room, the roof leaked, and Old Grouch always took the dry side. When the wind blew from the north there might as well have been no roof at all. One afternoon while Jerome was tramping in the woods, snug in oilskins and rubber boots, she moved her babies into the house. Helping herself to the stuffing in his mattress, she made a nest in the oven. She had long ago learned how to open the oven door. The smell of the oven pleased her. It had a faint food smell which was elegant. She could feed her babies and lick the oven walls, nibbling bits of burned meat as she came to them.

Jerome discovered the family at once because the oven door was open. He did not scold about the mattress when she showed him her brood of silky raccoons. But he was hungry and this was Saturday afternoon. Jerome always fixed a beef roast for Saturday supper. Once a week the mailman left the meat in his mailbox at the foot of the hill. Jerome got a wooden box and put it in a corner; then he moved the family. Mrs. Grouch was miffed, but she accepted the change with a sly smile. Later she would slip her family back into the oven.

Old Grouch stamped up on the porch and seated himself in the open doorway. He scolded his wife in proper style; he glared at Jerome and tossed a few nasty cracks at him. Between growls he kept sniffing the roast cooking in the oven, and shaking his fur to get the raindrops off it. With a final warning to his wife he turned about, climbed the redwood trunk, and got into his nest. The wind was from the north, and his wife was not there to keep the rain off his back. He stayed in the nest for half an hour, then he climbed back down the tree trunk and walked to the door. Jerome grinned at him. He was cutting the roast. He sliced off a piece and laid it on a saucer. He set the saucer on the floor.

Old Grouch looked at the saucer. This was dangerous business. Going into a cabin was like stepping into a box trap. But he was wet and cold; his wife had walked out on him. He needed food and warmth. Ruffling his scruff, he walked into the house. He paused at the saucer and sniffed the good smell of the roast. He took a bite. When Mrs. Grouch scurried across the floor to share with him, he caught up the piece of meat in his forepaws. He sat up and glowered at her. Then he began munching the roast. His wife sniffed eagerly. She looked up at Jerome. He handed her a slice of meat. She took it and seated herself beside her husband. They sat there eating very much like humans, using their small hands to tear bits of meat from the large pieces, then stuffing the bits into their mouths.

By the time Jerome had finished his supper Old Grouch had made up his mind. He had marched to the door three times, and each time the cold rain had spattered into his face. He knew his wife and babies were going to sleep warm and dry inside the cabin. She had already returned to the box, where she sat with her small black eyes just above the edge. Old Grouch felt he could do with some more roast, too. He was still a bit hungry. He would stay in the cabin.

After the dishes were washed Jerome lighted his pipe. He was faced with a new problem. He had been trying for weeks to get Old Grouch into the cabin. Now that the old fellow and his family had moved in he dared not close the door. If he closed the door it was hard to say what Old Grouch would do. Jerome was sure it would be pretty wild.

But the night air was growing chilly. The wind was blowing into the room, wet and cold. Even if he did chase Old Grouch out into the rain he couldn't put Mrs. Grouch and the babies out. Jerome got to his feet. Old Grouch took one look at Jerome towering above him, then scuttled out into the night.

Jerome set the gasoline mantel lamp on the table so the white light would flood the door. He got his tool chest from under the bed. Mrs. Grouch kept her eyes just above the edge of the box. Jerome cut a small door in the bottom of his big door. He swung the small door by a pair of butterfly hinges and bored three holes in it.

As he gathered up his saw and auger and screw driver Jerome realized that the little door would offer welcome to any and all who roamed. It would mean keeping open house to all, except, of course, those neighbors too big to squeeze through the little door. He had never been able to make friends; it might be that the little door would change everything. He took the lamp and examined the chimney of his fireplace. The little skunks were not sleeping on the damper, so he lighted the fire he had laid earlier in the day. Pulling his padded chair up to the fireplace, he set his tobacco jar on the chair arm. As an afterthought he got a saucer and stacked a few squares of roast on it. He set the saucer on the floor beside the chair.

Jerome puffed slowly on his pipe. He watched the red tongues of flame lick around the oak and madroña logs in the fireplace. The beating warmth made him feel drowsy. He was on his second pipe when Old Grouch solved the mystery of the little door. He had peeped in through the three holes and discovered that Jerome had turned out the gasoline lamp, that his wife was snug and dry in the box with the babies. He sniffed and caught the rich smell of roast beef. He was wet and cold. He eased through the little door just as his wife hopped from the box, carrying one of the babies. She had her teeth set in the scruff. Shaking the water from his fur, he watched her put the youngster into the oven. He scowled at her, but he didn't make a sound. The warmth of the fireplace and the smell of the roast in the saucer drew him. He moved warily toward the fire. His experience with men had made him wary. But he was cold and he had an idea he could eat some more. Seating himself in the deep shadows near the chair, he stretched his snout toward the dish. He kept his eyes on Jerome. When Jerome did not move Old Grouch eased forward and picked up a piece of meat. He sat up and began munching it.

Mrs. Grouch had finished transferring her babies to the oven. She sat on the door for a while, watching the two males at the fireplace. Shaking her head, she turned her back upon them and curled up with her brood.

Jerome had never been able to talk with people. He had always known he was missing a great deal, but he had never been able to say the weather was nice or that the weather was bad when people came into his shop. He set his pipe on the arm of the chair and tossed another log on the fire. Old Grouch ducked into a patch of deep shadow, but he came out again and got another piece of meat. The warmth of the fire was beating against his fur. He felt contented and happy. Jerome leaned back and spoke out loud. When he spoke the sound of his voice startled even himself. Old Grouch, now gorged with roast and sleepy from the heat, toppled off the hearth and had to make quite an effort to right himself. Mrs. Grouch thrust her head out of the oven and stared at Jerome wildly. If it had not been for her babies she would have fled into the night.

"When I came up here I was licked," Jerome had said. It was as though a stranger had spoken to him; he heard his own voice so seldom. He felt called upon to answer the stranger.

"And were you licked?"

Old Grouch batted his eyes fearfully. He looked all around the room but saw no human being except Jerome, whom he had ceased to consider a man, because Jerome never shouted or whistled or talked at all.

"I've spent a lifetime carving cherubs and angels on tombstones. I've cut many a nice sentiment on a gravestone, but never was able to recite a single line before company." Jerome pointed his pipestem toward the fire. "It's a sad business dealing with sad people, and not being able to say a word to comfort them."

Old Grouch braced himself and let his stomach ease down until he was resting comfortably. He had room for a bite or two more, and the fire was very nice. Jerome smiled down at him. Old Grouch looked like a small bandit with the black patches which circled his eyes and extended along his cheeks like black bands, making a perfect mask against the lighter coloring of his fur. He cocked his head. He was in a mellow mood. His stomach was full to bursting; his furry hide was warm. He felt like singing.

He started out with a soft "Shur-r-r-r," then went into a deeper note, a long-drawn, tremulous "Whoo-oo-oo," not unlike the call of a screech owl, only softer and sweeter, much more mellow. Jerome's smile widened. He had never dared venture a note himself. In all of the hundreds of times he had sat alone in his pew in church he had never dared open his mouth and sing.

"I have missed much," he said.

"Whoo-oo-oo," Old Grouch sang, his head swaying sleepily.

From the oven door came an answering trill. Never had Mrs. Grouch heard her husband put so much tenderness, so much romance into his song. It touched her deeply, so deeply she closed her eyes and sang back to him. Jerome laid down his pipe.

Turning to catch the high soprano from the oven, Jerome noticed that the little door was bobbing back and forth. He fixed his attention upon it. A small head with black shoe-button eyes appeared. The head moved into the room, followed by a slim body. A moment later another slim body moved through the door. Two tall white plumes lifted. The little spotted skunks had come visiting. Papa waved his plume and stamped his feet; Mama waved her plume and stamped her feet. Like a good host, Jerome arose from his chair. Instantly the two little skunks vanished through the door. Jerome filled a saucer with canned milk and set it near the door, then he went back to his chair before the fire.

Almost at once the little door opened and the skunks marched in. They sat down and began lapping eagerly. When Mrs. Grouch hopped off the oven door and started toward the saucer, Papa elevated his plume and stamped his forefeet. He rushed at her, did a handstand, flipped his hind feet down again, then stamped some more. Mrs. Grouch knew what that meant, as did every other living thing in the woods. She hastily retreated to the oven door. Papa went back to his milk.

Jerome leaned back in his chair. Old Grouch was in full voice now; his whoo-oo-oo was deep and bell-like. Jerome tried an experimental note himself. He was amazed at its quality. It was a baritone note with feeling and depth in it. But it sent Mrs. Grouch scrambling back into the oven; Papa and Mama left without waiting to stamp their feet. Only Old Grouch was not startled at all. He just sat and swayed back and forth and sang. He seemed to have caught the fine flavor of Jerome's baritone. Jerome tried a few more notes. Mrs. Grouch stayed in the oven; the spotted skunks stayed under the floor. Old Grouch picked up the last square of roast and ate it slowly. When he swallowed it his stomach bulged bigger. He cocked an eye at Jerome. Jerome tried a few hymns he remembered. Old Grouch joined in. He had only one song, but it blended well with any hymn.

After a bit Jerome began to feel sleepy. He was sleepy and he was happy. He leaned back and closed his eyes. Old Grouch yawned. He ambled toward the oven door. After two tries he managed to hop up on the door. Easing into the oven, he curled up with his family. Jerome sighed deeply. Here among friends he could talk about things he had always wanted to talk about, and he could sing when he felt like it. He got to his feet and took his flannel nightgown from its hook. He smiled as he got ready for bed.

The Dog of Pompeii

LOUIS UNTERMEYER

Tito and his dog Bimbo lived (if you could call it living) under the city wall where it joined the inner gate. They really didn't live there; they just slept there. They lived anywhere. Pompeii was one of the gayest of the old Roman towns, but although Tito was never an unhappy boy, he was not exactly a merry one. The streets were always lively with shining chariots and bright red trappings; the open-air theaters rocked with laughing crowds; sham battles and athletic sports were free for the asking in the great stadium. Once a year the emperor visited the pleasure city, and the fireworks and other forms of entertainment lasted for days.

But Tito saw none of these things, for he was blind—had been blind from birth. He was known to everyone in the poorer quarters. But no one could say how old he was; no one remembered his parents; no one could tell where he came from. Bimbo was another mystery. As long as people could remember seeing Tito—several years at least—they had seen Bimbo. The dog never left his side. He was not only a watchdog, but mother and father to Tito.

Did I say Bimbo never left his master? (Perhaps I had better say "comrade," for if anyone was the master, it was Bimbo.) I was wrong. Bimbo did trust Tito alone exactly three times a day. It was a custom understood between boy and dog since the beginning of their friendship, and the way it worked was this:

Early in the morning, shortly after dawn, while Tito was still dreaming, Bimbo would disappear. When Tito awoke, Bimbo would be sitting quietly at his side, his ears cocked, his stump of a tail tapping the ground, and a fresh-baked loaf of bread—more like a large round roll—at his feet. Tito would stretch himself, Bimbo would yawn, and they would breakfast.

At noon, no matter where they happened to be, Bimbo would put his paw on Tito's knee, and the two of them would return to the inner gate. Tito would curl up in the corner (almost like a dog) and go to sleep, while Bimbo, looking quite important (almost like a boy), would disappear again. In a half-hour he would be back with their lunch. Sometimes it would be a piece of fruit or a scrap of meat; often it was nothing but a dry crust. But sometimes there would be one of those flat, rich cakes, sprinkled with raisins and sugar, that Tito liked so much.

At suppertime the same thing happened, although there was a little less of everything, for things were hard to snatch in the evening with the streets full of people.

But whether there was much or little, hot or cold, fresh or dry, food was always there. Tito never asked where it came from, and Bimbo never told him. There was plenty of rain water in the hollows of soft stones; the old egg-woman at the corner sometimes gave him a cupful of strong goat's milk; in the grape season the fat wine-maker let him have drippings of the mild juice. So there was no danger of going hungry or thirsty. There was plenty of everything in Pompeii if you knew where to find it—and if you had a dog like Bimbo.

As I said before, Tito was not the merriest boy in Pompeii. He could not romp with the other youngsters or play hare-and-hounds and I-spy and follow-your-master and ball-against-the-building and jackstone and kings-and-robbers with them. But that did not make him sorry for himself. If he could not see the sights that delighted the lads of Pompeii, he could hear and smell things they never noticed. When he and Bimbo went out walking, he knew just where they were going and exactly what was happening.

As they passed a handsome villa, he'd sniff and say, "Ah, Glaucus Pansa is giving a grand dinner here tonight. They're going to have three kinds of bread and roast pigling and stuffed goose and a great stew—I think bear stew—and a fig pie." And

Bimbo would note that this would be a good place to visit to-morrow.

Or "H'm," Tito would murmur, half through his lips, half through his nostrils. "The wife of Marcus Lucretius is expecting her mother. She's airing all the linens; she's going to use the best clothes, the ones she's been keeping in pine needles and camphor, and she's got an extra servant cleaning the kitchen. Come, Bimbo, let's get out of the dust!"

Or, as they neared the forum, "Mm'm! What good things they have in the market place today! Dates from Africa and salt oysters from sea caves and cuttle-fish and new honey and sweet onions and—ugh!—water-buffalo steaks. Come let's see what's what in the forum." And Bimbo, just as curious as his comrade, hurried on. Being a dog, he, too, trusted his ears and nose more than his eyes, and so the two of them entered the center of Pompeii.

The forum was the part of the town to which everybody came at least once during each day. Everything happened there. There were no private houses; all was public—the chief temples, the gold and red bazaars, the silk shops, the town hall, the booths belonging to the weavers and the jewel merchants, the wealthy woolen market. Everything gleamed brightly here; the buildings looked new. The earthquake of twelve years ago had brought down all the old structures; and since the citizens of Pompeii were ambitious to rival Naples and even Rome, they had seized the opportunity to rebuild the whole town. Hence there was scarcely a building that was older than Tito.

Tito had heard a great deal about the earthquake, although, since he was only about a year old at the time, he could hardly remember it. This particular quake had been a light one, as earthquakes go. The crude houses had been shaken down, and parts of the outworn wall had been wrecked, but there had been little loss of life. No one knew what caused these earthquakes. Records showed they had happened in the neighborhood since the beginning of time. Sailors said that it was to teach the lazy cityfolk a lesson and make them appreciate those who risked the dangers of the sea to bring them luxuries and to protect their town from invaders. The priests said that the gods took this way of showing their anger to those who refused to worship properly or failed to bring enough sacrifices to the altars. The tradesmen said that the foreign merchants had corrupted the ground and it was no longer safe to traffic in imported goods that came from strange places and carried a curse upon them. Everyone had a different explanation, and everyone's explanation was louder and sillier than his neighbor's.

People were talking about it this afternoon as Tito and Bimbo came out of the side street into the public square. The forum was crowded. Tito's ears, as well as his nose, guided them to the place where the talk was loudest.

"I tell you," rumbled a voice which Tito recognized as that of bathmaster Rufus, "there won't be another earthquake in my lifetime or yours. There may be a tremble or two, but earthquakes, like lightning, never strike twice in the same place."

"Don't they?" asked a thin voice Tito had never heard before. It had a high, sharp ring to it, and Tito knew it as the accent of a stranger. "How about the two towns in Sicily that have been ruined three times within fifteen years by the eruptions of Mount Etna? And were they not warned? And does that column of smoke above Vesuvius mean nothing?"

"That?" Tito could hear the grunt with which one question answered another. "That's always there. We use it for our weather guide. When the smoke stands up straight, we know we'll have fair weather, when it flattens out, it's sure to be foggy; when it drifts to the east——"

"Very well, my confident friend," cut in the thin voice, which now sounded curiously flat. "We have a proverb: 'Those who will not listen to man must be taught by the gods.' I say no more. But I leave a last warning. Remember the holy ones. Look to your temples. And when the smoke tree above Vesuvius grows to the shape of an umbrella pine, look to your lives!"

Tito could hear the air whistle as the speaker drew his toga about him, and the quick shuffle of feet told him that the stranger had gone.

"Now what," said Attilio, the cameo-cutter, "did he mean by that?"

"I wonder," grunted Rufus. "I wonder."

Tito wondered, too. And Bimbo, his head at a thoughtful angle, looked as if he were doing a heavy bit of pondering. By nightfall the argument had been forgotten. If the smoke had increased, no one saw it in the dark. Besides, it was Caesar's birthday, and the town was in a holiday mood. Tito and Bimbo were among the merrymakers, dodging the charioteers, who shouted at them. But Tito never missed his footing. He was thankful for his keen ears and quick instinct—most thankful of all for Bimbo.

They visited the open-air theater; then went to the city walls, where the people of Pompeii watched a sham naval battle in which the city, attacked from the sea, was saved after thousands of flaming arrows had been burned. Though the thrill of flaring ships and lighted skies was lost to Tito, the shouts and cheers excited him as much as anyone.

The next morning there were two of the beloved raisin cakes for his breakfast. Bimbo was unusually active and thumped his bit of a tail until Tito was afraid he would wear it out. Tito couldn't imagine whether Bimbo was urging him to some sort of game or was trying to tell him something. After a while he ceased to notice Bimbo. He felt drowsy. Last night's late hours had tired him. Besides, there was a heavy mist in the air—no, a thick fog rather than a mist—a fog that got into his throat and made him cough. He walked as far as the marine gate to get a breath of the sea. But even the salt air seemed smoky.

Tito went to bed before dusk, but he did not sleep well. . . . He awoke early. Or rather, he was pulled awake, Bimbo doing the pulling. The dog had dragged Tito to his feet and was urging the boy along. Where, Tito did not know. His feet stumbled uncertainly; he was still half asleep. For a while he noticed nothing except the fact that it was hard to breathe. The air was hot and heavy, so heavy that he could taste it. The air, it seemed, had turned to powder, a warm powder that stung his nostrils and burned his sightless eyes.

Then he began to hear sounds, peculiar sounds. Like animals under the earth. Hissings and groanings and muffled cries. There was no doubt of it now. The noises came from underneath. He not only heard them—he could feel them. The earth twitched; the twitching changed to an uneven shrugging of the soil. Then, as Bimbo half pulled, half coaxed him along, the ground jerked away from his feet and he was thrown against a stone fountain.

The water—hot water!—splashing in his face revived him. He got to his feet, Bimbo steadying him, helping him on again. The noises grew louder; they came closer. The cries were even more animal-like than before, but now they came from human throats. A few people began to rush by; a family or two, then a group, then, it seemed, the whole city of people. Tito, bewildered though he was, could recognize Rufus' voice as he bellowed like a water buffalo gone mad.

It was then the crashing began. First a sharp crackling, like a monstrous snapping of twigs; then an explosion that tore earth and sky. The heavens, though Tito could not see them, were shot through with continual flickerings of fire. Lightnings above were answered by thunders beneath. A house fell. Then another. By a miracle the two companions had escaped the dangerous side streets and were in a more open space. It was the forum. They rested here awhile; how long the boy did not know.

Tito had no idea of the time of day. He could *feel* it was black—an unnatural blackness. Something inside, perhaps the lack of breakfast and lunch, told him it was past noon. But it didn't matter. Nothing seemed to matter. He was getting drowsy, too drowsy to walk. But walk he must. He knew it. And Bimbo knew it; the sharp tugs told him so. Nor was it a moment too soon. The sacred ground of the forum was safe no longer. It began to rock, to pitch, then to split. As they stumbled out of the square, the earth wriggled like a caught snake, and all the columns of the Temple of Jupiter came down. It was the end of the world, or so it seemed.

To walk was not enough now. They must run. Tito, too frightened to know what to do or where to go, had lost all sense of direction. He started to go back to the inner gate; but Bimbo, straining his back to the last inch, almost pulled his clothes from him. What did the dog want? Had he gone mad?

Then suddenly he understood. Bimbo was telling him the way out. The sea gate, of course. The sea gate—and then the sea, far from falling buildings, heaving ground. He turned, Bimbo guiding him across open pits and dangerous pools of bubbling mud, away from buildings that had caught fire and were dropping their burning beams.

New dangers threatened. All Pompeii seemed to be thronging toward the marine gate, and there was the chance of being trampled to death. But the chance had to be taken. It was growing harder and harder to breathe. What air there was choked him. It was all dust now, dust and pebbles as large as beans. They fell on his head, his hands—pumice stones from the black heart of Vesuvius! The mountain was turning itself inside out. Tito remembered what the stranger had said in the forum two days ago: "Those who will not listen to men must be taught by the gods." The people of Pompeii had refused to heed the warnings; they were being taught now, if it was not too late.

Suddenly it seemed too late for Tito. The red-hot ashes blistered his skin; the stinging vapors tore his throat. He could not go on. He staggered toward a small tree at the side of the road and fell. In a moment Bimbo was beside him. He coaxed, but there was no answer. He licked Tito's hands, his feet, his face. The boy did not stir. Then Bimbo did the thing he least wanted to do. He bit his comrade, bit him deep in the arm. With a cry of pain, Tito jumped to his feet, Bimbo after him. Tito was in despair, but Bimbo was determined. He drove the boy on snapping at his heels, worrying his way through the crowd, barking, baring his teeth, heedless of kicks or falling stones.

Sick with hunger, half dead with fear and sulphur fumes, Tito plodded on, pursued by Bimbo. How long he never knew. At last he staggered through the marine gate and felt soft sand under him. Then Tito fainted.

Someone was dashing sea water over him. Someone was carrying him toward a boat.

"Bimbo!" he called. And then louder, "Bimbo!" But Bimbo had disappeared.

Voices jarred against each other. "Hurry! Hurry!" "To the boats!" "Can't you see the child's frightened and starving?" "He keeps calling for someone!" "Poor child, he's out of his mind." "Here, boy, take this!"

They tucked him in among them. The oarlocks creaked; the oars splashed; the boat rode over the toppling waves. Tito was safe. But he wept continually. "Bimbo!" he wailed. "Bimbo! Bimbo!"

He could not be comforted.

Eighteen hundred years passed. Scientists were restoring the ancient city; excavators were working their way through the stones and trash that had buried the entire town. Much had already been brought to light—statues, bronze instruments, bright mosaics, household articles, even delicate paintings which had been preserved by the ashes that had taken over two thousand lives. Columns were dug up, and the forum was beginning to emerge.

It was at a place where the ruins lay deepest that the director paused.

"Come here," he called to his assistant. "I think we've discovered the remains of a building in good shape. Here are four huge millstones that were most likely turned by slaves or mules, and here is a whole wall standing, with shelves inside it. Why, it must have been a bakery! And here is a curious thing—the skeleton of a dog!"

"Amazing!" gasped his assistant. "You'd think a dog would have had sense enough to run away at that time. What is that flat thing he's holding between his teeth? It can't be a stone."

"No. It must have come from this bakery. Do you know, it looks to me like some sort of cake, hardened with the years. And bless me, if those little black pebbles aren't raisins! A raisin cake almost two thousand years old! I wonder what made him want it at such a moment?"

"I wonder," murmured his assistant.

FROM

Jimmie, the Story of a Black Bear Cub

HAROLD BAYNES

Jimmie Arrives in New Hampshire

Pᴇᴄᴋ's bad boy was a super-cherub compared with Jimmie. The hunter who sent him to me from Parry Sound said that he was the "bad egg" of a family of three, and frankly admitted that that was why he had sent him, though what I had done to incur the enmity of a man at Parry Sound I have never learned to this day.

The mother of these cubs had been killed in her den by Indian hunters, and the white trapper who was with them had rescued the babies and taken them home to his own cabin for company.

Jimmie's baby brothers, it seems, were very good—that is for little bears—and one cuff on the ear was enough to make either of them lie down and be quiet. But Jimmie would stand up on his hind legs and put up a fight that would have been dangerous had the fighter's weight and reach been in proportion to his courage and determination.

So one day the trapper, with his thumb done up in a white rag, and the back of his right hand looking like a contour map of the Rocky Mountains done in red ink, picked up a small and screaming black bear cub, dropped it into a stout wooden box, carried it to the nearest railway station and addressed it to me.

I never shall forget Jimmie's arrival. It was late afternoon on a peaceful summer day and we were not expecting him. We were living at the "Haven Cottage," seven miles north of Newport, New Hampshire, and we were all seated on the piazza, looking out over a sunlit daisy field and listening to the song of a hermit thrush. I happened to glance down the road, and far away I could see a cloud of dust. It heralded the coming of the stage which brought our mail and express packages. Even at that distance I could hear strange sounds which did not harmonize with the song of the hermit thrush. Finally the stage drove up and the driver dumped a wooden box into the middle of the lawn. From the inside of that box was coming a perfectly awful noise. There was a continuous and frantic scratching at the woodwork and a vocal sound which seemed to grow louder every moment.

"Wow! Wow! WOW!" yelled an angry voice.

"No! No! NO-O-O!" it wailed.

I said to the stage driver, "What in the world have you got in that box?"

But the stage driver had been sitting alongside that noise for seven miles and was in no humor for talk. So he climbed to his seat, whipped up his lathering horses, and left me to find out for myself what was in the box. I took a hammer and a chisel and pried off a corner of it, and out of the hole I made there was thrust a little, black, furry face with a tawny muzzle, round, furry ears, a pair of beady black eyes, and the most impudent expression I have ever seen on the face of any animal. I recognized my guest at once as a black bear cub. He stepped out on to the lawn, and deliberately looked around as if in search of the man who was responsible for his discomfort. Then his anger gave way to sobs and wails of grief.

There was a sentimental lady calling on us at the time and at a glance she saw that the little stranger needed comforting. She ran down the steps, snapped the bear cub into her arms and murmured, "Oh, the poor little dear." Now "the poor little dear" had been in that box for several days, he was looking for something more substantial than love murmurings, and his naturally short temper was not quite as long as usual. With a savage little growl he bit the sentimental arm, and with a raking stroke of his sturdy hind legs he tore a long rent in the lady's dress. She promptly dropped him and rushed back to her place on the piazza. In the meantime our housekeeper, Lucy, had looked upon the scene. No kinder person lived than she, but her kindness to animals was based on knowledge and common sense. She knew that, no matter what the anatomists might tell you, the way to the heart of a hungry little bear was right down through his "tummy," and she lost no time in getting to his tummy. With the aid of a bowl of crackers and milk she found his heart, badly bent but not quite broken, and it was hers forevermore.

Haven Cottage, where Jimmie came to us, stands on the eastern border of the Blue Mountain Forest. This great game preserve comprises about forty square miles of beautiful wild country, surrounded by a high fence and stocked with buffalo, elk, white-tailed deer, and many other wild creatures both native and introduced. Down the middle of it, roughly north and south, like a mighty backbone, stretches the spruce-clad Croydon range —the "Blue Mountain" which gives the place its name. In the hilly country round about "the Park," as the country folk call it, lie old farms with white, green-shuttered, maple-shaded houses, gray barns, gnarled apple trees, and scrub-grown, rock-studded cattle pastures. Here and there may be found more prosperous homesteads, with well-kept lawns and flower beds, painted out-buildings, and herds of thoroughbred cattle. It was in this farm-ing country and in the Blue Mountain Forest itself that the little bear passed his New Hampshire days.

His life with us was one long series of humorous adventures —humorous for Jimmie, for us, or our neighbors, according to the point of view. But it made no difference what he did, Lucy always defended him with her tongue at least, and with the fire irons if necessary. If the paint were scratched off the front door, if all the strawberry jam in the pantry were eaten, if the coverlet of a bed were decorated with paw-painted bear tracks done in muddy water colors, it was the tame deer that did these things. Or, if the deer could prove an alibi, it was the wolves, the foxes, the opossums, or even the skunks—any living thing on the face of the landscape except Jimmie Bear; he never did anything wrong. And whenever we succeeded in actually "pinning it on him," she would either remind us that "we're all human, you know," or make us feel that somehow we were trying to take advantage of an infant who had no parents to stand up for him. Once when I caught him on the kitchen dresser, sitting among the fragments of some china he had pulled from a shelf above, I called the housekeeper and remarked sternly, "Well, I suppose you'll admit he did that?"

Now Lucy had been in our family for a long time, and had served my father and mother before us. Looking from me to the culprit bear and then at me again, her mind flashed back a score of years. Straightening to her full height and folding her arms she said reminiscently and half reproachfully: "Well, Master Harold, I don't think you should be so hard on him. Please remember you were a boy yourself once." And of course I remembered and did not press her for details.

Jimmie differed somewhat from the little girl who had a curl right in the middle of her forehead, for—

> "When he was fed he was never very good,
> But when he was hungry he was horrid."

When that comfortable feeling which followed a meal began to wear off, the cub would let us know it by mutterings and grumblings, low and unobtrusive at first, like the warnings of a miniature volcano about to become active. Unless the growing fires of his hunger were quenched with milk or something equally good, the rumblings grew deeper and louder, until at last there came an uncontrolled outpouring of ursuline profanity which told us that the volcano was in full eruption. At such a time it was quite useless to try and divert his attention. He was hungry and wanted his food and no one could persuade him that he didn't. If he were loose, he would probably make for the screen door of the kitchen and, opening it deftly with the aid of his sharp claws, march straight to the sink. Standing on his hind legs he would stretch until he reached the edge with his forefeet, and with a single hoist he would reach his goal. Here he was likely to find a pail of fresh drinking water, which might occupy his attention for a moment, though he would probably be grumbling all the time he was drinking. Then turning round he would let himself down backward until his hind feet touched the floor.

By this time Lucy would be preparing a basin of bread and milk. Jimmie would see her and at once start to hurry things by dancing on his hind legs in front of her, clasping her about the knees, biting and tugging at her skirts. She was not in the least afraid of him, and sometimes in order to try his patience, or rather his impatience, a little more, she would hold the coveted

basin just above his reach. Shrieking with rage, he would dance around her, wildly snatching at the food. Finally one swift paw would "make connections" and then the game began to go his way. His claws hung on to the rim of the basin like so many iron hooks, and if it were lifted any higher Jimmie went with it. Then Lucy would carry him out dinner and all, and set the basin on the lawn, whereupon we were treated to a moving picture showing the real meaning of the expression "as hungry as a bear." Lying flat on his tummy before the food, and with forearms wrapped around the basin right and left, he would thrust his muzzle, almost to the eyes, into the bread and milk, which rapidly disappeared to a combination of sounds showing greed, satisfaction, and distrust.

When he had licked the vessel so clean that it needed no further washing, he seemed to feel much better, and the time had come for play. He would roll about on the lawn, turn somersaults, and scramble up the piazza posts, seemingly as much to his own delight as to that of the neighbors' children who often gathered to see him. And here I might add that never before or since have we had so much attention from those children as we had when Jimmie was our guest. Before he arrived we had our

milk delivered once a day. Now it came twice a day, and a contribution to our standing order for eggs was made, it seemed,
every time a hen gave a declaratory cackle. Wide-eyed youngsters
were always coming to inquire if we needed any maple sugar or
fresh butter, whether we would like to sell our hay, or if we
wanted someone to saw the wood. Of course the inquirer never
left the premises until Jimmie had been seen, whether our needs
were urgent or not at all. Jimmie evidently enjoyed his young
visitors and seemed to make special efforts for their amusement.

Some of the grown-ups were not quite so much amused.
Among these were men who drove daily past our house. Horses
are affected differently by the odor of a bear, but many of them
dislike it intensely, and a few at least are thrown into paroxysms
of fear. Usually a spirited horse would begin to manifest uneasiness when he came within a few hundred yards of our place,
and the uneasiness, accompanied by snorting, pricked ears, and
sidelong glances, increased until he drew close to the house, when
the tendency was to bolt. This tendency was greatly increased
if the bear was actually in sight or giving vocal evidence of his
presence.

One morning a farmer neighbor, driving a mettlesome young
horse, was passing the house, and, seeing the bear, drew up to
have a better look at him. But the horse, which had been ex-
hibiting great nervousness, now went wild with fear, and leaping
into the air, came down upon his side. With the nimbleness of
a cat the man sprang clear and seized the horse by the head, and
a moment later the animal was on his feet again, fortunately
unhurt. The driver, a good sport, asked me to bring the cub close
up, as he wished his horse to become used to the sight and smell
of it. I turned round to look for Jimmie, but apparently he had
not liked the behavior of the horse, for he had climbed to the
top of a near-by tree, where he now sat calmly munching a cluster
of green wild cherries. It was fifteen minutes before he saw fit to
come down and be introduced, and then it was with an air of
conferring an honor upon the horse.

Jimmie loved farms and never tired of exploring them. The
odors of orchards and dairies seemed to tickle his nostrils
pleasantly, and of course there was always a fair chance of find-

ing something to tickle his palate as well. Then there was the fun of frightening things—hens, ducks, and sheep—and the greater fun of chasing them afterwards.

Sometimes even the owners of the farms were the victims of his pranks. One of our neighbors, who sleeps on the first floor, has a rare, almost extinct, passion for fresh air. One day the cub climbed through his open window, and when that night the man got into bed in the dark, he thought somebody had been setting a steel trap for him. It was only Jimmie who resented being disturbed at that late hour, and who bit one great toe so badly that it had to be carried in a sling.

Lucy seemed to think it was her duty to give him a personal introduction to all the other animals round about. Usually this was not at all necessary from his standpoint because Jimmie had no difficulty in becoming acquainted with anyone he cared to meet. He simply walked right up and introduced himself. Possibly she thought that there would be fewer misunderstandings if she were present, and in this no doubt she was right. But if he didn't want to be introduced not even her kindly offices could persuade him to extend the friendly paw. Once, I remember, she wished to introduce him to a fine, tri-colored collie dog named Bruce. She sat on the lawn beside the dog and tried to call Jimmie to her side. The cub refused to come. He walked around in circles regarding Bruce with a suspicious eye and finally went away leaving Lucy and the visitor to make the best of their own company. Lucy did not understand this behavior but I had seen a previous meeting. A few days before, a young Scotch farmer, the owner of Bruce, drove up in a buggy, with the dog at his side. Bruce jumped out and there was Jimmie standing on the lawn. The two eyed one another for a moment and then Jimmie advanced, rising to his hind legs and putting out his arms. The smell of bear was a new one to the collie and he retreated, growling, under the buggy. He seemed ashamed of his caution, but here was a queer new creature—a very dangerous one for all he knew—and Bruce was a canny dog. Had he known a little more about bear cubs he would not have been the least afraid; if Jimmie had known a little more about dogs he would have been more cautious. Just then Bruce's owner stepped out of the buggy. Now a dog by himself is one dog, but a dog backed by a real man whom he loves and trusts is three dogs, and three dogs are not to be daunted by one bear cub no matter how dangerous he may look. As the Scotchman's foot touched the ground, it seemed to release a spring which hurled Bruce from between the buggy wheels straight at the black and furry thing before him. Jimmie turned several somersaults backward and when he stopped rolling he was wrong side up with the collie astride of him.

"Bruceie!"

The Scotchman's voice was low but the tone of disapproval was perfectly understood, and, the dog, crestfallen, trotted back to his side.

"Na! Na! Ye mauna hoort the wee cub, Bruceie. He wadna hoort yew."

Bruce didn't seem at all sure of this. But his god had spoken, and the bear cub was safe even if it should try to chew the dog's tail off. But Jimmie didn't understand. He didn't know that dogs have gods and that it was to Bruce's god that he owed his life. All that Jimmie knew was that he had been scared almost to death and that the thing which scared him was to be avoided in future. Hence Lucy's failure to effect a formal introduction.

But Jimmie's disapproval of Bruce did not necessarily extend to other dogs, and he had some very intimate canine friends.

One of these was a cur of low degree named Bingo, who lived at a farm half a mile away. Sometimes Jimmie went to call on him, but usually Bingo came to our house. Bingo was of no particular breed—or as someone put it he was of many unparticular breeds. Nevertheless, he was a very lovable dog. He was black and tan in color, and his eyes and tail seemed to vie with one another in appearing happy and friendly. All the small boys for miles around

made a pal of Bingo. He was the dog they took with them when they went fishing or berrying or when they went to round up the cows. There was only one youngster whom Bingo liked better than these—that was Jimmie. The two seemed to have a complete understanding and I have seldom seen two animals have such glorious times together. They ran side by side through the fields, played tag around the barn, and when they were so winded that they didn't seem able to run another yard they would lie on the lawn about a foot apart and just gaze at one another until they recovered their breath. Then perhaps they would wrestle, each animal rising on his hind legs in an effort to down his opponent. Usually they would keep up the wrestling match until Jimmie was tired. Sometimes Bingo seemed to be tired first, but if Jimmie had a good hold on him, that didn't make any difference—they went straight on with the game. If, as occasionally happened, Bingo continued to be strenuous after Jimmie had had enough, the bear would try to escape by climbing a tree. In this he was seldom successful, for although the dog could not climb, he could jump beautifully. Just as the cub seemed to be safe, Bingo would leap after him and, seizing his short tail or hind foot, bring him tumbling to the ground again.

Jimmie wanted but little here below; in fact he wanted nothing but his own way. And he usually had it because it made life easier for the rest of us—not much easier, just easier. One thing he was very particular about was the milk he drank for breakfast —it had to be "this morning's" milk. It was of no use to offer him "last night's" milk, no matter how cool it had been kept or how sweet it was. Jimmie was a connoisseur of milk. He would detect the "fraud" at once and set up a wail which we were glad to stop at almost any price. As soon as the new milk was set before him he almost wallowed in it and the wailing ceased automatically. After he had absorbed all the milk and crackers he wanted, he was ready to play. He would roll about, on the lawn, biting his own feet, and then for no apparent reason he would dash straight up a tree. His method of climbing was interesting and different from that used by most animals. He ascended a trunk by a series of leaps, digging his hind toes in below him, springing from them, throwing his sturdy forearms upward and around the tree to get a fresh and loftier hold after every jump. He mounted with an agility one hardly would have accredited him. Coming down was a much more serious business, at least in the early days. Later he became more skillful and could even slide, but at first he would come down very slowly, and with almost unbelievable caution, like an elderly gentleman descending a precipice. Tail first he would come, stopping frequently to look down as though seeking a new foothold, and sometimes grumbling a little as if to let us know that he realized the horrible danger he was in. But he always reached the ground in safety, and at once was ready for another adventure.

Next to feeding, his greatest pleasure was bathing; so, soon after breakfast we would bring out a large washtub, fill it with water, and into it he would get. Sometimes before getting in he would walk around it on his hind legs, dipping in his forepaws as though to see if the temperature was all right. Or, perhaps, he would dance around it like a young Indian, scooping up the water with his little "hands" and dashing it over everything and everybody within reach. Then he would get into the tub and sit down on his haunches, or if the water was not too deep, he would roll around on his back and wash his face with his wet paws. After he had splashed as much as he cared to, he would suddenly jump out of his bath, and with water squirting from his long coat at every leap, chase anyone who happened to be near. If it were a woman, so much the better, because she would probably scream and that always seemed to add to the fun. It was quite useless for the pursued to try to climb out of his reach; climbing was Jimmie's long suit. The only safety was behind a closed door—a door with a latch. A door which closed simply with a spring, he could open as well as I could. First he would pull it ajar with one of his forepaws, and then insert his muzzle. In the kitchen there was a screen door which closed with a spring in this way, and he knew how to open this door at once. Whether he had done the trick before or not, I don't know. At the front hall there was another screen door, and it so happened that while the kitchen door opened at the right, the front door opened at the left.

Here was a chance to test the little bear's knowledge of doors, so, when I saw that he was very anxious to enter the house, I latched the kitchen door, and let him go around to the front. At once it was evident that he had had no experience with doors which opened at the left, for he devoted all his energies to the right-hand side, and for many minutes worked hard at the crack close to the springs and hinges. After he had given it up as a bad job, I brought him back, and opened the door just an inch or two. In a moment he inserted his nose, and ever afterwards he was able to open that door as easily as the other one.

As soon as Jimmie was considered big enough to go for a walk with me, he went. I took one black paw in my right hand and for a short distance he walked along like a little man. But he soon got tired of the upright position and I let him go on all fours. The world was very new and full of interest for him, and apparently he wanted to see it all that very day. He chewed the grass and sniffed the wild flowers and made clumsy attempts to catch the butterflies which hovered over them. He entered all the deserted houses, climbed into the cupboards, looked carefully

up the chimneys, and acted generally as if he were thinking of
renting a place for the summer. Once he had a fearful adventure.
In the yard of one of the houses was an old-fashioned well sweep
and Jimmie, after eyeing the tall, slanting pole decided to climb
it. It was stiff from disuse and never moved until he reached
the very top, when to his surprise and horror it tipped over and
brought him to the ground with a bump. Luckily the well itself
had been boarded up. But young bears are very strongly made
and he was much more scared than hurt. A few minutes later
he seemed to have forgotten all about it. At any rate he shinned
to the top of the next signpost we came to, very much to the
amusement of a passing rustic who remarked with a grin, "I guess
that b'ar wants to see how fur he is from hum."

Along the country road we went, Jimmie galloping gaily, now
in front, now behind, and making frequent excursions into the
woods on either hand to satisfy his curiosity, or to pick wild
raspberries, of which he was very fond. When he came to a
raspberry bush, he would first eat those which hung near the
ground, and then, standing on his hind legs, he would pull the
tall branches down to him with his forepaws. The amount of
energy he displayed was remarkable. He never seemed to know
what it was to be tired even after the most violent exertion.
After galloping perhaps a hundred yards to catch up, he would
make a playful run at me, biting at my legs and giving me a
vigorous hug and shake with his forepaws, breaking away only
to dash up a tree to a point perhaps fifty feet from the ground,
without so much as a twig to aid him in his ascent. Here he would
probably chew the green leaves for a moment, and then he would
come sliding down, tail first, and at once break into a gallop to
make up for the ground he had lost. He would march boldly
along the tops of stone walls, walk slowly and cautiously on
wobbly rail fences, and rush up the trunks of trees when there
was nothing more exciting on hand. Sometimes he would remain up a tree so long that I got far ahead of him on the road, or
sometimes I would hide in the long grass and call him to see
what he would do. Apparently he seldom followed my trail by
scent, as a dog would have done, but relied on his ears and eyes,
and chiefly on the latter. At the sound of my voice, he would

stand straight up on his hind legs, and I would see him peering in my direction, over the tops of the grass blades. If I called again, or if he caught sight of me, down he would drop, and, taking the general direction, he would gallop toward me. Then, as soon as he was in doubt, up on his hind legs he would go to get his bearings again. When at last he found me, he seemed satisfied, but showed not the least sign of affection, such as a fox or even a wolf would have shown, but simply ran along as before.

After that Jimmie went walking with me almost every day. Indeed, it was by no means an easy matter to leave him at home even if I wanted to. If he were loose he would go with me whether he was invited or not, and if I shut him up—well, I had no one to blame but myself. I tried it once, and the hole he chewed in the door was almost as big as the noise he made. I didn't hear the noise, because I was away, but I heard other things when I returned, and the orders from headquarters were that in future Jimmie was to accompany me everywhere except to church unless there was some awfully good reason why he shouldn't. So I had a great deal of his company that summer, and I enjoyed it immensely. There was nothing monotonous about him, he was always doing something different.

I shall never forget the first time he saw a cow. There were several grazing in a field next to the road and Jimmie stood up on his hind legs at a fence post to watch them. Presently the cows looked up and saw him standing there, and no doubt he was just as strange a sight to them as they were to him. So one of them, overcome by curiosity, I suppose, walked over to get a better look at him. When she got reasonably near she stopped, and Jimmie, as if willing to meet her halfway, ducked under the barbed wire and walked straight up to her. Then when they were face to face, he stood erect. He seemed to be especially attracted by her ears—the largest, the hairiest, the most interesting ears he had ever seen. He put out his paws and began to examine one of them. This was a liberty which the cow resented promptly. Charging like a battering ram, she knocked him spinning under the barbed wire fence and for twenty feet among the clover and buttercups on the other side. With a disgusted "Wow!" the cub picked himself up, and came running to me, muttering and grumbling as if he thought I was to blame for his discomfiture. Perhaps he came only for sympathy, in which case he got what he came for, because after all he was only a baby and the cow had been very rough!

A few days later we were going through a pasture where there was a cow with a small calf. As soon as she saw Jimmie, she seemed to remember an appointment she had with him. She threw her tail in the air and started for him at her very best pace, but Jimmie had had one painful experience with a cow quite recently and he wasn't going to have another one right away if he could help it. The fence around the pasture was a high one, and he ran for it just as hard as he could hump his little back. The cow followed in hot pursuit. Jimmie got there first and quickly scrambled up a fence post out of reach. Bossy, seeing him safe, stopped about ten feet away and looked up at him. The cub, from the top of the post looked down at the cow. Then, as if a bright idea had occurred to him, he scrambled down again and walked slowly out to meet the enemy. The cow seemed to realize that her chance was coming and she lowered her head, all ready to rush in and toss him over the fence the moment she was sure of him. But Jimmie had a surprise in store for her. Instead of walking right up as he did to the other cow, he stopped a little short of this one, and arose on his sturdy hind legs. Then, without preliminaries, he "squared off" like a flyweight prize fighter, swung for her jaw with a "right" and "left," and landed twice. Then, with something very like a sneer on his impudent little face, he scrambled back up the fence post before the cow could recover from her astonishment.

Jimmie Says Good-Bye

The following spring, after long deliberation, we decided that Jimmie was getting too large for private use. Good-natured as he was, he was growing very strong, and quite too strenuous and demonstrative for the liking of some of the people he made it his business to meet. If he saw a man coming up the road, that man was in for a wrestling match whether he was in training or not, and if his apparel happened to be quite unsuitable for work "on the mat" it made not the slightest difference to the black imp who challenged him. A very nice young man walked all the way from Lebanon one day to try to sell us a copy of "To Heaven through Nature." Jimmie happened to meet him a quarter of a mile down the road, and by the time I was able to respond to his very vigorous call for help, he looked as if he had been trying to hurry through a series of barbed wire entanglements. We simply had to ask him to lunch, and Lucy spent most of the afternoon mending his trousers. As he was leaving, her eyes twinkled and she called to him, "When you get out a new edition of your book, don't forget to have a chapter on bears."

Even Lucy was no longer sure that she could hold her own against Jimmie. One day he caught her away from the house and in his playful, bearish way tore her skirt and apron and at last, to her great mortification, she was obliged to call for help.

But the climax was reached one evening, when, as Mrs. Baynes was coming home from a walk, Jimmie seized her, and in spite of all she could do to prevent him, tripped her up and threw her on to the snow. Of course it was in fun from his point of view, but from hers it was becoming serious, and she called to me. I ran as fast as I could, but by the time I got there he had taken the knot of her hair in his mouth and pushed her head into a soft snowbank. He was getting too funny to laugh at, and I determined to find a new home for him.

That was not entirely easy. When he was very little everybody wanted him, but as he had grown larger and stronger the offers which were made for him grew fewer and fewer. One friend, when asked if he didn't want a nice young bear about Jimmie's size, answered, "No thanks—what have I done to you?"

But at last I learned that the New York Zoological Society wanted a Canadian black bear, and the Director kindly wrote to me offering to buy him. I could not accept the offer, as I have always made it a point never to sell an animal which has been a member of my household. But I promptly presented him, and I confess it was with mingled feelings. Next morning we went for our last walk together, and when I marked his height as he stood on his hind legs and felt the strength of his arms and the grip of his teeth when he closed with me for a wrestling bout, I knew that we had not made our decision too soon. But that afternoon when he walked out on to the piazza, stood up at one of the posts, and with a strangely sad expression on his face looked away across those blue hills and valleys which he was never to see again, there came a choky feeling in our throats. And when a little later he picked up a much beloved rag doll which Mrs. Baynes had made for him, sat down with it in his lap, licked its face all over for the last time and then carried it off to bed with him, we couldn't help feeling very sorry that little bears grow up into big ones. Of course our intelligence told us that he had no idea that he was going away, that his standing at the piazza post that particular afternoon was merely an interesting coincidence, and that the sadness of his expression was probably in our own imagination. Nevertheless, these things all tended to emphasize the fact that he was about to leave us and we were genuinely sad to think that we were going to lose him.

Early next morning a sledge drawn by two big black oxen stopped at our door. They were headed toward Lebanon, our nearest railroad station, eight miles away. After we had all let Jimmie give us a parting hug, I led him to a crate which had been made for him, and a few moments later the crate, with the bear inside it, was lifted on to the sledge.

"Gee!" cried the driver, and the great black oxen swung to the right, breaking out the runners and sending glittering ice splinters in all directions.

"Huish!" The powerful brutes lunged forward into the yoke, the sledge moved northward over the rough and frozen roads, and Lucy, her apron held to her face, stood crying as if her heart would break.

Two months later I went to New York, and naturally the first person I called on was Jimmie. I wanted to see if he remembered me—to know whether he could distinguish me from the thousands of other people who went past those bear dens every day. I told the director and he consented to go with me and help me to make a test of it. From a distance we could see Jimmie lying in a corner of the den, his head on his left paw and evidently fast asleep. According to agreement, the director went to the corner which was farthest from the sleeping cub and began to call him by name.

"Jimmie!" he shouted. "Jimmie! Jimmie! Come along, Jimmie! Come! Come!"

But the bear never moved. Of course he must have heard the sound, but the voice meant nothing to him. Then the director stepped back, and I began to call. Instantly Jimmie's head came up from his arm, and he scrambled to his feet. Then he came trotting along the inside of the pen and when he got opposite me he stood up on his hind legs and I gave him my hand through the bars. He grabbed it in both his forepaws and fairly gasped in his excitement.

"Ooah! Ooah!—Ooooah!"

Then he gave way to that queer, continuous, bubbling sob he often made when greatly stirred.

"Ubble-uble-uble-uble-uble-uble," he blubbered, and he kept it up until I thought I should cry myself.

It was very hard to leave him, but, of course, it had to be. Slowly I took my hand from between his clinging paws and walked away, leaving him sobbing softly to himself.

About a year later I went to see him again. He had grown much larger and was easily holding his own with several other young bears who were occupying the same den with him. When I arrived some small boys, in defiance of the rules, were throwing peanuts through the bars. All the bears in the den were on the alert for them, but it is safe to say that Jimmie was getting three out of five.

I went as near as the guard rail would let me and called him by name. Again he came up, but with a look quite different from the one he had given me a year ago. He stood up on his hind legs and looked at me with a puzzled expression which seemed to say, "It seems to me that I have met you somewhere before, but I'll be hanged if I can remember just where it was or who you are."

The last time I saw Jimmie—and it was not so long ago—he was still at the Zoo. He had outstripped all his companions both in size and good looks, and was really a superb specimen. As he arose on his hind legs he was tall and straight, his eyes were bright, and his coat was long and healthy. He was the largest and handsomest black bear in the New York Zoological Park.

Stickeen

JOHN MUIR

In the summer of 1880, I set out from Fort Wrangel in a canoe to continue the exploration of the icy region of southeastern Alaska begun in the fall of 1879. After the necessary provisions, blankets, etc. had been collected and stowed away, and my Indian crew were in their places ready to start, while a crowd of their relatives and friends on the wharf were bidding them good-bye and good luck, my companion, the Rev. S. H. Young, for whom we were waiting, at last came aboard, followed by a little black dog, that immediately made himself at home by curling up in a hollow among the baggage. I like dogs, but this one seemed so small and worthless that I objected to his going, and asked the missionary why he was taking him.

"Such a little helpless creature will only be in the way," I said; "you had better pass him up to the Indian boys on the wharf, to be taken home to play with the children. This trip is not likely to be good for toy dogs. The poor silly thing will be in rain and snow for weeks or months, and will require care like a baby."

But his master assured me that he would be no trouble at all; that he was a perfect wonder of a dog, could endure cold and hunger like a bear, swim like a seal, and was wondrous wise and cunning, etc.; making out a list of virtues to show he might be the most interesting member of the party.

Nobody could hope to unravel the lines of his ancestry. In all the wonderfully mixed and varied dog tribe, I never saw any creature very much like him, though in some of his sly, soft, gliding motions and gestures he brought the fox to mind. He was short-legged and bunchy-bodied, and his hair, though

smooth, was long and silky and slightly waved, so that when the
wind was at his back it ruffled, making him look shaggy. At
first sight his only noticeable feature was his fine tail, which was
about as airy and shady as a squirrel's, and was carried curling
forward almost to his nose. On closer inspection you might notice his thin sensitive ears, and sharp eyes with cunning tan spots
above them. Mr. Young told me that when the little fellow was
a pup about the size of a wood rat he was presented to his wife
by an Irish prospector at Sitka, and that on his arrival at Fort
Wrangel he was adopted with enthusiasm by the Stickeen Indians as a sort of new good-luck totem, was named "Stickeen"
for the tribe, and became a universal favorite; petted, protected,
and admired wherever he went, and regarded as a mysterious
fountain of wisdom.

On our trip he soon proved himself a queer character—odd,
concealed, independent, keeping invincibly quiet, and doing
many little puzzling things that piqued my curiosity. As we
sailed week after week through the long intricate channels and
inlets among the innumerable islands and mountains of the
coast, he spent most of the dull days in sluggish ease, motionless, and apparently as unobserving as if in deep sleep. But I discovered that somehow he always knew what was going on.
When the Indians were about to shoot at ducks or seals, or when
anything along the shore was exciting our attention, he would
rest his chin on the edge of the canoe and calmly look out like
a dreamy-eyed tourist. And when he heard us talking about making a landing, he immediately roused himself to see what sort
of a place we were coming to, and made ready to jump over-
board and swim ashore as soon as the canoe neared the beach.
Then, with a vigorous shake to get rid of the brine in his hair,
he ran into the woods to hunt small game. But though always
the first out of the canoe, he was always the last to get into it.
When we were ready to start he could never be found, and refused to come to our call. We soon found out, however, that
though we could not see him at such times, he saw us, and from
the cover of the briers and huckleberry bushes in the fringe of the
woods was watching the canoe with wary eye. For as soon as we
were fairly off he came trotting down the beach, plunged into

the surf, and swam after us, knowing well that we would cease rowing and take him in. When the contrary little vagabond came alongside, he was lifted by the neck, held at arm's length a moment to drip, and dropped aboard. We tried to cure him of this trick by compelling him to swim a long way, as if we had a mind to abandon him; but this did no good: the longer the swim the better he seemed to like it.

Though capable of great idleness, he never failed to be ready for all sorts of adventures and excursions. One pitch-dark, rainy night we landed about ten o'clock at the mouth of a salmon stream when the water was phosphorescent. The salmon were running, and the myriad fins of the onrushing multitude were churning all the stream into a silvery glow, wonderfully beautiful and impressive in the ebon darkness. To get a good view of the show I set out with one of the Indians and sailed up through the midst of it to the foot of a rapid about half a mile from camp, where the swift current dashing over rocks made the luminous glow most glorious. Happening to look back down the stream, while the Indian was catching a few of the struggling fish, I saw a long spreading fan of light like the tail of a comet, which we thought must be made by some big, strange animal that was pursuing us. On it came with its magnificent train, until we imagined we could see the monster's head and eyes; but it was only Stickeen, who, finding I had left the camp, came swimming after me to see what was up.

When we camped early, the best hunter of the crew usually went to the woods for a deer, and Stickeen was sure to be at his heels, provided I had not gone out. For, strange to say, though I never carried a gun, he always followed me, forsaking the hunter and even his master to share my wanderings. The days that were too stormy for sailing I spent in the woods, or on the adjacent mountains, wherever my studies called me; and Stickeen always insisted on going with me, however wild the weather, gliding like a fox through dripping huckleberry bushes and thorny tangles of panax and rubus, scarce stirring their rain-laden leaves; wading and wallowing through snow, swimming icy streams, skipping over logs and rocks and the crevasses of glaciers with the patience and endurance of a determined mountaineer, never tiring or getting discouraged. Once he followed me over a glacier the surface of which was so crusty and rough that it cut his feet until every step was marked with blood; but he trotted on with Indian fortitude until I noticed his red track, and, taking pity on him, made him a set of moccasins out of a handkerchief. However great his troubles he never asked help or made any complaint, as if, like a philosopher, he had learned that without hard work and suffering there could be no pleasure worth having.

Yet none of us was able to make out what Stickeen was really good for. He seemed to meet danger and hardships without anything like reason, insisted on having his own way, never obeyed an order, and the hunter could never set him on anything, or make him fetch the birds he shot. His equanimity was so steady it seemed due to want of feeling; ordinary storms were pleasures to him, and as for mere rain, he flourished in it like a vegetable. No matter what advances you might make, scarce a glance or a tail wag would you get for your pains. But though he was apparently as cold as a glacier and about as impervious to fun, I tried hard to make his acquaintance, guessing there must be something worth-while hidden beneath so much courage, endurance, and love of wild-weathery adventure. No superannuated mastiff or bulldog grown old in office surpassed this fluffy midget in stoic dignity. He sometimes reminded me of a small, squat, unshakable, desert cactus. For he never displayed a single trace of the merry, tricksy, elfish fun of the terriers and collies that we all know, nor of their touching affection and devotion. Like children, most small dogs beg to be loved and allowed to love; but Stickeen seemed a very Diogenes, asking only to be let alone: a true child of the wilderness, holding the even tenor of his hidden life with the silence and serenity of nature. His strength of character lay in his eyes. They looked as old as the hills, and as young, and as wild. I never tired of looking into them: it was like looking into a landscape; but they were small and rather deep-set, and had no explaining lines around them to give out particulars. I was accustomed to look into the faces of plants and animals, and I watched the little sphinx more and more keenly as an interesting study. But there is no estimating the wit and wisdom concealed and latent in our lower fellow mortals until made manifest by profound experiences; for it is through suffering that dogs as well as saints are developed and made perfect.

After exploring the Sumdum and Tahkoo fiords and their glaciers, we sailed through Stephen's Passage into Lynn Canal and thence through Icy Strait into Cross Sound, searching for unexplored inlets leading toward the great fountain ice fields of the Fairweather Range. Here, while the tide was in our favor, we were accompanied by a fleet of icebergs drifting out to the ocean from Glacier Bay. Slowly we paddled around Vancouver's Point, Wimbledon, our frail canoe tossed like a feather on the massive heaving swells coming in past Cape Spenser. For miles the Sound is bounded by precipitous mural cliffs, which, lashed with wave spray and their heads hidden in clouds, looked terribly threatening and stern. Had our canoe been crushed or upset we could have made no landing here, for the cliffs, as high as those of Yosemite, sink sheer into deep water. Eagerly we scanned the wall on the north side for the first sign of an opening fiord or harbor, all of us anxious except Stickeen, who dozed in peace or gazed dreamily at the tremendous precipices when he heard us talking about them. At length we made the joyful discovery of the mouth of the inlet now called "Taylor Bay," and about five o'clock reached the head of it and encamped in a spruce grove near the front of a large glacier.

While camp was being made, Joe the hunter climbed the mountain wall on the east side of the fiord in pursuit of wild goats, while Mr. Young and I went to the glacier. We found that it is separated from the waters of the inlet by a tide-washed moraine, and extends, an abrupt barrier, all the way across from wall to wall of the inlet, a distance of about three miles. But our most interesting discovery was that it had recently advanced, though again slightly receding. A portion of the terminal moraine had been plowed up and shoved forward, uprooting and overwhelming the woods on the east side. Many of the trees were down and buried, or nearly so, others were leaning away from the ice cliffs, ready to fall, and some stood erect, with the bottom of the ice plow still beneath their roots and its lofty crystal spires towering high above their tops. The spectacle presented by these century-old trees standing close beside a spiry wall of ice, with their branches almost touching it, was most novel and striking. And when I climbed around the front, and a little way up the west side of the glacier, I found that it had swelled and increased in height and width in accordance with its advance, and carried away the outer ranks of trees on its bank.

On our way back to camp after these first observations, I planned a far-and-wide excursion for the morrow. I awoke early, called not only by the glacier, which had been on my mind all night, but by a grand floodstorm. The wind was blowing a gale from the north and the rain was flying with the clouds in a wide, passionate horizontal flood, as if it were all passing over the country instead of falling on it. The main perennial streams were booming high above their banks, and hundreds of new ones, roaring like the sea, almost covered the lofty gray walls of the inlet with white cascades and falls. I had intended making a cup of coffee and getting something like a breakfast before starting, but when I heard the storm and looked out I made haste to join it; for many of Nature's finest lessons are to be found in her storms, and if careful to keep in right relations with them, we may go safely abroad with them, rejoicing in the grandeur and beauty of their works and ways, and chanting with the old Norsemen, "The blast of the tempest aids our oars, the hurricane is our servant and drives us whither we wish to go." So, omitting breakfast, I put a piece of bread in my pocket and hurried away.

Mr. Young and the Indians were asleep, and so, I hoped, was Stickeen; but I had not gone a dozen rods before he left his bed in the tent and came boring through the blast after me. That a man should welcome storms for their exhilarating music and motion, and go forth to see God making landscapes, is reasonable enough; but what fascination could there be in such tremendous weather for a dog? Surely nothing akin to human enthusiasm for scenery or geology. Anyhow, on he came, breakfastless, through the choking blast. I stopped and did my best to turn him back. "Now don't," I said, shouting to make myself heard in the storm, "now don't, Stickeen. What has got into your queer noddle now? You must be daft. This wild day has nothing for you. There is no game abroad, nothing but weather. Go back to camp and keep warm, get a good breakfast with your master, and be sensible for once. I can't carry you all day or feed you, and this storm will kill you."

But Nature, it seems, was at the bottom of the affair, and she gains her ends with dogs as well as with men, making us do as she likes, shoving and pulling us along her ways, however rough, all but killing us at times in getting her lessons driven hard home. After I had stopped again and again, shouting good warning advice, I saw that he was not to be shaken off; as well might the earth try to shake off the moon. I had once led his master into trouble, when he fell on one of the topmost jags of a mountain and dislocated his arm; now the turn of his humble companion was coming. The pitiful little wanderer just stood there in the wind, drenched and blinking, saying doggedly, "Where thou goest, I will go." So at last I told him to come on if he must, and gave him a piece of the bread I had in my pocket; then we struggled on together, and thus began the most memorable of all my wild days.

The level flood, driving hard in our faces, thrashed and washed us wildly until we got into the shelter of a grove on the east side of the glacier near the front, where we stopped awhile for breath and to listen and look out. The exploration of the glacier was my main object, but the wind was too high to allow excursions over its open surface, where one might be dangerously shoved while balancing for a jump on the brink of a crevasse. In the meantime the storm was a fine study. Here the end of the glacier, descending an abrupt swell of resisting rock about five hundred feet high, leans forward and falls in ice cascades. And as the storm came down the glacier from the north, Stickeen and I were beneath the main current of the blast, while favorably located to see and hear it. What a psalm the storm was singing, and how fresh the smell of the washed earth and leaves, and how sweet the still small voices of the storm! Detached wafts and swirls were coming through the woods, with music from the leaves and branches and furrowed boles, and even from the splintered rocks and ice crags overhead, many of the tones soft and low and flutelike, as if each leaf and tree, crag and spire were a tuned reed. A broad torrent, draining the side of the glacier, now swollen by scores of new streams from the mountains, was rolling boulders along its rocky channel, with thudding, bumping, muffled sounds, rushing toward the bay with tremendous energy, as if in haste to get out of the mountains; the waters above and beneath calling to each other, and all to the ocean, their home.

Looking southward from our shelter, we had this great torrent and the forested mountain wall above it on our left, the spiry ice crags on our right, and smooth gray gloom ahead. I tried to draw the marvelous scene in my notebook, but the rain blurred the page in spite of all my pains to shelter it, and the sketch was almost worthless. When the wind began to abate, I traced the east side of the glacier. All the trees standing on the edge of the woods were barked and bruised, showing high-ice mark in a very telling way, while tens of thousands of those that had stood for centuries on the bank of the glacier farther out lay crushed and being crushed. In many places, I could see down fifty feet or so beneath the margin of the glacier mill, where trunks from one to two feet in diameter were being ground to pulp against outstanding rock ribs and bosses of the bank.

About three miles above the front of the glacier I climbed to the surface of it by means of ax steps made easy for Stickeen. As far as the eye could reach, the level, or nearly level, glacier stretched away indefinitely beneath the gray sky, a seemingly boundless prairie of ice. The rain continued, and grew colder, which I did not mind, but a dim snowy look in the drooping clouds made me hesitate about venturing far from land. No trace of the west shore was visible, and in case the clouds should settle and give snow, or the wind again become violent, I feared getting caught in a tangle of crevasses. Snow crystals, the flowers of the mountain clouds, are frail, beautiful things, but terrible when flying on stormwinds in darkening, benumbing swarms or when welded together into glaciers full of deadly crevasses. Watching the weather, I sauntered about on the crystal sea. For a mile or two out I found the ice remarkably safe. The marginal crevasses were mostly narrow, while the few wider ones were easily avoided by passing around them; and the clouds began to open here and there.

Thus encouraged, I at last pushed out for the other side; for Nature can make us do anything she likes. At first we made rapid progress, and the sky was not very threatening, while I took bearings occasionally with a pocket compass to enable me to find my way back more surely in case the storm should become blinding; but the structure lines of the glacier were my main guide. Toward the west side we came to a closely crevassed section in which we had to make long, narrow tacks and doublings, tracing the edges of tremendous transverse and longitudinal crevasses, many of which were from twenty to thirty feet wide, and perhaps a thousand feet deep—beautiful and awful. In working a way through them I was severely cautious, but Stickeen came on as unhesitating as the flying clouds. The widest crevasse that I could jump he would leap without so much as halting to take a look at it. The weather was now making quick changes, scattering bits of dazzling brightness through the wintry gloom; at rare intervals, when the sun broke forth wholly free, the glacier was seen from shore to shore with a bright array of encompassing mountains partly revealed, wearing the clouds as garments, while the prairie bloomed and sparkled with irised light from myriads of washed crystals. Then suddenly all the glorious show would be darkened and blotted out.

Stickeen seemed to care for none of these things, bright or dark, nor for the crevasses, wells, moulins, or swift flashing streams into which he might fall. The little adventurer was only about two years old, yet nothing seemed novel to him, nothing daunted him. He showed neither caution nor curiosity, wonder nor fear, but bravely trotted on as if glaciers were playgrounds. His stout, muffled body seemed all one skipping muscle, and it was truly wonderful to see how swiftly and, to all appearance, heedlessly he flashed across nerve-trying chasms six or eight feet wide. His courage was so unwavering that it seemed to be due to dullness of perception, as if he were only blindly bold; and I kept warning him to be careful. For we had been close companions on so many wilderness trips that I had formed the habit of talking to him as if he were a boy and understood every word.

We gained the west shore in about three hours; the width of the glacier here being about seven miles. Then I pushed northward in order to see as far back as possible into the fountains of the Fairweather Mountains, in case the clouds should rise. The walking was easy along the margin of the forest, which, of course, like that on the other side, had been invaded and crushed by the swollen, overflowing glacier. In an hour or so, after passing a massive headland, we came suddenly on a branch of the glacier, which, in the form of a magnificent ice cascade two miles wide, was pouring over the rim of the main basin in a westerly direction, its surface broken into wave-shaped blades and shattered blocks, suggesting the wildest updashing, heaving, plunging motion of a great river cataract. Tracing it down three or four miles, I found that it discharged into a lake, filling it with icebergs.

I would gladly have followed the lake outlet to tidewater, but the day was already far spent, and the threatening sky called for haste on the return trip to get off the ice before dark. I decided therefore to go no farther and, after taking a general view of the wonderful region, turned back, hoping to see it again under more favorable auspices. We made good speed up the cañon of the great ice torrent, and out on the main glacier until we had left the west shore about two miles behind us. Here we got into a difficult network of crevasses, the gathering clouds began to drop misty fringes, and soon the dreaded snow came flying thick and fast. I now began to feel anxious about finding a way in the blurring storm. Stickeen showed no trace of fear. He was still the same silent, able little hero. I noticed, however, that after the storm darkness came on he kept close up behind me. The snow urged us to make still greater haste, but at the same time hid our way. I pushed on as best I could, jumping innumerable crevasses, and, for every hundred rods or so of direct advance, traveling a mile in doubling up and down in the turmoil of chasms and dislocated ice-blocks. After an hour or two of this work we came to a series of longitudinal crevasses of appalling width, and almost straight and regular in trend, like immense furrows.

These I traced with firm nerve, excited and strengthened by the danger, making wide jumps, poising cautiously on their dizzy edges, after cutting hollows for my feet, before making the spring, to avoid possible slipping or any uncertainty on the farther sides, where only one trial is granted—exercise at once frightful and inspiring. Stickeen followed seemingly without effort.

Many a mile we thus traveled, mostly up and down, making but little real headway in crossing, running instead of walking most of the time as the danger of being compelled to spend the night on the glacier became threatening. Stickeen seemed able for anything. Doubtless we could have weathered the storm for one night, dancing on a flat spot to keep from freezing, and I faced the threat without feeling anything like despair; but we were hungry and wet, and the wind from the mountains was still thick with snow and bitterly cold, so of course that night would have seemed a very long one. I could not see far enough through the blurring snow to judge in which general direction the least dangerous route lay, while the few dim, momentary glimpses I caught of mountains through rifts in the flying clouds were far from encouraging either as weather signs or as guides. I had simply to grope my way from crevasse to crevasse, holding a general direction by the ice structure, which was not to be seen everywhere, and partly by the wind. Again and again I was put to my mettle, but Stickeen followed easily, his nerve apparently growing more unflinching as the danger increased. So it always is with mountaineers when hard beset. Running hard and jumping, holding every minute of the remaining daylight, poor as it was, precious, we doggedly persevered and tried to hope that every difficult crevasse we overcame would prove to be the last of its kind. But on the contrary, as we advanced they became more deadly trying.

At length our way was barred by a very wide and straight crevasse, which I traced rapidly northward a mile or so without finding a crossing or hope of one; then down the glacier about as far, to where it united with another uncrossable crevasse. In all this distance of perhaps two miles there was only one place where I could possibly jump it, but the width of this jump was the utmost I dared attempt, while the danger of slipping on the farther side was so great that I was loath to try it. Futhermore, the side I was on was about a foot higher than the other, and even with this advantage the crevasse seemed dangerously wide. One is liable to underestimate the width of crevasses where the magnitudes in general are great. I therefore stared at this one mighty keenly, estimating its width and the shape of the edge on the farther side, until I thought that I could jump it if necessary, but that in case I should be compelled to jump back from the lower side I might fail. Now, a cautious mountaineer seldom takes a step on unknown ground, which seems at all dangerous, that he cannot retrace in case he should be stopped by unseen obstacles ahead. This is the rule of mountaineers who live long, and, though in haste, I compelled myself to sit down and calmly deliberate before I broke it.

Retracing my devious path in imagination as if it were drawn on a chart, I saw that I was recrossing the glacier a mile or two farther upstream than the course pursued in the morning, and that I was now entangled in a section I had not before seen. Should I risk this dangerous jump, or try to regain the woods on the west shore, make a fire, and have only hunger to endure while waiting for a new day? I had already crossed so broad a stretch of dangerous ice that I saw it would be difficult to get back to the woods through the storm before dark, and the attempt would most likely result in a dismal night-dance on the glacier; while just beyond the present barrier the surface seemed more promising, and the east shore was now perhaps about as near as the west. I was therefore eager to go on. But this wide jump was a dreadful obstacle.

At length, because of the dangers already behind me, I determined to venture against those that might be ahead, jumped and landed well, but with so little to spare that I more than ever dreaded being compelled to take that jump back from the lower side. Stickeen followed, making nothing of it, and we ran eagerly forward, hoping we were leaving all our troubles behind. But within the distance of a few hundred yards we were stopped by the widest crevasse yet encountered. Of course I made haste to explore it, hoping all might yet be remedied by finding a bridge or a way around either end. About three-fourths of a mile upstream I found that it united with the one we had just crossed, as I feared it would. Then, tracing it down, I found it joined the same crevasse at the lower end also, maintaining throughout its whole course a width of forty to fifty feet. Thus to my dismay I discovered that we were on a narrow island about two miles long, with two barely possible ways of escape: one back by the way we came, the other ahead by an almost inaccessible sliver bridge that crossed the great crevasse from near the middle of it!

After this nerve-trying discovery I ran back to the sliver bridge and cautiously examined it. Crevasses, caused by strains from variations in the rate of motion of different parts of the glacier and convexities in the channel, are mere cracks when they first open, so narrow as hardly to admit the blade of a pocket knife, and gradually widen according to the extent of the strain and the depth of the glacier. Now some of these cracks are interrupted, like the cracks in wood; and in opening, the strip of ice between overlapping ends is dragged out, and may maintain a continuous connection between the sides, just as the two sides of a slivered crack in wood that is being split are connected. Some crevasses remain open for months or even years, and by the melting of their sides continue to increase in width long after the opening strain has ceased; while the sliver bridges, level on top at first and perfectly safe, are at length melted to thin, vertical, knife-edged blades, the upper portion being most exposed to the weather; and since the exposure is greatest in the middle, they at length curve downward like the cables of suspension bridges. This one was evidently very old, for it had been weathered and wasted until it was the most dangerous and inaccessible that ever lay in my way. The width of the crevasse was here about fifty feet, and the sliver crossing diagonally was about seventy feet long; its thin knife-edge near the middle was depressed twenty-five or thirty feet below the level of the glacier, and the upcurving ends were attached to the sides eight or ten feet below the brink. Getting down the nearly vertical wall to the end of the sliver and up the other side were the main difficulties, and they seemed all but insurmountable. Of the many perils encountered in my years of wandering on mountains and glaciers, none seemed so plain and stern and merciless as this. And it was presented when we were wet to the skin and hungry, the sky dark with pick driving snow, and the night near. But we were forced to face it. It was a tremendous necessity.

Beginning, not immediately above the sunken end of the bridge, but a little to one side, I cut a deep hollow on the brink for my knees to rest in. Then, leaning over, with my short-handled ax I cut a step sixteen or eighteen inches below, which on account of the sheerness of the wall was necessarily shallow. That step, however, was well made; its floor sloped slightly inward and formed a good hold for my heels. Then, slipping cautiously upon it, and crouching as low as possible, with my left side toward the wall, I steadied myself against the wind with my left hand in a slight notch, while with the right I cut other similar steps and notches in succession, guarding against losing balance by glinting of the ax, or by wind gusts, for life and death were in every stroke and in the niceness of finish of every foothold.

After the end of the bridge was reached I chipped it down until I had made a level platform six or eight inches wide, and it was a trying thing to poise on this little slippery platform while bending over to get safely astride of the sliver. Crossing was then comparatively easy, by chipping off the sharp edge with short, careful strokes, and hitching forward an inch or two at a time, keeping my balance with my knees pressed against the sides. The tremendous abyss on either hand I studiously ignored. To me the edge of that blue sliver was then all the world. But the most trying part of the adventure, after working my way across inch by inch and chipping another small platform, was to rise from the safe position astride and to cut a stepladder in the nearly vertical face of the wall—chipping, climbing, holding on with feet and fingers in mere notches. At such times one's whole body is eye, and common skill and fortitude are replaced by power beyond our call or knowledge. Never before had I been so long under deadly strain. How I got up that cliff I never could tell. The thing seemed to have been done by somebody else. I never have held death in contempt, though in the course of my explorations I have oftentimes felt that to meet one's fate on a noble mountain, or in the heart of a glacier, would be blessed as compared with death from disease, or from some shabby low-land accident. But the best death, quick and crystal-pure, set so glaringly open before us, is hard enough to face, even though we feel gratefully sure that we have already had happiness enough for a dozen lives.

But poor Stickeen, the wee, hairy, sleekit beastie, think of him! When I had decided to dare the bridge, and while I was on my knees chipping a hollow on the rounded brow above it, he came behind me, pushed his head past my shoulder, looked down and across, scanned the sliver and its approaches with his mysterious eyes, then looked me in the face with a startled air of surprise and concern, and began to mutter and whine; saying as plainly as if speaking with words, "Surely, you are not going into that awful place." This was the first time I had seen him gaze deliberately into a crevasse, or into my face with an eager, speaking, troubled look. That he should have recognized and appreciated the danger at the first glance showed wonderful sa-gacity. Never before had the daring midget seemed to know that ice was slippery or that there was any such thing as danger any-where. His looks and tones of voice when he began to complain and speak his fears were so human that I unconsciously talked to him in sympathy as I would to a frightened boy, and in try-ing to calm his fears perhaps in some measure moderated my own. "Hush your fears, my boy," I said, "we will get across safe, though it is not going to be easy. No right way is easy in this rough world. We must risk our lives to save them. At the worst we can only slip, and then how grand a grave we will have, and by and by our nice bones will do good in the terminal moraine."

But my sermon was far from reassuring him: he began to cry, and after taking another piercing look at the tremendous gulf, ran away in desperate excitement, seeking some other crossing. By the time he got back, baffled of course, I had made a step or two. I dared not look back, but he made himself heard; and when he saw that I was certainly bent on crossing, he cried aloud in despair. The danger was enough to daunt anybody, but it seems wonderful that he should have been able to weigh and appreciate it so justly. No mountaineer could have seen it more quickly or judged it more wisely, discriminating between real and apparent peril.

When I gained the other side, he screamed louder than ever, and after running back and forth in vain search for a way of escape, he would return to the brink of the crevasse above the bridge, moaning and wailing as if in the bitterness of death. Could this be the silent, philosophic Stickeen? I shouted encouragement, telling him the bridge was not so bad as it looked, that I had left it flat and safe for his feet, and he could walk it easily. But he was afraid to try. Strange so small an animal should be capable of such big, wise fears. I called again and again in a reassuring tone to come on and fear nothing; that he could come if he would only try. He would hush for a moment, look down again at the bridge, and shout his unshakable conviction that he could never, never come that way; then lie back in despair, as if howling, "O-o-oh! what a place! No-o-o, I can never go-o-o down there!" His natural composure and courage had vanished utterly in a tumultuous storm of fear. Had the danger been less, his distress would have seemed ridiculous. But in this dismal, merciless abyss lay the shadow of death, and his heartrending cries might well have called Heaven to his help. Perhaps they did. So hidden before, he was now transparent, and one could see the workings of his heart and mind like the movements of a clock out of its case. His voice and gestures, hopes and fears, were so perfectly human that none could mistake them; while he seemed to understand every word of mine. I was troubled at the thought of having to leave him out all night, and of the danger of not finding him in the morning. It seemed impossible to get him to venture. To compel him to try through fear of being abandoned, I started off as if leaving him to his fate, and disappeared back of a hummock; but this did no good; he only lay down and moaned in utter hopeless misery. So, after hiding a few minutes, I went back to the brink of the crevasse and in a severe tone of voice shouted across to him that now I must certainly leave him, I could wait no longer, and that, if he would not come, all I could promise was that I would return to seek him next day. I warned him that if he went back to the woods the wolves would kill him, and finished by urging him once more by words and gestures to come on, come on.

He knew very well what I meant, and at last, with the courage of despair, hushed and breathless, he crouched down on the brink in the hollow I had made for my knees, pressed his body against the ice as if trying to get the advantage of the friction of every hair, gazed into the first step, put his little feet together and slid them slowly, slowly over the edge and down into it, bunching all four in it and almost standing on his head. Then, without lifting his feet, as well as I could see through the snow, he slowly worked them over the edge of the step and down into the next and the next in succession in the same way, and gained the end of the bridge. Then, lifting his feet with the regularity and slowness of the vibrations of a seconds pendulum, as if counting and measuring *one-two-three*, holding himself steady against the gusty wind, and giving separate attention to each little step, he gained the foot of the cliff, while I was on my knees leaning over to give him a lift should he succeed in getting within reach of my arm. Here he halted in dead silence, and it was here I feared he might fail, for dogs are poor climbers. I had no cord. If I had had one, I would have dropped a noose over his head and hauled him up. But while I was thinking whether an available cord might be made out of clothing, he was looking keenly into the series of notched steps and fingerholds I had made, as if counting them, and fixing the position of each one of them in his mind. Then suddenly up he came in a springy rush, hooking his paws into the steps and notches so quickly that I could not see how it was done, and whizzed past my head, safe at last!

And now came a scene! "Well done, well done, little boy! Brave boy!" I cried, trying to catch and caress him; but he would not be caught. Never before or since have I seen anything like so passionate a revulsion from the depths of despair to exultant, triumphant, uncontrollable joy. He flashed and darted hither and thither as if fairly demented, screaming and shouting, swirling round and round in giddy loops and circles like a leaf in a whirlwind, lying down, and rolling over and over, sidewise and heels over head, and pouring forth a tumultuous flood of hyster-

ical cries and sobs and gasping mutterings. When I ran up to
him to shake him, fearing he might die of joy, he flashed off two
or three hundred yards, his feet in a mist of motion; then, turning suddenly, came back in a wild rush and launched himself at
my face, almost knocking me down, all the time screeching
and screaming and shouting as if saying, "Saved! saved! saved!"
Then away again, dropping suddenly at times with his feet in
the air, trembling and fairly sobbing. Such passionate emotion
was enough to kill him. Moses' stately song of triumph after
escaping the Egyptians and the Red Sea was nothing to it. Who
could have guessed the capacity of the dull, enduring little fellow
for all that most stirs this mortal frame? Nobody could have
helped crying with him!

But there is nothing like work for toning down excessive fear
or joy. So I ran ahead, calling him in as gruff a voice as I could
command to come on and stop his nonsense, for we had far to
go and it would soon be dark. Neither of us feared another trial
like this. Heaven would surely count one enough for a lifetime.
The ice ahead was gashed by thousands of crevasses, but they
were common ones. The joy of deliverance burned in us like fire,
and we ran without fatigue, every muscle with immense rebound
glorying in its strength. Stickeen flew across everything in his
way, and not till dark did he settle into his normal foxlike trot.
At last the cloudy mountains came in sight, and we soon felt
the solid rock beneath our feet, and were safe. Then came weakness. Danger had vanished, and so had our strength. We tottered
down the lateral moraine in the dark, over boulders and tree
trunks, through the bushes and devil-club thickets of the grove
where we had sheltered ourselves in the morning, and across the
level mud slope of the terminal moraine. We reached camp about
ten o'clock, and found a big fire and a big supper. A party of
Hoona Indians had visited Mr. Young, bringing a gift of porpoise
meat and wild strawberries, and Hunter Joe had brought in a
wild goat. But we lay down, too tired to eat much, and soon
fell into a troubled sleep. The man who said, "The harder the
toil, the sweeter the rest," never was profoundly tired. Stickeen
kept springing up and muttering in his sleep, no doubt dreaming
that he was still on the brink of the crevasse; and so did I, that

night and many others long afterwards, when I was overtired.

Thereafter Stickeen was a changed dog. During the rest of the trip, instead of holding aloof, he always lay by my side, tried to keep me constantly in sight, and would hardly accept a morsel of food, however tempting, from any hand but mine. At night, when all was quiet about the campfire, he would come to me and rest his head on my knee with a look of devotion as if I were his god. And often as he caught my eye he seemed to be trying to say, "Wasn't that an awful time we had together on the glacier?"

Nothing in after years has dimmed that Alaska storm day. As I write, it all comes rushing and roaring to mind as if I were again in the heart of it. Again I see the gray flying clouds with their rain floods and snow, the ice cliffs towering above the shrinking forest, the majestic ice cascade, the vast glacier outspread before its white mountain fountains, and in the heart of it the tremendous crevasse—emblem of the valley of the shadow of death—low clouds trailing over it, the snow falling into it; and on its brink I see little Stickeen, and I hear his cries for help and his shouts of joy. I have known many dogs, and many a story I could tell of their wisdom and devotion; but to none do I owe so much as to Stickeen. At first the least promising and least known of my dog friends, he suddenly became the best known of them all. Our storm battle for life brought him to light, and through him as through a window I have ever since been looking with deeper sympathy into all my fellow mortals.

None of Stickeen's friends knows what finally became of him. After my work for the season was done I departed for California, and I never saw the dear little fellow again. In reply to anxious inquiries, his master wrote me that in the summer of 1883 he was stolen by a tourist at Fort Wrangel and taken away on a steamer. His fate is wrapped in mystery. Doubtless he has left this world—crossed the last crevasse—and gone to another. But he will not be forgotten. To me Stickeen is immortal.

An Elephant Never Forgets

DON LANG

OLD Roger? He was what they call a bad elephant. I mean really bad, not just mischievous and full of fun as any elephant might be, but downright bad. That was his reputation, and he did everything he could to live up to it.

Roger belonged to one of the old-time circuses, and the owners of the circus seemed to delight in his badness. He was advertised everywhere as the world's largest and meanest elephant. And every time he went off on a rampage or did some damage, it was all played up in flashy billboard signs bragging about what an old rogue he was and how dangerous, just so that more people would come to the circus to see him. He was a great attraction, a real headliner for that circus.

But they had a time with Roger, those circus people. There were only two men in the business who could handle him. One of them was his keeper, an old English clown. While the other one, the only other man who could handle him without trouble, was a man by the name of Tex Bell.

Now Tex was in charge of the canvas part of the circus, the tents. He didn't have a thing to do with the menagerie, but he and Roger just happened to get acquainted accidentally and they took a shine to each other. No matter how busy Tex was, whenever he passed Roger, staked there on the picket line with the rest of the herd, he'd always find time to stop a minute or two, to pet him and talk to him, give him a lump of sugar or some peanuts or something. And that old rascal appreciated it.

Those two men, they were old Roger's only friends. He had no use in this world for anybody else, not a soul. Why, he'd attack a person quick as a wink, if they hadn't kept him chained and shackled. Now, there must have been a reason (of course there's no way to be certain), but it seems likely that from the very first, ever since he was captured, people must have bullied Roger, and instead of being patient and kind to him, they probably clouted him every time they had a chance. So what could be expected? He just naturally hated the sight of people, all except those two men, his regular keeper and Tex Bell.

Then one day Tex left and went to work for another circus. That was a blow to Roger. He missed Tex, missed him plenty. He missed those lumps of sugar, those little acts of kindness and understanding. As the days went by, he grieved and grieved for Tex and things got steadily worse and worse. He got more unruly, more vicious and dangerous, till finally he was so dangerous that the circus was afraid to keep him.

And so he was sold, sold to another circus, the very same circus where Tex Bell was working. They wanted a famous elephant for their own advertising purposes, so they bought Roger. They decided to take a chance on him. Of course, Tex didn't know a thing about it, not a thing. He had no idea that Roger had been bought by his show. On his new job, he never had a chance to go through the menagerie or come in contact with the elephant herd. So, naturally, he never saw Roger.

But when Roger was transferred to the new show, it was the last straw. This change meant separation from his one remaining friend, the old English clown. And worse than that even, he didn't like his new keeper. He didn't like him a bit.

In the first place, he didn't trust the man. But he tried to behave himself because there was always a club or an elephant hook threatening him the minute he looked cross-eyed at anything. So he just made it his business to put up with his keeper and get along with him the best he could. He knew, regardless of everything, that he had to perform. He had to go through with his stunts no matter how he felt.

However, every once in a while something would happen. Something would make him especially mad, and then he couldn't control himself. He would rampage around perfectly furious.

And in return he'd be more abused than ever. And so it went on like that, day after day, year in and year out. That was Roger's life. And more and more he hated the very sight of a human being.

Then one night, it was in 1898, the circus was in winter quarters at Argentine, Kansas. It was the middle of the night, and everything around the lot was dead quiet. Just then, Roger's keeper came rushing into the elephant's quarters with some of his friends, shouting and singing.

Down the picket line came the keeper. Stopping in front of an elephant, he'd slap it across the trunk, shout and swear at it a second, then pass on to the next one. Chains began to rattle and clang, big, clumsy feet paddled the ground as the awakened elephants swayed and tossed from side to side in fear and trembling.

Soon, the keeper came to Roger. Roger eyed him, his great trunk swinging carelessly from right to left. The man bullied and shouted at Roger, then bragged and boasted to his friends about what a bad elephant Roger was and how he was the only person who could handle him, how he could make Roger do anything he wanted him to do.

So just to prove it, just to be showing off, he shouted a command to Roger, a command to do a stunt that Roger did in the ring as part of his performance. Roger never moved, just kept his trunk switching from side to side. He'd done that stunt in the afternoon during his training hour and he wasn't going to do it again at two o'clock in the morning, not for anybody like that. He never moved. He never budged. He just stood there staring.

That keeper was furious when Roger didn't pay any attention to his command. He, the big boss, the great elephant trainer! And his friends stood there jeering at him. He was wild! But instead of reaching for an elephant hook, the hook that Roger was used to, he ran his hand in his pocket, fished out his penknife, opened it, and jabbed it to the hilt in Roger's trunk.

Roger screamed with pain. Never before had he felt anything like it. Every ounce of hate in his huge body rose up as he reached out, wrapped his trunk around the keeper, lifted him high in the air and shook him. Then, with a furious bellow, he tossed the lifeless body to one side, gave a terrific lunge, jerked and strained. Every chain snapped and he was free!

Again and again that terrible trumpet sounded, as he started off on a wild rampage. Pandemonium broke loose. Every elephant understood and recognized that fearful challenge of the killer.

Down past the long line of cringing, squealing, frightened elephants Roger lumbered, straight on up to the massive stockade fence built to hold back a whole herd of elephants. It rose directly in his path and threatened to stop him, as it was supposed to do. But he stopped only an instant, just long enough to place his head against it, and then down it crashed. And on he plunged.

A siren shrieked through the crisp, night air its warning call to every man to be up and armed, for tragedy was at hand. A dangerous elephant was on the loose. Men came from every direction, excited and yelling.

The hate in Roger's heart burned to an insane rage as that shouting mob gave chase, shooting and firing. Every man was his enemy now. Everyone was bent on destroying him. But on he went, down to the Santa Fe Railroad yards. Then down the track he went, as fast as he could, still screaming his anger and defiance. As bullet after bullet buried itself in his huge body, the pain of that knife wound grew keener and the hate in his heart more and more. And on each side of him as he traveled down that track, appeared great freight cars. Harmless they might be, yet each and every one of them was something to be destroyed. And, as more of those bullets thudded and plowed into his body, more and more of those box cars toppled over on their sides and crashed to splinters, victims of his furious onslaught.

Suddenly there came to him a different sound. His ears caught it distinctly. It was the sound of a horse's hoofs beating a steady tattoo on the wooden railroad ties. Louder and louder that sound came. It was catching up to him. Mysteriously the shooting and the noise of the mob had faded out. But the new enemy, the danger of those hoof beats, threatened him. They kept coming nearer, gaining on him.

Realizing he couldn't get away, he stopped short, right there in the middle of the track. He wheeled around to face this new enemy and destroy it as he'd destroyed that man, that fence, and those freight cars. With a frightful bellow of rage, he challenged his oncoming foe.

Roger waited, his uplifted trunk ready to strike. Every muscle taut, he waited for the attack. It came! First a shadow, then the outline of a horse and rider dashing up to him. The horse wheeled to a stop, the rider slid to the ground and started toward him fearlessly. That trunk slashed wickedly down. Down! But something stopped it halfway in midair, stopped it short. It was a gentle, coaxing voice, pleading with him.

"Come on, Roger! What's the trouble, ol' boy? Aw, come on!"

Instantly Roger recognized that kind, sympathetic command. He hadn't heard it for years, but he recognized it. It was the voice of a friend, the man he loved. His trunk dropped limp, then reached out to fondle his old pal, Tex Bell. Tex put his arm around that trunk which could slash so wickedly and for a long time they remained there, the man and the elephant, renewing a great friendship, while the old elephant tried to tell a story that only his friend could understand. It was a story of mobs, bullets, clubs, and hooks. He had conquered them all one by one, only in turn to be conquered himself by a few soft words and a memory of love and kindness.

The next morning, very early, a tired old man could be seen slowly trudging down the railroad track. On one side of him was a riderless horse with reins flung loosely over his head. On the other side, his great ears flapping backward and forward, his long, powerful trunk switching lazily from right to left, was a thoroughly docile and contented elephant. It was Roger, old Roger, going back to the circus, to live the remaining years of his life and become famous once more, famous as a good elephant.

FROM

The Call of the Wild

JACK LONDON

No dog ever loved his master more than Buck loved John Thornton. Thornton was a Klondike fur trapper who had saved the big dog's life—and since then the two had become inseparable. Buck seemed to understand everything his master said to him and their relationship was so close as to be almost human. Jack London's tale of a dog and a man is one of the most stirring stories about an animal's devotion.

For the Love of a Man

Wʜᴇɴ John Thornton froze his feet in the previous December, his partners had made him comfortable and left him to get well, going on themselves up the river to get out a raft of saw logs for Dawson. He was still limping slightly at the time he rescued Buck, but with the continued warm weather even the slight limp left him. And here, lying by the river bank through the long spring days, watching the running water, listening lazily to the songs of birds and the hum of nature, Buck slowly won back his strength.

A rest comes very good after one has traveled three thousand miles, and it must be confessed that Buck waxed lazy as his wounds healed, his muscles swelled out, and the flesh came back to cover his bones. For that matter, they were all loafing—Buck, John Thornton, and Skeet and Nig—waiting for the raft to come that was to carry them down to Dawson. Skeet was a little Irish setter who early made friends with Buck who, in a dying condition, was unable to resent her first advances. She had the doctor trait which some dogs possess, and as a mother cat washes her kittens, so she washed and cleansed Buck's wounds. Regularly, each morning after he had finished his breakfast, she performed her self-appointed task, till he came to look for her ministrations as much as he did for Thornton's. Nig, equally friendly, though less demonstrative, was a huge black dog, half bloodhound and half deerhound, with eyes that laughed and a boundless good nature.

To Buck's surprise these dogs manifested no jealousy toward him. They seemed to share the kindliness and largeness of John Thornton. As Buck grew stronger they enticed him into all sorts of ridiculous games, in which Thornton himself could not forbear to join, and in this fashion Buck romped through his convalescence and into a new existence. Love, genuine passionate love, was his for the first time. This he had never experienced at Judge Miller's down in the sun-kissed Santa Clara Valley. With the Judge's sons, hunting and tramping, it had been a working partnership; with the Judge's grandsons, a sort of pompous guardianship; and with the Judge himself, a stately and dignified friendship. But love that was feverish and burning, that was adoration, that was madness, it had taken John Thornton to arouse.

This man had saved his life, which was something; but, further, he was the ideal master. Other men saw to the welfare of their dogs from a sense of duty and business expediency; he saw to the welfare of his as if they were his own children, because he could not help it. And he saw further. He never forgot a kindly greeting or a cheering word, and to sit down for a long talk with them ("gas" he called it) was as much his delight as theirs. He had a way of taking Buck's head roughly between his hands, and resting his own head upon Buck's, of shaking him back and forth, the while calling him ill names that to Buck were love names. Buck knew no greater joy than that rough embrace and the sound of murmured oaths, and at each jerk back and forth it seemed that his heart would be shaken out of his body so great was his ecstasy. And when, released, he sprang to his feet, his mouth laughing, his eyes eloquent, his throat vibrant with unuttered sound, and in that fashion remained without movement, John Thornton would reverently exclaim, "God! you can all but speak!"

Buck had a trick of love expression that was akin to hurt. He would often seize Thornton's hand in his mouth and close so fiercely that the flesh bore the impress of his teeth for some time afterward. And as Buck understood the oaths to be love words, so the man understood this feigned bite for a caress.

For the most part, however, Buck's love was expressed in adoration. While he went wild with happiness when Thornton touched him or spoke to him, he did not seek these tokens. Unlike Skeet, who was wont to shove her nose under Thornton's hand and nudge and nudge till petted, or Nig, who would stalk up and rest his great head on Thornton's knee, Buck was content to adore at a distance. He would lie by the hour, eager, alert, at Thornton's feet, looking up into his face, swelling upon it, studying it, following with keenest interest each fleeting expression, every movement or change of feature. Or, as chance might have it, he would lie farther away, to the side or rear, watching the outlines of the man and the occasional movements of his body. And often, such was the communion in which they lived, the strength of Buck's gaze would draw John Thornton's head around, and he would return the gaze, without speech, his heart shining out of his eyes as Buck's heart shone out.

For a long time after his rescue, Buck did not like Thornton to get out of his sight. From the moment he left the tent to when he entered it again, Buck would follow at his heels. His transient masters since he had come into the Northland had bred in him a fear that no master could be permanent. He was afraid that Thornton would pass out of his life as Perrault and François and the Scotch half-breed had passed out. Even in the night, in his dreams, he was haunted by this fear. At such times he would shake off sleep and creep through the chill to the flap of the tent, where he would stand and listen to the sound of his master's breathing.

But in spite of this great love he bore John Thornton, which seemed to bespeak the soft civilizing influence, the strain of the primitive, which the Northland had aroused in him, remained alive and active. Faithfulness and devotion, things born of fire and roof, were his; yet he retained his wildness and wiliness. He was a thing of the wild, come in from the wild to sit by John Thornton's fire, rather than a dog of the soft Southland stamped with the marks of generations of civilization. Because of his very great love, he could not steal from this man, but from any other man, in any other camp, he did not hesitate an instant; while the cunning with which he stole enabled him to escape detection.

His face and body were scored by the teeth of many dogs, and he fought as fiercely as ever and more shrewdly. Skeet and Nig were too good-natured for quarrelling—besides, they belonged to John Thornton. But the strange dog, no matter what the breed or valor, swiftly acknowledged Buck's supremacy or found himself struggling for life with a terrible antagonist. And Buck was merciless. He had learned well the law of club and fang, and he never forewent an advantage or drew back from a foe he had started on the way to Death. He had lessoned from Spitz, and from the chief fighting dogs of the police and mail, and knew there was no middle course. He must master or be mastered; while to show mercy was a weakness. Mercy did not exist in the primordial life. It was misunderstood for fear, and such misunderstandings made for death. Kill or be killed, eat or be eaten, was the law; and this mandate, down out of the depths of Time, he obeyed.

He was older than the days he had seen and the breaths he had drawn. He linked the past with the present, and the eternity behind him throbbed through him in a mighty rhythm to which he swayed as the tides and seasons swayed. He sat by John Thornton's fire, a broad-breasted dog, white-fanged and long-furred; but behind him were the shades of all manner of dogs, half-wolves and wild wolves, urgent and prompting, tasting the savor of the meat he ate, thirsting for the water he drank, scenting the wind with him, listening with him and telling him the sounds made by the wild life in the forest, dictating his moods, directing his actions, lying down to sleep with him when he lay down, and dreaming with him and beyond him and becoming themselves the stuff of his dreams.

So peremptorily did these shades beckon him that each day mankind and the claims of mankind slipped farther from him. Deep in the forest a call was sounding, and as often as he heard this call, mysteriously thrilling and luring, he felt compelled to turn his back upon the fire and the beaten earth around it, and to plunge into the forest, and on and on, he knew not where or why; nor did he wonder where or why, the call sounding imperiously, deep in the forest. But as often as he gained the soft unbroken earth and the green shade, the love for John Thornton drew him back to the fire again.

Thornton alone held him. The rest of mankind was as nothing. Chance travelers might praise or pet him; but he was cold under it all, and from a too demonstrative man he would get up and walk away. When Thornton's partners, Hans and Pete, arrived on the long-expected raft, Buck refused to notice them till he learned they were close to Thornton; after that he tolerated them in a passive sort of way, accepting favors from them as though he favored them by accepting. They were of the same large type as Thornton, living close to the earth, thinking simply and seeing clearly; and ere they swung the raft into the big eddy by the sawmill at Dawson, they understood Buck and his ways, and did not insist upon an intimacy such as obtained with Skeet and Nig.

For Thornton, however, his love seemed to grow and grow. He, alone among men, could put a pack upon Buck's back in the summer traveling. Nothing was too great for Buck to do when Thornton commanded. One day (they had grub-staked themselves from the proceeds of the raft and left Dawson for the headwaters of the Tanana) the men and dogs were sitting on the crest of a cliff which fell away, straight down, to naked bed-rock three hundred feet below. John Thornton was sitting near the edge, Buck at his shoulder. A thoughtless whim seized Thornton, and he drew the attention of Hans and Pete to the experiment he had in mind. "Jump, Buck!" he commanded, sweeping his arm out and over the chasm. The next instant he was grappling with Buck on the extreme edge, while Hans and Pete were dragging them back into safety.

"It's uncanny," Pete said, after it was over and they had caught their speech.

Thornton shook his head. "No, it is splendid, and it is terrible, too. Do you know, it sometimes makes me afraid."

"I'm not hankering to be the man that lays hands on you while he's around," Pete announced conclusively, nodding his head toward Buck.

"Py jingo!" was Hans' contribution. "Not mineself either."

It was at Circle City, ere the year was out, that Pete's apprehensions were realized. "Black" Burton, a man evil-tempered and malicious, had been picking a quarrel with a tenderfoot at the bar, when Thornton stepped good-naturedly between. Buck, as was his custom, was lying in a corner, head on paws, watching his master's every action. Burton struck out, without warning, straight from the shoulder. Thornton was sent spinning, and saved himself from falling only by clutching the rail of the bar.

Those who were looking on heard what was neither bark nor yelp, but a something which is best described as a roar, and they saw Buck's body rise up in the air as he left the floor for Burton's throat. The man saved his life by instinctively throwing out his arm, but was hurled backward to the floor with Buck on top of him. Buck loosed his teeth from the flesh of the arm and drove in again for the throat. This time the man succeeded only in partly blocking, and his throat was torn open. Then the crowd was upon Buck, and he was driven off; while a surgeon checked the bleeding, he prowled up and down, growling furiously, attempting to rush in, and being forced back by an array of hostile clubs. A "miners' meeting," called on the spot, decided that the dog had sufficient provocation, and Buck was discharged. But his reputation was made, and from that day his name spread through every camp in Alaska.

Later on, in the fall of the year, he saved John Thornton's life in quite another fashion. The three partners were lining a long and narrow poling-boat down a bad stretch of rapids on the Forty-Mile Creek. Hans and Pete moved along the bank, snubbing with a thin Manila rope from tree to tree, while Thornton remained in the boat, helping its descent by means of a pole, and shouting directions to the shore. Buck, on the bank, worried and anxious, kept abreast of the boat, his eyes never off his master.

At a particularly bad spot, where a ledge of barely submerged rocks jutted out into the river, Hans cast off the rope, and, while Thornton poled the boat out into the stream, ran down the bank with the end in his hand to snub the boat when it had cleared the ledge. This it did, and was flying downstream in a current as swift as a millrace, when Hans checked it with the rope and checked too suddenly. The boat flirted over and snubbed into the bank bottom up, while Thornton, flung sheer out of it, was carried downstream toward the worst part of the rapids, a stretch of wild water in which no swimmer could live.

Buck had sprung in on the instant, and at the end of three hundred yards, amid a mad swirl of water, he overhauled Thornton. When he felt him grasp his tail, Buck headed for the bank, swimming with all his splendid strength. But the progress shoreward was slow; the progress downstream amazingly rapid. From below came the fatal roaring where the wild current went wilder and was rent in shreds and spray by the rocks which thrust through like the teeth of an enormous comb. The suck of the water as it took the beginning of the last steep pitch was frightful, and Thornton knew that the shore was impossible. He scraped furiously over a rock, bruised across a second, and struck a third with crushing force. He clutched its slippery top with both hands, releasing Buck, and above the roar of the churning water shouted: "Go, Buck! Go!"

Buck could not hold his own, and swept on downstream, struggling desperately, but unable to win back. When he heard Thornton's command repeated, he partly reared out of the water, throwing his head high, as though for a last look, then turned obediently toward the bank. He swam powerfully and was dragged ashore by Pete and Hans at the very point where swimming ceased to be possible and destruction began.

They knew that the time a man could cling to a slippery rock in the face of that driving current was a matter of minutes, and they ran as fast as they could up the bank to a point far above where Thornton was hanging on. They attached the line with which they had been snubbing the boat to Buck's neck and shoulders, being careful that it should neither strangle him nor impede his swimming, and launched him into the stream. He struck out boldly, but not straight enough into the stream. He discovered the mistake too late, when Thornton was abreast of him and a bare half-dozen strokes away while he was being carried helplessly past.

Hans promptly snubbed with the rope, as though Buck were a boat. The rope thus tightening on him in the sweep of the current, he was jerked under the surface, and under the surface he remained till his body struck against the bank and he was hauled out. He was half drowned, and Hans and Pete threw themselves upon him, pounding the breath into him and the water out of him. He staggered to his feet and fell down. The faint sound of Thornton's voice came to them, and though they could not make out the words of it, they knew that he was in his extremity. His master's voice acted on Buck like an electric shock. He sprang to his feet and ran up the bank ahead of the men to the point of his previous departure.

Again the rope was attached and he was launched, and again he struck out, but this time straight into the stream. He had miscalculated once, but he would not be guilty of it a second time. Hans paid out the rope, permitting no slack, while Pete kept it clear of coils. Buck held on till he was on a line straight above Thornton; then he turned, and with the speed of an express train headed down upon him. Thornton saw him coming, and, as Buck struck him like a battering ram, with the whole force of the current behind him, he reached up and closed with both arms around the shaggy neck. Hans snubbed the rope around the tree, and Buck and Thornton were jerked under the water. Strangling, suffocating, sometimes one uppermost and sometimes the other, dragging over the jagged bottom, smashing against rocks and snags, they veered in to the bank.

Thornton came to, belly downward and being violently propelled back and forth across a drift log by Hans and Pete. His first glance was for Buck, over whose limp and apparently lifeless body Nig was setting up a howl, while Skeet was licking the wet face and closed eyes. Thornton was himself bruised and battered, and he went carefully over Buck's body, when he had been brought around, finding three broken ribs.

"That settles it," he announced. "We camp right here." And camp they did, till Buck's ribs knitted and he was able to travel.

That winter, at Dawson, Buck performed another exploit, not so heroic, perhaps, but one that put his name many notches higher on the totem pole of Alaskan fame. This exploit was particularly gratifying to the three men; for they stood in need of the outfit which it furnished and were enabled to make a long-desired trip into the virgin East, where miners had not yet appeared. It was brought about by a conversation in the Eldorado Saloon, in which men waxed boastful of their favorite dogs. Buck, because of his record, was the target for these men, and Thornton was driven stoutly to defend him. At the end of half an hour one man stated that his dog could start a sled with five hundred pounds and walk off with it; a second bragged six hundred for his dog; and a third seven hundred.

"Pooh!" said Thornton. "Buck can start a thousand pounds."

"And break it out and walk off with it for a hundred yards," demanded Matthewson, a Bonanza King, hc of the seven hundred vaunt.

"And break it out and walk off with it for a hundred yards," John Thornton said coolly.

"Well," Matthewson said, slowly and deliberately, so that all could hear, "I've got a thousand dollars that says he can't. And there it is." So saying, he slammed a sack of gold dust of the size of a bologna sausage down upon the bar.

Nobody spoke. Thornton's bluff, if bluff it was, had been called. He could feel a flush of warm blood creeping up his face. His tongue had tricked him. He did not know whether Buck could start a thousand pounds. Half a ton! The enormousness of it appalled him. He had great faith in Buck's strength and had often thought him capable of starting such a load; but never, as now, had he faced the possibility of it, the eyes of a dozen men fixed upon him, silent and waiting. Further, he had no thousand dollars; nor had Hans or Pete.

"I've got a sled standing outside now, with twenty fifty-pound sacks of flour on it," Matthewson went on with brutal directness, "so don't let that hinder you."

Thornton did not reply. He did not know what to say. He glanced from face to face in the absent way of a man who has lost the power of thought and is seeking somewhere to find the thing that will start it going again. The face of Jim O'Brien, a Mastodon King and oldtime comrade, caught his eyes. It was as a cue to him, seeming to rouse him to do what he would never have dreamed of doing.

"Can you lend me a thousand?" he asked, almost in a whisper.

"Sure," answered O'Brien, thumping down a plethoric sack by the side of Matthewson's. "Though it's little faith I'm having, John, that the beast can do the trick."

The Eldorado emptied its occupants into the street to see the test. The tables were deserted, and the dealers and gamekeepers came forth to see the outcome of the wager and to lay odds. Several hundred men, furred and mittened, banked around the sled within easy distance. Matthewson's sled, loaded with a thousand pounds of flour, had been standing for a couple of hours, and in the intense cold (it was sixty below zero) the runners had frozen fast to the hard-packed snow. Men offered odds of two to one that Buck could not budge the sled. A quibble arose concerning the phrase "break out." O'Brien contended it was Thornton's privilege to knock the runners loose, leaving Buck to "break it out" from a dead standstill. Matthewson insisted that the phrase included breaking the runners from the frozen grip of the snow. A majority of the men who had witnessed the making of the bet decided in his favor, whereat the odds went up to three to one against Buck.

There were no takers. Not a man believed him capable of the feat. Thornton had been hurried into the wager, heavy with doubt; and now that he looked at the sled itself, the concrete fact, with the regular team of ten dogs curled up in the snow before it, the more impossible the task appeared. Matthewson waxed jubilant.

"Three to one!" he proclaimed. "I'll lay you another thousand at that figure, Thornton. What d'ye say?"

Thornton's doubt was strong in his face, but his fighting spirit was aroused—the fighting spirit that soars above odds, fails to recognize the impossible, and is deaf to all save the clamor for battle. He called Hans and Pete to him. Their sacks were slim, and with his own the three partners could rake together only two hundred dollars. In the ebb of their fortunes, this sum was their total capital; yet they laid it unhesitatingly against Matthewson's six hundred.

The team of ten dogs was unhitched, and Buck with his own harness, was put into the sled. He had caught the contagion of the excitement, and he felt that in some way he must do a great thing for John Thornton. Murmurs of admiration at his splendid appearance went up. He was in perfect condition, without an ounce of superfluous flesh, and the one hundred and fifty pounds that he weighed were so many pounds of grit and virility. His furry coat shone with the sheen of silk. Down the neck and across the shoulders, his mane, in repose as it was, half bristled and seemed to lift with every movement, as though excess of vigor made each particular hair alive and active. The great breast and heavy forelegs were no more than in proportion with the rest of the body, where the muscles showed in tight rolls underneath the skin. Men felt these muscles and proclaimed them hard as iron, and the odds went down to two to one.

"Gad, sir! Gad, sir!" stuttered a member of the latest dynasty, a king of the Skookum Benches. "I offer you eight hundred for him, sir, before the test, sir; eight hundred just as he stands."

Thornton shook his head and stepped to Buck's side.

"You must stand off from him," Matthewson protested. "Free play and plenty of room."

The crowd fell silent; only could be heard the voices of the gamblers vainly offering two to one. Everybody acknowledged Buck a magnificent animal, but twenty fifty-pound sacks of flour bulked too large in their eyes for them to loosen their pouch-strings.

Thornton knelt down by Buck's side. He took his head in his two hands and rested cheek on cheek. He did not playfully shake him, as was his wont, or murmur soft love curses; but he whispered in his ear. "As you love me, Buck. As you love me," was what he whispered. Buck whined with suppressed eagerness.

The crowd was watching curiously. The affair was growing mysterious. It seemed like a conjuration. As Thornton got to his feet, Buck seized his mittened hand between his jaws, pressing in with his teeth and releasing slowly, half-reluctantly. It was the answer, in terms, not of speech, but of love. Thornton stepped well back.

"Now, Buck," he said.

Buck tightened the traces, then slacked them for a matter of several inches. It was the way he had learned.

"Gee!" Thornton's voice rang out, sharp in the tense silence.

Buck swung to the right, ending the movement in a plunge that took up the slack and with a sudden jerk arrested his one hundred and fifty pounds. The load quivered, and from under the runners arose a crisp crackling.

"Haw!" Thornton commanded.

Buck duplicated the manoeuvre, this time to the left. The cracking turned into a snapping, the sled pivoting and the runners slipping and grating several inches to the side. The sled was broken out. Men were holding their breaths, intensely unconscious of the fact.

"Now, MUSH!"

Thornton's command cracked out like a pistol shot. Buck

threw himself forward, tightening the traces with a jarring lunge. His whole body was gathered compactly together in the tremendous effort, the muscles writhing and knotting like live things under the silky fur. His great chest was low to the ground, his head forward and down, while his feet were flying like mad, the claws scarring the hard-packed snow in parallel grooves. The sled swayed and trembled, half-started forward. One of his feet slipped, and one man groaned aloud. Then the sled lurched ahead in what appeared a rapid succession of jerks, though it never really came to a dead stop again . . . half an inch . . . an inch . . . two inches. . . . The jerks perceptibly diminished; as the sled gained momentum, he caught them up, till it was moving steadily along.

Men gasped and began to breathe again, unaware that for a moment they had ceased to breathe. Thornton was running behind, encouraging Buck with short, cheery words. The distance had been measured off, and as he neared the pile of firewood which marked the end of the hundred yards, a cheer began to grow and grow, which burst into a roar as he passed the firewood and halted at command. Every man was tearing himself loose, even Matthewson. Hats and mittens were flying in the air. Men were shaking hands, it did not matter with whom, and bubbling over in a general incoherent babel.

But Thornton fell on his knees beside Buck. Head was against head, and he was shaking him back and forth. Those who hurried up heard him cursing Buck, and he cursed him long and fervently, and softly and lovingly.

"Gad, sir! Gad, sir!" spluttered the Skookum Bench king. "I'll give you a thousand for him, sir, a thousand, sir—twelve hundred, sir."

Thornton rose to his feet. His eyes were wet. The tears were streaming frankly down his cheeks. "Sir," he said to the Skookum Bench king, "no, sir. You can go to hell, sir. It's the best I can do for you, sir."

Buck seized Thornton's hand in his teeth. Thornton shook him back and forth. As though animated by a common impulse, the onlookers drew back to a respectful distance; nor were they again indiscreet enough to interrupt.